BALLAD OF
A GHETTO POET

BALLAD OF
A GHETTO POET

A. J. WHITE

A
SBI
PUBLICATION

A STREBOR BOOKS INTERNATIONAL LLC PUBLICATION
DISTRIBUTED BY SIMON & SCHUSTER, INC.

Published by

SBI

Strebor Books International LLC
P.O. Box 1370
Bowie, MD 20718

ISBN 0-7394-4776-9
LCCN

Cover design: www. mariondesigns.com

Manufactured and Printed in the United States

DEDICATION

To all my young brothers and sisters in Richmond, Virginia.
In Church Hill, Northside, Southside, and my hood
roots, Highland Park, who are struggling, crying, dying,
fighting, yet still are scratching at that wall, trying to reach that door
that opens up to that place called the American Dream.
Don't give up.
There will be another day...

ACKNOWLEDGMENTS

There is always one book that is your baby, that defines the reason you write and the love for the pen that you have inside you. For me, *Ballad of a Ghetto Poet* is that book. Even though this is not my first published novel, it is the first novel I ever wrote. That alone places it in a special spot in my heart. There are also many who, by their encouragement, belief, and influence, have a special place in my heart, and I want to thank them all.

First, I would like to thank my mother, who is not only my best friend, but also my biggest fan. My siblings for boosting me up and being proud of my efforts and encouraging me to keep on rolling. My publicist, Tonya Howard, for her hard work, trust, and enthusiasm in all I do. My agent, Sara Camilli, for continuing to push my books to get to the highest level. Zane, thank you for trusting the unknown. Simon and Schuster, for getting my books out there and in the stores for readers to enjoy. Shonell Bacon, my buddy and partner till the end. Virginia, for reading and critiquing *Ballad* at its infancy, and letting me know it was off the hook.

V. Anthony Rivers, Brandon Massey, Trey Brashears, Darrien Lee, Cookie, The Nubian Chronicles family, Radio One, Hot 99 Radio Station, 104.7 Radio, Pssst Book Club, APOOO, Raw Sistaz, Waldenbooks at Virginia Center Commons, Karibu Books, and many others who have been there, done that, and continue to encourage me.

One Luv...

Prayed many prayers to Allah…
Cried silent tears to Jah…
So lost inside a brotha's world
The sun can't reach my heart…

"They dead, they all dead!"

Aileen Mayes recoiled back at the pain-filled voice that screamed over the phone line. She didn't have to see Elizabeth Grayson's face to know that it was reddened and streaked with tears. The emotion in her voice was almost tangible.

"Who's dead? Who's dead, Elizabeth?" Aileen asked in a fearful whisper.

"The boys, Candy! They all dead! They all shot, at the house, at the house! Oh, God, I can't breathe, I can't take this...I can't!" she wailed pitifully.

Aileen's heart hammered loudly. Her worse fear, her worse nightmare was being announced as a reality at that very moment. She loved her students, and had worked so hard to instill in them a desire to fulfill their dreams. A desire to be more than what the streets in the Church Hill part of Richmond, Virginia had to offer them. She had her stars. Students whose futures shined like the luminaries that lit up the sky over Maymount Park. Sean Grayson had been one of those stars, although he didn't know it. But Aileen did. She saw it every time she read his work. The spirit, energy and power he would put in every poem, every bit of prose he would pen.

The wailing continued, turning into deep, beckoning howls. A mother's cry.

"How...how?" Aileen asked as her own tears gathered in her eyes.

"They come to my house; hurt my children. Shooting and fighting and fighting and..." Elizabeth paused, choking on her sobs.

Aileen could hear voices in the background telling Elizabeth Grayson to hurry, that they were leaving for the hospital. A hope filled her. If they were going to the hospital, then maybe, just maybe the children were not dead!

"Are you sure they're dead, Elizabeth? Are you certain?" Aileen asked. Silence cried back at her. "Elizabeth?" she called out again, panicking.

"I have to go. We're leaving now," Elizabeth said. "We're at MCV!"

"Okay, but what about Chico? Elizabeth? Elizabeth?"

Aileen heard music, but it was the sound of the dial tone, letting her know that Elizabeth Grayson had hung up. She hung up her own receiver and rushed to get her purse and keys. As she quickly made her way out to her car, she couldn't help but wonder how it had come to this. Teenagers and street violence were nothing new to the urban communities of Richmond. But it was a totally different feeling when it came to children whom you were close to, had taught and had high hopes for.

Every bad ending has a beginning. This one started, six months ago...

CHAPTER ONE
LIFE IS JUST A SONG...

Six months prior…

"Nicca, wha!"

"Nicca, who!" Chico sung back at Malcolm, laughing.

Malcolm pushed his way through the crowded bus. Loads of tired people grumbled and scowled, seemingly aggravated at his coarse tone and loudness. But it was nothing unusual for Malcolm when it came to being just plain loud and raw.

"Nicca, slide yo ass over on this chair; that's what you betta do!" Malcolm continued.

"Yea, whateva." Chico smiled broadly. "So wassup, dawg?" he asked, as his long time homie plopped down beside him.

"Not a damn thing, man. Shit, it's hot as a mutha' out there! This bus took forever. I started to walk or take the Church Hill Three down further. So what about you? Where you been hiding, yo?"

"I ain't been hiding, just taking care of bidness, ya know?" Chico smirked.

"Uh huh, I know about that *bidness;* spit it out, jigga, don't play!"

Chico gave Malcolm a knowing grin, and then grabbed his crotch suggestively. "Dis' wassup."

Malcolm looked around at the people sitting behind them and frowned slightly. "Don't be doing that; peeps be thinking we gay and shit!"

Chico laughed. "Yea, but you know what this means. I got tap lessons."

Malcolm's eyes lit up as he looked at Chico with admiration. "You lyin'. You lyin', boy, you ain't hit that."

"Again and again and again," Chico bragged, feeling proud of himself.

Malcolm's smile grew wider when he saw Chico's cocky grin. "You one lucky nicca, man! How you manage to work that out?"

"Well, you know, I had to throw a lil sumpin-sumpin on her. And, Malcolm…" He leaned closer, sliding down a bit in his chair, "she sucks, too; know what I mean? Whoa! Umm…umm…umm; made me scream like a bitch. And when I got up in that bush, she was so tight and sweet. Like a tangerine, my brotha..." he bragged, goaded on by the rapturous expression on Malcolm's face.

"Ahh, damn..." Malcolm's mouth flew open like Chico knew it would. Chico smiled to himself when he saw it. "Um...What about Candy? She find out you messing around you may lose that sweet thang."

"Yeah, like I'm s'pose to tell her? That ho ain't mean nuttin to me anyhow. Candy is my boo, you know this."

"Right, so if she's your boo then why was you all up in Alisha? Don't front, you know I got ya numba," Malcolm joked. He looked at Chico with one eye-brow cocked, waiting for a comeback.

"Well, just keep this to yourself, aight?"

"Word. You ain't gotta worry about that," Malcolm said.

Chico reached up and pulled the thick, black cord, prompting the bus driver that he wanted the next stop. Malcolm yanked on his sleeve.

"Wait, before you go just tell me one thing. *How was the grip?*"

Chico paused a second before it hit him what Malcolm meant. "Man, get outta here wit' your stoopid ass." Chico laughed as he quickly made his way to the exit door. "I'll kick it wit' you later, ya non-coochie-gettin' mofo."

"Yea, fuck you, Chico!"

"Love you, too, son!" Chico spat out, laughing, and turned quickly to make his way down the littered sidewalk. He laughed to himself, ignoring the curses of his friend through the bus window.

It was a typical day with a typical laziness, and nothing to do. A typical life of being black, poor and living in the hood. Sean Grayson, better known as Chico to his boys, was a tall, butterscotch complexioned, hazel-eyed hood rat. His world consisted of himself, his mom and sister, and the homies round the way that he considered closer than brothers. Born and raised in Richmond, Virginia to a single mother, life had never been easy for them, and dealing with the extra blows that came their way. Chico had long learned his own way of dealing with those blows, and trying to come out on top. Not that anyone would consider how they lived as being on top, but like his mom always would remind him and Asha, they had food in their bellies, clothes on their backs, a roof over their heads, and nobody was dying from any dreaded disease. With all that to compare to, they weren't doing bad at all. But even with the common sense of his mother's words, Chico couldn't help but feel that the American dream had somehow escaped them. Especially when he knew that it didn't have to be that way. Especially when he thought about how good his dad was living. Whenever he thought about his dad Chico would grow cold inside. No matter the weather, that cold feeling never failed to consume him. So to counteract it he would switch his mind to something more pleasant. Like chicks, or dreams of money.

◆◆◆

The evening sun blazed. Hot wind blew through the broken cracks in the window. The smell of bad crabs filled the room. It was evidence that somebody had used the alley as a garbage dump again. It wasn't surprising. A bunch of stanky hoochies lived across the way. They were the type of chicks who would never leave the house with their hair undone, yet kept their babies in dirty diapers, and snotty noses. And of course they were *always* looking for a new man. They always did Chico the favor of reminding him of the type of girls he wouldn't wanna screw with.

"Sean!" Liz Grayson's voice sung out in a shrilling tone.

The sudden banging on his bedroom door woke Chico from his evening nap. He sat up abruptly, quickly bringing his hand up to his nose, trying to block the strong, rotten crab smell that radiated.

"Why didn't you take the trash out?!" his mom screamed. "Where is Asha? How come you got this door locked? Are you smoking weed? Is that gal in there? Why ain't you answering me? Sean! Sean!"

Sighing a little, Chico got ready for the daily questions that always came from his mama. But he really didn't mind. If there was one thing he was sure of in this life it was that his mom had mad love for him and his twin sister Asha. She was a hard-working lady. He couldn't remember a time when she hadn't worked two jobs to support them. He unlocked the door to see her standing there. She was a short, dark, pleasantly plump woman, and to him the most beautiful lady in the world. He couldn't help but think, but wish, he could take her out of this madness, out of the projects. He knew that his mom wasn't brought up poor, but instead was raised in the country in Stony Creek, Virginia. She and his Aunt Delores never wanted for anything, and had both finished high school and college. Well, almost. Liz Grayson ending up dropping out her sophomore year after she discovered she was pregnant. But even with all that, Chico knew that things didn't have to be so bad for his mom. If things were right, she wouldn't have to work so hard, and they wouldn't be living on a street littered with crack vials and beer cans. He was still unable to slow the bile that always filled his throat whenever he thought of the man he blamed for this. The so-called father he never really knew, whmo he would only hear from on those occasional times when he just so happened to call, or rather...when their phone just so happened to still be connected.

"Why did you have the door locked?" his mother asked him again.

"I was sleep. I just lock it automatically sometimes," he answered back.

"Well, don't lock it no more. There are no private domains around here. And where is Asha? Why didn't she do them dishes like I told her to?"

"I don't know, dang...she ain't here," Chico huffed. He got up, stretched, and then started straightening up his clothes. Liz Grayson's rantings continued. She kicked angrily at the collection of socks that were in front of his bureau.

"You need to clean this room. It's filthy! And I don't even know why Asha went out. She knew I needed her to do some things around here. I don't have time to do everything. I have to go back to work. You're just gonna have to do those dishes."

"I don't feel like doin' no dishes," Chico grumbled.

Elizabeth's eyes narrowed. "You think I feel like going to work again? There's a lot that I don't feel like doing that I do anyhow. You two could really help me more around here, Sean, and you know it!"

"Well, I was gonna take out the trash."

Liz crossed her arms and looked at Chico from across the room as he picked up the socks she had kicked. As always he had the same defiant look on his face.

"Then why didn't you?"

"'Cuz I was just tired. I just took a nap is all. I was gon' do it. Besides, why you gotta go back to work? Forget those white folks. Let 'em cook their own dinner!"

"Cooking for those white folks puts dinner on the table for you as you well know."

Chico grumbled quietly to himself.

"What did you say? Sorry, mister, I didn't hear you. What was that?" his mother asked with raised eyebrows.

Chico was quiet for a second before blurting, "Thing is, you shouldn't have to work so hard. Thing is, you should be getting help from you know who. Thing is, I could even get a full-time job and help out; just get my GED and chill with that."

"Oh, I don't think so. You're going to college, Sean. I've already told you that."

"Why?" he asked. "I mean, you went, and you still gotta work, cleaning and cooking and stuff like that. What good does it do?"

Liz closed her eyes before speaking, and sighed. She always felt this guilt whenever she talked to her twins about college, because she had not finished. Still she was not going to allow her example to be an excuse for them not to pursue higher learning. She wanted better for them. She wanted better for herself, too. Maybe it was too late for that, although her goal had always been to return to school herself once she got them their grants and hopefully scholarships that would help them along the way.

"I know I didn't finish," she said quietly, "which is one of the reasons we struggle so hard now. But I don't want that for you; things can be better for you two, and will be."

"Yeah but..."

"No buts! Look, I don't have time to argue with you over this. I do what I have to do, okay? And I don't want to hear any more about you leaving school because it's not gonna happen, Sean, not as long as I'm alive to stop it. And when Asha gets here you tell her to wash those dishes, and to stay in tonight please. You, too! You two are always gone and I don't know what y'all be doing out in them streets. And here," she said, handing over a wad of food stamps. "Go get something to eat, and get milk, too, okay?"

She kissed him quickly, not missing the look of protest on her son's face. "Don't even say it, Sean. Just do what I tell you."

His mom hurried out the door, and headed to her room to get ready. Chico frowned as she left. To him his mother's working all the time was only one step down from indentured slavery. He also noticed that she avoided the subject of his dad, like always. It seemed that the older he got, the more pain he saw his mama in, the wider his eyes opened.

Placing the food stamps on the end table, he picked up his zebra spiral notepad. It was his haven, the uncool part of Chico. It was his thought tablet. Words always seemed to come easily to him, especially when he was feeling stressed, or angry. When they did, he always was sure to pen them down in his thought tablet. It was therapeutic.

His closed his eyes as he felt *Lyric* whispering, that poetic spirit coming over him, and felt the hidden emotions coming out through his pen. Feelings that he rarely let anyone outside himself see, or even know he had.

While flowing through this place called life, and all its hidden paths...
I sometimes have to stop, exhale, and have a shaky laugh...
Things aren't always the way they seem, no life is not that clear...
Sometimes inside my hidden soul, I feel this quake of fear...
I cover, hide it from the world, so people just don't see...
The fear, the pain that tore up kid hiding inside of me...
Those little things there from the past, those memories, those scars...
The depth, the richness of my heart I hide them in the dark...
One thing that helps my soul escape from all that's done it wrong...
Is music, tempo, melody...cuz life is just a song...

Chico closed his tablet, staring blankly as in deep thought. Slipping his Nikes back on, he quickly headed out into the darkness of the night.

CHAPTER TWO:
SOMEONE JUST LIKE ME...

Have you ever caught sight of someone like me?
With leather-bound Jordans caressing his feet?
Did you get scared? Did you run for cover?
Did you fail to recognize that he was your brotha?
Have you bought into the hype, the black stereotype?
Would you hold your purse so tight if the brotha was white?
Would your heart beat so fast, sweat blanketing your face?
Thinking crime is only an adjective for a dude of his race?
Have you ever thought to give him the benefit of the doubt?
That maybe he's defected cuz he's always gone without?
Would you ever give a hand to one resembling me?
Helping him become a man, and helping him to become free?
Don't you know it only takes just one person like you?
To save a young man from the streets, to show him what to do?
As you answer these questions search your heart,
Dig real deep, ask yourself
If you have the power to share and give emotional need.
The answers may astound you; bring you crashing to your knees,
For surprisingly, the one you fear...is someone, just like me...

Asha's eyes shot heated arrows at Peanut's back. He was ignoring her as always when she wanted to talk about anything deeper than the next NFL superstar, or whatever he was interested in for the moment.

"Peanut!"

"What?!" he screamed. He still would not look up at her from the Playstation Two game that he was so involved in.

"I'm talking to you. Why won't you look at me?"

"I told you I'm busy. Now get off my fuckin' back!" he shouted, then whispered, "Bitch..."

Asha growled, then picked up Peanut's size-eleven Nike and threw it at him. Her aim landed right at the back of his head. "Your mama is a bitch!"

Within seconds Asha realized that once again she had gone too far. She saw Peanut charging toward her. She bounced, slipping as she ran for the door. Falling face first to the floor, she banged her chin on the end table. But before she could even cry out, she felt Peanut's weight atop her, his big hand slapping her soundly across the face. She flung back at him, punching him in the lip.

"Oh, you wanna play?" he shouted, grabbing her by the throat, and then banging her head hard against the floor.

She choked out, "Stop it, Peanut! Ouch, stop!"

He slapped her again.

Peanut stood and watched Asha's bawling face turn redder and redder. "Get up, girl! You always make me do this, Asha. You always gotta play too much, and keep running your big mouth. I don' told you before, stop fuckin' with me, dammit!"

Asha lay still while Peanut got up and started straightening up the mess they had made fighting. She whimpered quietly to herself.

"Get up, I said. You know damn well I ain't hurt you."

"Yes you did. You hurt my face," she cried, as she sat up.

The fighting between Peanut and Asha was nothing new. It was like a love-hate thing. But the thin line that stretched between love and hate was wearing out next to none with them lately. But even with the pain, love had cast a blind spell over Asha that was impenetrable. Even when her common sense told her that Peanut was no good for her, her foolish heart would crush her common sense every time. Crush it with the same strength that Peanut's fist would plow into her face.

Asha walked slowly to the door. Tears blinded her eyes.

"Asha?" Peanut called out. She stalled before turning around. "Asha?" he called out again as she faced him.

"What?" she whispered.

Peanut zoned in at the slight swell to her cheek. Asha knew what he was thinking. She made him do it, that she always made him do it.

"I'm sorry, aight? I didn't mean it."

Asha kept walking out into the warm summer air. "I love you," Peanut called out to her. "I'm sorry, Asha; I didn't mean it…"

She wrapped her arms around herself, and kept walking.

As he made his way quickly down the street, Chico hoped in vain that no one he knew would spot him heading for the store. He hated with a passion using food stamps. To him it was just an embarrassing way of showing that they were some poor ass black folk. And to him the food stamps were nothing but a government handout.

He stuck his hands deep inside his jean pockets and was about to turn the corner leading to Cal's Grocer when he spotted Malcolm. He let out a deep sigh, thinking Malcolm would have to show his mug at the wrong time. Speeding up his steps, he hoped Malcolm wouldn't see him.

"Chico! Hold up, man, I gotta holla at cha!" Malcolm screamed.

Chico finally slowed down and turned around with a frown.

Malcolm Tyler was his best friend since that day in third grade at Woodville Elementary when a couple of fifth–graders decided they wanted someone to pick on and chose Chico. Malcolm had stood up for him, he being the bigger of the two, and they had been tight ever since. The two were as tight as twins yet still different as night and day. Chico sported long light–brown cornrows that hung past his shoulders and almost matched the color of his eyes. Malcolm, one of the darker-hued brothas, preferred to keep his do long and wild the way he wore it now, all over his head. They both agreed on one thing, though: The baggie jeans off the butt hip-hop style of dress—to the dismay of Chico's mother and Malcolm's grandmother, of course.

"Yo, you heard about that dude that's been rolling on Q Street, right? This nicca named Marco."

"Yea, and what about 'em?" Chico asked, walking fast again.

"Well…" Malcolm walked in double strides to meet his friend's fast steps. "Damn, cuz, hold up! What you rushing for? This is serious, yo!"

"Aight then." Chico walked a little slower. "What about him?"

"He's lookin' to do some recruiting, man. He got plans for Creighton and Jackson Ward, so he lookin' for some real niccas, you know what I'm sayin'?"

"So what does that got to do with us?" Chico asked, shaking his head.

Malcolm huffed, looking Chico up and down like he just knew his boy wasn't hearing clearly.

"What you mean what does it has to do with us? Datz us, man. We the ones. We can work with him; help him run this joint. And I'm not talking about pennies either. Marco told me he pullin' some real green up in this joint."

"Like what, drugs?" Chico raised a brow.

"Naw, man. That's too damn easy. I'm not sure what it's all about, but I do know it's not about no drugs. Marco says it's a business deal. A proposition he got for us."

Chico stopped walking, slipped his hands in his back pockets, and looked at Malcolm suspiciously. "This kat from Brooklyn, ain't he?"

"So?"

"So? If he's from BK he's probably bangin', and I don't want no parts of that shit, Malcolm. I don' told you that once before. We been doin' our own lil gigs around here. We don't need that shit he talking."

"What gigs, Chico?" Malcolm pressed. "What, grabbing a couple of TVs? Jewelry? That ain't no money, dawg, and you know it ain't. And how you know what shit he talking if you ain't even heard it? I know you don't want to get too deep into nuttin' and I don't either. But this ain't a gang type of activity. Marco, yo he's a businessman. Serious business." Malcolm jerked on Chico's sleeve, trying to get his point across. "Look, Chico, I don't know all that's involved, but here's an opportunity. We can at least talk to him, right?"

"I don't know," Chico said hesitantly.

"Come on. Don't make me look bad now. I told him you would be down for it, and you know I don't make a move without you." He brought his closed fist to his chest in the ultimate salute of hood love. "One love, man, remember? Holla at me, I know you down." An earnest look filled Malcolm's eyes.

Chico looked hard at Malcolm. He still felt the instinct to say no, but they had never done anything apart. If you saw one, you saw the other—Chico and Malcolm, Malcolm and Chico. They stuck like glue. "I don't know, Malcolm. Let me think on this, okay?"

"There is no time to think about it. I told him we would meet and talk to him today; all we have to do is go pick up Junnie."

"I guess," Chico said slowly.

Maybe, just maybe it would be something worth his time. He wasn't sure, but he suddenly pictured the way his mom had looked earlier, all tired and beat-down. If he could start making some real money she wouldn't have to slave for the man all the time the way she did. He smiled at that thought. This could be the writing on the wall, their big break, their opportunity. Besides, talking to somebody didn't necessarily make one involved. He'd talk, just talk to this dude with Malcolm and see what he was all about. If he didn't feel it, he'd just say no, easy as that.

"Okay, but all we are gonna do is talk, aight? Nothing more than that."

Malcolm crossed his heart. "I swear to God, that's it, nuttin' more, nuttin' less. We can head on over there right now, aight? I told him I needed to talk to you and then we'd be over to talk biz. And hell you know if both of us are cool with it Junnie gon' be down."

Chico nodded. He still wasn't sure, but Malcolm sounded convinced. He looked to answer Malcolm who was still yappin' when suddenly both of them froze in their tracks at the sight of the lone figure walking slowly up the street toward them.

"Asha?" Chico called as he recognized his twin sister. "What you doing still out, girl? Ma was trying to get me to do your damn dishes…" His words froze on his lips when she got closer, and he saw the deep purple bruise on her cheek, and the slight swell underneath her tearstained, hazel eyes.

"What the hell!" Chico exclaimed at the sight of his sister's face. "Peanut been hitting on you?"

"Nooo…" she stammered, "I fell and hit my face on the end table."
Chico raised Asha's face up by her chin. She jumped at the pressure.

"Girl, that ain't no end-table bruise. That's a whip!"

Asha's facial expression quickly turned to a look of guilt, then fear. She spoke quickly. "Move, Chico, I don't even feel like talking to you about this. I'm going home."

"You crazy, you know that?!" Chico screamed. "Where he at? Where that nicca at! He must don' lost his damn mind! And you? How you gonna let some nicca hit up on you wit' yo stupid ass!"

"That's not what happened!" Asha insisted, but her brother wasn't hearing her.

As he rushed off to find his source of anger, Chico could only think of how he wanted to kill the salty bitch. This was the second time he had seen Asha with bruises that he knew were due to her boyfriend, Peanut. He was determined it would be the last!

"Man, where that punk ass nicca at?" Malcolm stormed, equally pissed off.

With both he and Chico almost running toward Peanut's place, the best Asha could do was to run behind them and try to keep up with their pace.

"Chico, please don't hurt him. He ain't do nuttin'. Come on, pleassssseee!"

She grabbed his arm. Chico's off as they hook her walked into the building.

The sounds of 2Pac's old cut "I ain't mad at cha" filled the putrid hallway. Peanut's voice was loud and clear coming through his apartment door. An astounded look marred his dark, handsome features as the door came crashing open. Not getting a chance to speak another word, he felt a stinging blow to his chest as a familiar voice issued curses at him.

"Gonna whip yo ass, bitch!"

Hard blows flew through the air. Asha's cries and screams could be heard throughout the building as she witnessed the violent beating and kicking of her boyfriend. Blood dripped down the corner of his mouth.

Chico could not still the anger that filled him and felt lost in his own rage. Peanut's eyes became huge saucers as he looked up and saw Chico pulling out a .38. His screams became gurgled as Chico brought it swiftly across his face in a pistol whip.

In the midst of his anger he could hear Asha's cries of protest, and then Malcolm's. "Man, let's go; we don't wanna 'em, dawg! Come on, we need to get out of here before somebody calls Five-O!" Chico gave Peanut another hard kick. "Come on, Chico, we gotta roll!" Malcolm screamed again.

They both dashed from the apartment, pulling a screaming, protesting Asha along with them.

"Why'd you do that?" she cried, as the three stopped to catch their breath in the alleyway. "We only had a misunderstanding. You didn't have to beat him like that!"

Chico grabbed her roughly by her shoulders. "It's gon' be more than that, more than that, Asha, if he ever puts his hands on you again."

"Don't touch me!" she cried.

"You listen to me!" He shook her hard. "Don't you ever, ever let me hear that you be letting him put his hands on you again. You understand me, Asha?" Asha ignored him, still crying. "Do you hear me?!" he screamed yet again.

Malcolm watched silently as the two siblings faced one another. The tension between them was so thick it floated like invisible putty through the air.

"I hear you," Asha said quietly. "I hear you…"

"Yeah, you better."

Asha broke away from her twin brother's heated gaze and walked away. He looked at her blankly as she trailed down the street to their apartment…not at first hearing Malcolm as he roused him from his thoughts, reminding him that they had business to tend to, someone to meet.

CHAPTER THREE:
LOVE AIN'T S'POSE TO HURT...

"I don't understand you, girl."

Asha cringed as her mother Liz Grayson brought a warm washcloth to her face, pampering the swell under her eye. After she had left Chico and Malcolm, she had come home surprised to see her mother there, her having come home early with a headache.

"Yeah, you oughta jump. Any girls who would let a pissy-tail boy hit them should get their butts beat. And I should beat you myself for you being so stupid!"

"I'm not, Mama," Asha said with a sigh. "I told you already that I fell against the end table. I tried to tell Chico, too, but you should have seen how he and Malcolm were beating up on Peanut."

"Chico did right!" Liz hissed. She then took some oil-based, soothing balm medication and rubbed it under Asha's eye. "You're gonna have a black eye." She paused and examined the swelling. "You aren't to see that boy anymore, Asha Grayson, do you understand me?"

"But, Mom!"

"I mean it," Liz warned.

Asha's face read stubborn. Liz didn't have to hear her say it to know what she was thinking. Mothers never understand. Mothers don't know what it's like to be in love.

"It's not fair!" Asha cried. She stood up with her hands on her hips, ready to war. "Everybody is judging Peanut and trying to decide things for me. Y'all don't even know him. Y'all don't even know what we are about!"

"I don't have to know him to know he ain't about nothing, Asha. I mean put yourself in my place; how would you feel if you were me?"

Asha sniffed again, ignoring her mother's reasoning. "You just don't understand cuz you ain't got nobody that you love like that. If you had Daddy or someone else that you were dating, you would see how I feel, but you don't!"

A look of hot pain flashed across Liz's face at her daughter's words. "Oh, so now just because you have some silly lil boy beating your ass you know more than me? You're a woman now, right?"

"That's not what I meant…" Asha broke in. She pulled back at her mother's anger. Liz Grayson never ever cursed unless she was angry.

"No, you go on. I am too tired, and I can't spend my off time worrying about you and your brother. You like having somebody slapping you all up in your face so just go for it. After all, he loves you, right?"

Asha was quiet. More tears welled up in her eyes, causing Liz's anger to dissipate. She sighed sadly at her daughter's tearful disposition and continued to speak.

"You have no clue what I have dealt with in my life, Asha. You don't know a thing about your father and me, or whom I have dated or what I have been doing. And it is way out of line for you to even open your mouth to me like that…"

"I know, I know and I'm sorry…" Asha said quietly.

She backed toward the door, leading out of her mother's bedroom. Liz sat quietly, fighting hard not to allow her own doubts and fears of love to color her words to her daughter. It was very hard for her, always had been. She knew that she hadn't been a perfect example for Asha, not when it came to loving, and being loved by a man. Asha was right; she didn't have one, she wasn't with their father, and she had no prospects either. Not that she was dying to meet Mr. Right. Mr. Right usually would turn into Mr. Wrong in the blink of an eye or slap of the hand the way it had with Asha. She just didn't want her baby to go through all of that drama.

"I do know how you feel, Asha. You think I don't because you're at that age where you don't realize that everything you are going through all women have gone through it at one time or another, in one form or another. And I know you love him." She watched slow tears trail down Asha's face, and felt her own starting to gather, emotion tightening her throat. "Love ain't s'pose to hurt, baby. Love ain't s'pose to make you feel like nothing. I learned that long ago and never forgot it. I hope you never will either."

Asha wrapped her arms around herself as she leaned back against the door. "I just love him, Mama. I can't just let it go. I have to at least try."

Liz opened her mouth to speak, then realized as she watched her daughter that at this point nothing she had to say would get through. Asha would have to see; experience things for herself. She only prayed that her quest for knowledge didn't lend her more black eyes and bruises along the way.

Marco hadn't been home for their so-called meeting the day before. That was funny to Chico, especially since Malcolm had made such a big deal with his excitement about filling them in on his business proposition. After contacting him later, Marco had told Malcolm that they should meet up in a couple of days after he got some things squared away. That was okay with Chico. He knew he had to make up time with his baby girl, Candy. Yeah, he definitely owed her an explanation about where he had been, and why he hadn't been around a lot.

Rehearsing his words as he slowly made his way up the walkway to Candy's door, Chico tried to fix his mind on what he would say to her. Fortunately she hadn't gotten wind of the messin' he had been doing. At least he hoped she hadn't. He knew that the other girl meant nothing to him, but he also knew that Candy would not see it that way. She would see it for what it was. His cheating while they were supposed to be one on one. He could tell by the sound of her voice that she was upset with him when he had talked to her the evening before. Upset that he hadn't spent as much time with her lately. But he was mainly hoping that she wouldn't ask too many questions. She probably wouldn't like the answers.

Candy was from a different world than him. For one, she lived in the suburbs, and she had more balance, more focus, a complete family, traditions, and a dad who loved her. Yet, she had sought out a classic street thug like Chico. There was a connection that the two of them had that was unexplainable. Or maybe it just went back to the same ol', same ol': a so–called good girl fascinated by the bad–boy image.

The door opened abruptly. Candy stood there with a vexed expression on her face. She was a black/boricua beauty, a petite girl with sparkling amber eyes, small pretty face, and shoulder-length curly black hair. She was five four and a hundred pounds on a wet day. But had a mouth that could only be mildly described as *blaring*.

"Oh, so you've decided to grace me with your presence, huh?" she said in a dry, sarcastic tone. "Where have you been, Chico? You haven't called me or nothing!" An indignant pout coated her face.

"Aw come on, ain't you glad to see me? Gimme kiss, boo," Chico slipped his hands around her waist. He puckered up and bent his head forward toward her lips.

Candy sniffed as she watched his expectant lips, and his eyes sealed shut. "See, you trying to ignore my question. Where've you been? What you been doing?"

"Thinking about you, missing you," Chico said softly, caressing her hair. "Have I ever told you how much I love your hair?"

He could tell by the look in her eyes that she was starting to soften up and decided to take advantage of her moment of weakness. Pulling her closer to him, he whispered in her ear, "I've missed you, a lot. Is your mom home?"

"No, and Jose is at basketball camp," she said, referring to her younger brother.

She rolled her neck to the side at the feel of Chico's lips against it, moaning at the feel of it. Chico smiled inside at her reaction. He was always able to get her to soften up with just a brush of his lips. He began slowly sucking at her delicate skin.

"So…" He looked seductively at her, resting his eyes on the swell of her breast.

"So what, Chico?" Candy moaned. "I mean you know I want you, too. But you come up in here after not hearing a word from you in days. Now you want to kick it just like that, like I'm some booty call or sumpin'."

"See now you know it ain't even like that." He winked, trying to pull a smile out of her. When he saw her serious expression, he thought better of it. "Aight, let's talk." Taking her hand, they both settled comfortably on the L-shaped couch.

"Well, what have you been up to? Hanging out all night with Malcolm again?"

Chico nodded. "Not just hanging out with him, but trying to make some money. I told you I needed to start bringing some in to help my moms out with the bills and stuff, remember?"

"So where'd you get a job at?" Candy asked. "Now I know good and well you ain't at Burger King cuz I can't see you doing that."

"Hell naw, I ain't at no Burger King. Like how much could I make there? That's chump change. I'm looking for real money."

A slightly suspicious look entered Candy's eyes. "I just know you ain't dealing drugs, are you?"

"What?" Chico drew back. "Girl, what you smoking? You know I'm not about that; that ain't me. What you think I am? Some kind of thug or sumpin'?"

"I know you're a wannabe. But you're just a lil softee." She punched him on the side of his arm.

"For you." He winked. "But naw, ain't nuttin' going on like that. You talking about L.A. and Compton shit, baby. Or that Brooklyn war zone. This is Virginia, remember? *Virginia is for lovers...*" he sang, laughing to try and ease her doubts. "Come on, trust me, aight? I'm not gonna do nuttin' crazy. Trust me?"

He was softly caressing Candy's inner thigh, very thankful that she had on some daisy dukes, or bootie shorts and short halter-top. *DAMN*...she was a fine ass, he thought to himself. Working his hand in a circular motion, pretty soon he was squeezing and caressing at the swollen Y between her thighs.

"We...we still haven't finished talking yet." Candy sighed deeply as he rubbed harder and harder.

"You want me to stop, boo?"

Loosening the tiny snap of her halter-top, he soon had her small, yet shapely breasts open to his explorations. He slowly took one of her tiny nipples between his lips, sucklin' her as she moaned. Pretty soon he had the front of her daisy dukes loose. His hand eased down the front of her shorts and panties, then stroked the soft hair between her legs, feeling her heat and wetness.

"Ohhhh...Chico, that feels so good, boo," Candy moaned, moving her hips in a circle as he touched her and sucked at her breast. Her sighs and moans sung a song to Chico that she just loved her some him.

The sound of the front door unlocking jerked both of them from their passionate embrace. Candy jumped up quickly and made her way to the hall bathroom, leaving Chico alone to face her mother walking through the door.

"Hi, Chico. How are you, sweetie?" asked Mrs. Rosas. She offered a friendly smile.

"Hi, Mrs. Rosas. I'm fine, thank you."

"So where did Candy run off to?" she asked, looking around. "Oh, and how is your mother, dear? Is she still working all those cleaning jobs?"

An irritated feeling washed over Chico, not that he didn't like Candy's mother. But somehow she always made him feel that she was looking down on his mom. It always seemed like she didn't think he or his family were good enough to be connected with theirs.

"She's a cook. And yeah she's still hanging with it," came his flat reply.

"Oh, that's too bad. I can barely stand cooking for my own family." Mrs. Rosas hooted. "Well, you tell her I asked about her, you hear?"

Chico let out a deep breath as Candy's mom made her way down the hall. He frowned at Candy as she walked back into the living room.

"What are you frowning at? Don't you dare say anything about my mother." She gave him another playful slap on the arm.

"Oh, I'm not. She's just a trip is all. *I can barely stand cooking for my own family. Tell her I asked about her, ya heard?*" Chico said in a mocking tone.

"Oh, shuddup! I know good and well she didn't say *ya heard*; Ebonics is not her thang," she said laughingly. "Let's go, fool."

"Go where?"

"Is anyone at your place right now?" Candy slowly traced his lips with her finger.

"My mom is off today."

"Oh." Candy pouted. "Well, I guess we'll just have to go get a Rita's Icey or sumpin'."

"What you mean?"

"Well," she whispered, leaning close to whisper in his ear, "you don' lit a fire, baby boy. Obviously you can't put it out. So...let's get something cold to drink." She smiled mischievously.

"But...what about this?" He pulled her hand to the front of his jeans, moving it up and down.

"Boy! My mom been don' looked out that window."

Chico sighed. "Come on, Candy..."

"Well, do you think we can maybe sneak in? Creep into your room without your mama seeing or hearing us?"

Chico's eyes lit up at her suggestion, showing that was exactly what he wanted to do.

"Maybe..."

"You gotta finish what you start, baby. Is that gonna be a problem?"

"Only if you take too long to lead us down that sidewalk."

A smug expression covered Candy's face, as they walked outside, into the summer heat.

CHAPTER FOUR:
GETTING THAT RESPECT...

The following day Marco paged Malcolm to tell him that they needed to meet up and let him know something before he searched elsewhere. Chico still felt ambivalent about meeting him. But his doubts faded a bit once they were there. He looked around Marco's crib, noting its stylish furnishings, and especially the expensive stereo system that took up a whole wall in the living room. Straight up, the brotha had bank. This was Chico's dream, to have what Marco had. This is what he'd always hoped to accomplish someday. But maybe his dream wouldn't have to be that far in the future if he played his cards right.

"It's a gold mine out there," Marco said in a crafty voice, drawing Chico's attention back toward him. "Everybody wants a piece of the money pie; it's a matter of how hungry you are, how vicious."

A gold tooth glittered as the piercing, dark brown eyes of twenty-four-year-old Marco stared back at the three younger males in the room. He was an East Coast brotha from Brooklyn; a hard-core thug in every way. But he had somehow molded a sophisticated image of himself. He fancied himself as a black godfather type of character. There was always one or two in the crowd, the specials ones, the so-called born leaders. Marco saw himself as part of this special breed and never failed to let everyone else know it.

"See one thing I've noticed since I've been scoping out this territory is the possibilities. The market is rich in Creighton, Fairmount and Southside. Filled wit' a lot of brothas looking for inexpensive weapons. I've found some ways of manufacturing them, but I need workers who are reliable. I need people to sell and transport to other cities if necessary, and I need to not have my hands visibly in the bowl. That's where you kats come in."

Chico, Malcolm and Junnie sat staring at Marco. Junnie was another one of the Creighton homies from around the way—second only to Malcolm in being one of Chico's closest friends. He almost gave off the air of being Gothic. He had an earring in his brow, an earring in both ears, his nose, and his tongue.

Chico and Malcolm would joke that if he drunk too much water he would start looking like a seal, with water shooting out all the holes in his body. Still with all his oddities, Junnie was the most cautious of the three, and he did a pretty good job in keeping the other two in line—usually.

As Chico listened to Marco, he felt fascinated and scared at the same time, but decided to keep the latter feeling to himself. No use looking like some punk. He and Malcolm and Junnie had always done their thing and weren't Boy Scouts by any means. But this sounded different, yet exciting. Marco was hard to pin down though, even though Malcolm had come at him as if Marco was waiting for them to contact him. It appeared that he wanted to let them know that wasn't the case. He had spent the past few hours explaining things to them—what his plans were, and what he would need them to do for him. His eyes sparkled as he explained the large amount of money that could be made in Richmond. It was all illegal. And lots of thoughts flew through Chico's head as he listened. Ways to justify this, ways to make it okay. He didn't even have to wonder what his mom would think about the whole deal, because no matter how hard they had always struggled, he knew that she had never wanted him to become a gangbanger. But this wasn't gangbanging, he reasoned with himself; this was a job, a way to help pull in some extra cash. He was sure that either way she wouldn't be smiling over his decision, but something had to give. He was tired of sitting back and waiting. It was time for him to *make* things happen.

"So why us? Why exactly do you need us?" Chico inquired.

Marco coughed, looking at Chico cockily. "Need you? Hold the fuck up, yung. Marco don't *need* nobody. I'm doing your ass a favor, ya heard me?" He looked at Chico again, then shook his head. "What the hell have you ever done anyhow, outside of jackin' a few cars or some infantile shit like that? Y'all ain't got nothing that I need. But see Malcolm here said y'all were some real niccas, so I figured I would check y'all out, give you an opportunity."

"Yeah, we appreciate that, Marco," Malcolm said.

Chico frowned at his friend's kiss-ass attitude.

"You should, cuz see we talking real green here. Anybody can sell a lil weed, crack and shit like that, but the real money is in weapons. And from what I've been told they've been going to other hoods, other cities to find it. But now it's time to put the store in the South, right here. You get my point? There's a lot of competition going on and it's bigger than what people realize. I figure if I cut my prices I'll get those sales. People always come to you if they think they can save dollars, but peeps up North just haven't realized that shit yet."

Marco looked around at the three of them. "Now I don't want or need no bitches running my shit, so if either of you don't think you can handle what we talking about, speak up now. Let's not waste each other's time." He looked over at Malcolm. "What about you, yung? I know we been talking about this for a while now. You got the balls, or are you too bitchy?"

"Nope. It all sounds sweet to me. I'm down, yo," Malcolm said.

Both Chico and Junnie stared back at Marco cautiously. Both could sense that this was a truly dangerous brotha. Yet even with the sixth sense feeling they were getting, both were too entranced by the money possibilities to step away from what he was saying.

"You all got ya piece on you? You strapped?" Marco looked over at Malcolm.

"No doubt, always," Malcolm said, nodding his head slightly.

"What about you two ladies?" Marco asked again. This time he looked from Chico to Junnie. "Y'all mighty quiet, and you two seem a bit hesitant to me. Y'all got a problem with this little enterprise we trying to get going here?"

"I'm not hesitant at all," Chico said. "I'm just taking it in, observing and listening carefully. You know what I'm sayin'?" He met Marco's eye defiantly.

"Same here, I'm down for whatever," Junnie agreed, which surprised Chico and Malcolm at how quickly he responded.

Malcolm looked at both of his homies. He seemed to be silently begging them to chill and go with the flow. It was obvious that both Chico and Junnie were having second thoughts. Neither had ever been involved in anything like this before. But both had always voiced how if the chance for fast cash ever arrived, they would jump at it. Marco, however, was arrogant as hell.

"Then you ladies wouldn't mind a little test then, huh? I wanna see what you got. I got this nicca who's been fuckin' with my damn Gs. Don't nobody fuck with my money, ya heard me? So I want my new niccas to help me take care of it. Can y'all handle that?"

"What do you need us to do?" Chico queried.

"Do? You decide that. You do whatever the fuck you need to do. Exterminate his ass if necessary. Fat muthafucka trying to fuck me and Marco don't like to get fucked."

"What...what you mean, take him out? Junnie asked with more than a little surprise in his voice.

"What you think? If he don't have my money, that's right. It's all about getting that respect. This punk has disrespected me. Don't you need respect? You know how to get it?"

Everyone was quiet, so Marco continued.

"Now see y'all sitting here talking about you strapped. You ever used that thing before? I know how y'all lil niccas are. You wanna show and tell your shit but you too scurred to used it."

Chico knew as well as Malcolm and Junnie that neither one of them had ever really used the guns they had for anything. It was just a way of letting people know not to step to you. Yeah, they were ass–kickers and halfway troublemakers, but this was much bigger than anything they had ever done before. Marco was talking real money, and they all could use it, but he couldn't deny to himself that his mom's face was popping up all over the place. She would shit a brick if she knew he was even sitting around talking to a dude like Marco. Even moreso if she knew he was talking to him about selling weapons and actually using them, she would kick his ass.

Something—Chico didn't know what it was—but something would not let him back down from this, no matter the buzzing in his ear or the stomping that his conscience was giving him.

"Yea, I've used it," Chico lied. "I used it when I've had to. Ain't no problem, man, I'm witcha...if we gonna deal, then let's hit it." Chico stood up and pulled out his .38.

"Yeah, um, I have, too. No problem," stammered Junnie. He had a tongue-in-cheek sort of look on his nervous face.

"That's right," Malcolm said, as he high-fived his boys, Chico and Junnie. "I told you, man. We some 'bout-it muthafuckas. No doubt!"

Marco laughed a little, as if he knew they were frontin' big time.

Eyeing all three of his new Creighton prodigies, he flipped his ivory cane toward the door. "Well, all right then, you 'bout-it muthafuckas...let's see what you got. Let's go get that respect."

CHAPTER FIVE:
GOD'S GONNA ASK IT BACK FROM YOU...

The heat of the day betrayed the chilliness inside the dark blue Sentry. As Chico, Malcolm, Junnie and Marco made way for Chamberlayne Avenue in Northside Richmond, the streets were quiet. People were trying to stay cool in the ninety-nine-degree heat wave. Only the little kids seemed not to mind the intense heat as they took turns shooting each other with a Super Soaker. Marco looked around, then pointed toward a raggedy setup of pink apartments that should have been ripped down ages ago.

"Pull around the back, man. I know that nicca at home, but he's gonna try to play me. Just gonna surprise his fat ass," Marco said. "Now this is what I want y'all to do: Junnie, you stay with me; Malcolm, you and Chico go up there, knock on the door, and I want y'all to ask for this nicca named Wesley. Then you tell 'em, Marco wants to holla with 'em, aight?"

"Aight, that's cool," Malcolm said.

Chico was really quiet, not sure how he should respond to Marco. He glanced pensively at Malcolm as he pulled the car to a slow halt. After nodding to Marco they both got out the vehicle and made their way up the trash-cluttered, metal stairway.

"Man, what we doin' here? This ain't even our biz. This is just too wild for me," said Chico.

"Yeah, it is our biz. Marco is cool peeps; you just have to know how to deal wit' him, you know?"

"This ain't none of our business, I'm telling you," Chico insisted. "Besides, how would you know how to deal with him? You don't know him any better than I do."

Malcolm gestured for him to quiet down, then tapped on the door as they looked down to the balcony below. Chico noticed Marco and Junnie waiting for a signal, with Marco's ever-present ivory cane waiting on the sideline.

A heavyset, brown-skinned, baldheaded brotha opened the door. "Yeah? What can I do for ya?" he asked, as he eyed both guys suspiciously.

"Yo, we looking for this dude name Wesley. He here?" Malcolm asked.

"And who wants to know?"

"Marco wants to know," said Chico, noticing that this bruh fitted the slight description Marco had given them. "Would that be you?"

Suddenly with a loud bang, the door shut hard on Malcolm's hand.

"Oh shit! cried Malcolm, grabbing his smashed hand. "Get that nicca!"

Giving the door two hard-left kicks, Chico felt it give way with a loud thump. He worked his way in the apartment house, soon to hear Marco and Junnie running up the stairs behind them.

"What happened?" Marco asked. "Where'd he go?"

"He's in there," Chico nodded toward the inside of the apartment.

"Aight. See this fool wanna make things hard. Hey, where you at, Wesley?" Marco called out as he stepped inside the apartment. Malcolm, Chico and Junnie stood closely behind him. "Hey, Wes, you know wassup, man. I just wanna talk to you, aight? Don't play me, man; don't make me have to search for your ass."

All four guys looked around the quiet apartment, with no signs of Wesley. Suddenly a shadow from behind a curtain alerted them to his presence. The sound of a scuffle soon could be heard throughout the room, ending with Malcolm and Chico holding Wesley hard against the floor.

"Hold him tight." Marco said, as he quietly leaned down at Wesley. "See, what's so crazy about this is now I don't even have to ask you if you have my money or my product. 'Cuz I know you don't with you trying to run and all. Now I don' told you, not to fuck me. Do you realize how painful that is for a man?"

"I've been trying to get your money, Marco! Come on, you gotta give me more time, aight?!" Wesley begged. Fear caused his voice to rise and tremble.

Marco brought the shiny ivory cane up to Wesley's lips, motioning for Malcolm and Chico to hold him even tighter. With one swift movement of that cane, Wesley's mouth was a bloody pulp.

"I *gots* to give you more time? Pardna, the only *thang* Marco *gots* to do in this world is eat, piss, shit and die, you got that? And it's just so happens that your time is up, my brotha…so rest…in…peace."

Marco rose up with his eyes never leaving Wesley's. "Junnie, smoke this piece of shit."

Junnie's eyes widened as Chico's heart quickened.

"Man, what's wrong with you? Do it!" Marco screamed. "You got the heat. Nicca, do it!"

Junnie aimed at Wesley. His hands were shaking. Suddenly Marco grabbed the gun from him. "You slow as shit. I'll do it myself." He aimed.

Chico closed his eyes to what he knew was coming, then opened them when he instead heard nothing.

Marco laughed crazily at Wesley. "Silly, nicca, I was just fuckin' witcha! That piece ain't even loaded," he said to Junnie.

Junnie's hands were shaking. "I swear I thought I had loaded it!"

"Oh, you thought it was loaded?"

Suddenly Wesley jumped up and kicked Malcolm, hitting him with such force that he flew back and hit the floor with a thud. He then ran for the door. Malcolm was able to reach around and grab Wesley by the ankles, which brought him tumbling down like the Jolly Green Giant. Once he was grounded, Marco started beating him viciously with his cane.

"See, I told you I was just fuckin' with you, but you have to get all crazy, right?" Bringing the cane down hard against him, Marco screamed to Wesley, "Don't you ever play with my money again, you hear me?!"

Without warning Wesley grabbed the cane from Marco, then stabbed the sharp end into his upper arm. Marco screamed out. Chico jumped at the scream, and moved quickly to quiet him. Wesley grabbed Chico's hand that held his .38. They wrestled back and forth with it. Chico jerked at the loud pop sound. It was loud and deafening, and seemed to echo throughout the tiny apartment. It seemed to him that it had all happened in slow motion. Splattered blood and brains were everywhere. Smoke seemed to radiate from the hole in Wesley's head as his dead eyes looked blankly in Marco's face. He fell back with a thud.

Somehow Chico could hear voices coming from two different directions. He could hear Malcolm's voice as he said, "Oh, shit, Chico! Oh shit! That nicca is *FUCKED UP!*" He could also hear Marco's demanding voice saying, "Let's roll! Let's roll!"

Chico looked up at Junnie, who shook his head and looked back at him in utter disbelief before also rushing out the apartment. But the loudest voice he heard as he followed his boys down the stairway was the voice of Elizabeth Grayson, and the words he used to hear all the time growing up: *"God's gonna ask it back from you, baby; everything you do, God's gonna ask it back from you..."* Her words seemed to echo, again...and again in Chico's ears.

When they got back into the car, all was quiet. Hearts were beating fast. Everyone was trying to absorb individually what had happened.

Marco looked at Chico as they got in the car. "Damn! What happened, man? I hadn't really planned taking him out, but damn!" He pulled his bloodied hand back from his forearm, which was bleeding profusely.

"That looks bad, Marco. You need to have that looked at, yo," Malcolm said.

"Yea, imma do that." He sighed and laid his head back against the seat. "That shit was wild." He looked over at Junnie. "Junnie, you was funny as hell. *I thought it had bullets,*" he mocked. "And you should have seen the look on your face when I told you to kick it to ol' boy." Marco laughed, then cringed as pain from his wound flashed through his arm.

Junnie didn't look like he found it as funny. He shook his head at Marco, then looked toward Chico. "You aight, man?"

"Yea, he's okay, just all shook up. Right, bruh?" Malcolm said. "Yo! How did it feel to pop that nigga? That shit was straight outta *Scarface.* BAM!!" he said, mockingly moving his hands in a gun shape.

Chico was still silent.

"I gotta admit, you surprised me how quick and easy you did that. That's what I need, somebody who can be quick on his feet, and not chicken out when you have to do what you gotta do. Besides, that was Wes' fault for trying to take your piece from you," Marco said to Chico approvingly. He looked down at the blood and tissue covering Chico's clothes. "You look like you been in a war. Need to get you cleaned up before your mama sees ya."

The conversation seemed to go on without Chico thinking or feeling anything, only hearing his mama's words…

Long, long ago when I was small, I remember the solitude…
Swiping gummy balls at the mall…
He'll ask it back from you…
When throwing rocks at passing cars and lying of what you do…
Six words are heard unfailingly…
He'll ask it back from you…
A shrouded cheat sheet in my desk; the consequences that ensued…
Still left me illiterate to the fact,
He'll ask it back from you…
Older and older as I became…my sins they grew and grew…
To Mama's words I became enslaved…
He'll ask it back from you…
My disgrace has escalated; commandment number six is through…
For now my fear and trepidation tells me…
God will ask it back from you…

When the car stopped in front of Marco's townhouse, Chico looked down at his bloody clothes and suddenly began to vomit uncontrollably.

"Do you have mustard to go with this?" a customer asked Asha as she looked down at her freshly baked pretzel.

"Sorry, we ain't got no mustard."

"How y'all gonna sell hot pretzels with no mustard?" the woman grumbled, giving Asha a nasty look as she walked away.

"Old heffa," Asha mumbled to herself.

"Now that ain't no way to treat a customer."

Asha turned around at the familiar voice. She felt herself immediately stiffen. It was Peanut, smiling down at her as if nothing bad had ever happened between them. She turned back around and started refilling the pretzel carousel, trying her best to ignore him.

"So whas' been up, baby?" he said cheerfully.

"Nuttin' up."

"Nuttin' up? Aight. So, did you miss me?" Peanut leaned against the counter, giving Asha a heated stare.

She noticed that his face still held the bruises from his fight with Chico. Sighing as he watched her, Asha mistakenly dropped the sleeve of cups she was stacking.

"Oops!" Peanut said, smiling at her.

"Peanut, would you please leave? I'm at work and I have a lot to do, and I don't feel like talking to you right now."

"Girl, I've been trying to call you for the past two days, and your mama always saying you ain't at home, or you busy. Now either she lying for you or you don' found another nicca to take my place. So which one is it?"

Asha could tell Peanut was getting antsy. His voice rose and fell as he spoke. Just as she was about to answer him, a customer walked up. She felt relief flowing through her; she was happy for a reprieve.

"Can I help you?" she asked the short, white man, who took his place behind Peanut.

"I think he was first," the man said.

"Naw, it's okay," Asha assured him. "He don't want nuttin'."

"Yea, I do," Peanut announced. "I'll take a twelve-pack of pretzel sticks, with pizza sauce and nacho cheese."

"Aight." Asha swallowed hard, then got busy with the pretzel sticks. Her hands shook as she prepared them. She handed Peanut the pretzels sticks and sauce. "That's four dollars and seventy-five cents," she said.

"Damn, girl, that's steep!"

"Four dollars and seventy-five cents, please…" Asha's eyebrows rose.

The customer behind Peanut looked at both of them with amusement as if he could sense animosity.

"Here you go," Peanut said, as he handed Asha the money. His hand lingered a bit in hers.

"Hey, Asha, you can go home now. I'll finish cleaning up here," Asha's boss called from the back.

"All right. Let me finish up with this customer and I'm out."

Asha looked up at Peanut's smiling face. He pointed toward the benches down the mall floor. *"Be waiting for you,"* he mouthed.

After waiting on her final customer, and making sure she took her time to avoid Peanut as long as possible, Asha counted out her draw, and clocked out. The whole time her eyes kept being drawn to Peanut. She had promised herself that she was done with him, and was gonna move on and focus more on her senior year at school instead of dealing with his abusive ass. But even with the promises she had made to herself she couldn't slow down the fast beat of her heart whenever she thought of him. She couldn't keep her mind or eyes off him as he sat casually on the bench eating his pretzel sticks.

Peanut wasn't the best-looking guy she had ever dated, although he had a body that would put Shemar Moore to shame. But what had grabbed her most about him was the way he treated her. That is before he started slapping her around. It hadn't always been that way. She could vividly remember when they first met. She was at a party with her cousin Jenene. He had walked up to her, smiled and introduced himself as Tony Innis, but cockily announced that his friends called him Peanut. Jenene had laughed later, saying that with that big ass head she couldn't see why they called him Peanut, unless it had something to do with the size of his balls. Basically, Jenene never liked him. But Asha knew that if she had even an inkling of some of the things that had happened between them, her cousin would dislike him even more.

After grabbing her purse Asha closed the door to the pretzel bar. She took a deep breath and started toward Peanut. He stood up as she got nearer.

"Took you long enough," he said. "But that's aight, you're worth it."

Asha stopped in front of him, eyeing him suspiciously. "Peanut, why you trying to be all nice all of a sudden?"

"You mean why am I not pissed off that you sicced Chico and Malcolm on me?"

"I didn't sic anybody on you," Asha spat out.

Peanut laughed. "Yeah right. Anyhow, I'm always nice to you, Asha. I mean I know we have our bad times, but doesn't everyone?" He noted Asha's hard stance. "I love you, girl. You know I do."

"Love ain't s'pose to hurt, Peanut. Love ain't s'pose to make you feel like nothing…" Asha surprised herself as she repeated the words her mother had said to her days before. *Oh God*, she thought, *I'm turning into my mother!*

"Oh, so I make you feel like that?"

Asha closed her eyes. She loved him so much. Why couldn't she just be like her mom and make herself hate him? Her eyes stayed closed even as she felt Peanuts lips kissing slowly down her neck and his arms wrapped loosely around her waist.

"Peanut, we're in the mall, and people are looking at us," she whispered.

"Then let's go. Come on, Asha. I miss you and I'm sorry and it won't ever happen again. I promise, okay?"

She looked at him, feeling herself weakening. She knew she shouldn't believe him, but still, maybe, just maybe…She didn't want to be like her mom, old and alone, manless. Shoot, she was seventeen, this was prom year coming up, she loved Peanut, she…she…He kissed her again behind her ear, which was her hot spot.

She gave in.

CHAPTER SIX:
JUST LIKE THAT...

The late August air was suffocating and dense as Liz Grayson hung clothes out on the back line. Sweat dripped down her tired face. Her days were so long. Very rarely could she keep up with Asha long enough to get her to help much around the house. And Sean, she basically had just given up on him altogether when it came to housework. She hadn't seen her son in three days, and it had almost become a habit of always having to track him down just to know for sure that he was alive and breathing.

"Liz!" came an urgent shout from the project house next door. Liz sighed, feeling too tired to deal with the tirades of her longtime neighbor, Mrs. Warren. Not that she didn't appreciate all the times Mrs. Warren had kept her eyes on the kids while she worked. But sometimes she got the feeling that Asha and Sean were right when they said that Mrs. Warren got great pleasure out of exposing any wrongdoing she saw. Liz was torn between wanting to know when they did something wrong, but at the same time, felt the need to jump to their defense.

"Liz!" Mrs. Warren called out again. "Did you hear on the news about that drug bust in Highland Park? They rounded up about fifteen colored boys in the paddy wagon."

Liz had been listening to the radio, and the easy sounds of Smokey Robinson on the old school station. Usually nothing and nobody could pull her away from Smokey Robinson, but her ears perked up at Mrs. Warren's words.

"What did they arrest the boys for?" she asked, as she turned the radio down.

"Drugs. You know how those no good boys over there are. My cousin told me that even over on Chamberlayne they found this dead body in the apartments across the street from her. It's just getting bad I tell ya. Kids just don't care about nothing I tell ya."

"When did they find the body?" Liz asked.

"A few days ago. A young man, shot in the head." Mrs. Warren shook her head in disgust as she opened up her container of powdered snuff and sprinkled some on her tongue. Liz fought the desire to gag. Whenever she saw Mrs.

Warren using the powdered tobacco it reminded her of her grandmother from Stony Creek, and how she would always get her and Delores to empty her spit can as she gummed the foul substance.

"You outta keep betta tabs on that boy of yours, Liz. I haven't seen him around here for a while. You never know what kids getting into these days."

Liz cleared her throat, shook the pillowcase that she was about to hang on the line and turned her back slightly. "Well, Sean is fine," she mumbled.

"Hmph! Well, when I was raising my kids, we kept our boys busy working. They didn't have time to hang out in the streets, selling drugs or getting into God knows what other troubles."

"Well, thanks for you concern, Mrs. Warren, but as I said, Sean is fine. He's been staying with a friend of his overnight."

Liz knew that was a big lie. She actually had not a clue as to where her son was, but she'd be damned if she was gonna let Mrs. Warren know that. Looking over at Mrs. Warren, her face got heated at her knowing gaze. Just as she was about to reinforce her words, she could hear the sounds of a car pulling up around the front. She excused herself, then headed around to see who it was. When she saw Sean's butt poking out of a blue vehicle, she felt her foot burning to give it a swift kick!

"Hey, Ma," he sung out, as he walked toward the front door.

Liz quietly steamed inside like a tea kettle as he got closer. He seemed to walk slower than he normally did, watching her cautiously.

Along with her son was Malcolm Tyler, his best friend, whom she had known and watched grow along with Sean since they were both of a wee age. But right now she could feel no maternal affection for either of them, and was quite sure her eyes were letting them know that.

"Where in the world have you been?!"

"Aww, Ma, chill out. It's all good."

"Calm down?" A look of shock and rage swept over Liz Grayson's face. She was suddenly going upside Sean's head with a vengeance, screaming as she went. "Have you lost your dangone mind, boy?! Don't you ever in your life talk to me like that again!" she yelled, giving a slap per each word and syllable.

"Damn, aight. I'm sorry!" Chico covered his head with his hands.

"And don't you be damning the Lord!"

"I didn't damn no Lord. You trippin'. Dang I'm sorry!"

"Get in the house. Now! And you go home, Malcolm, 'cuz your grandma is looking for you, too. You boys think you so grown, think you know it all, and don't know nothing! What in the world can y'all be doing in the streets all...night...long, and never coming home?"

Chico frowned at Malcolm as he laughed. "Ah, man, look at your mama kickin' yo butt in public!" He tried to still his laugh at the look on Ms. Grayson's face. "Aight, Ma Grayson, I'm leaving now! Ah ha! Go get your whipping, boy!" He laughed as he jumped in the half-moving vehicle. "See ya!"

Chico walked quietly into his room, conscious of his mama slowly walking behind him.

"Who was that driving that car?" she asked.

"Just a friend of ours. This dude named Marco."

"Uh-huh...and just who is *this Marco?* Does he live around here?"

Taking a deep breath, he slowly removed his Nikes and socks. The bed gave way to his mom as she sat down beside him. He breathed deeply, as if knowing what was coming next.

"Sean..." she said. "What are you doing, honey? What have you and Malcolm been up to for the past couple of days?"

"Won't doin' nuttin."

"You weren't doing *anything?*"

"We weren't doing anything, aight? All right? I mean, we weren't doing anything. Dang..." Chico squirmed uncomfortably, looking from his mom to the key chain he was tossing around in his hands.

"You better calm down the attitude," she warned.

Liz looked at the braids trailing to Chico's shoulders, then reached out to finger the fine baby hair that peeped out from his hairline. She remembered well the curls that once graced his head as a child. She secretly wished back to those safe, innocent days when she always knew where he was and what he was up to. Back then the biggest problem she seemed to have was when he would dump all the cereal out of the box of Fruity Pebbles to get to that one little plastic top at the bottom of it. Then having to play referee as he and Asha fought over whose turn it was to get the toy. Those special yesterdays seemed to have disappeared... *just like that.*

"Don't you realize how much I worry about you? The streets are so dangerous, Sean. And Richmond is getting worse and worse. Every time you turn around some young boy or girl is found dead in the streets. Mrs. Warren was just telling me before you got here how they found someone dead in the apartments over on Chamberlayne Avenue."

Chico's eyes widened. "Yea?"

"Yes! And I don't want that to happen to you. Don't you realize how much I love you?" Liz sighed at the obstinate expression on her son's face. "I'm not stupid, Sean...I *feel* things. I know when something is not right with you. You are my child. Look at me!" she said, grabbing his chin to turn his face toward hers. "What is it out there that you want, Sean? Do you really think I don't know about the streets? That I'm that ignorant to what goes on? I have to know, because I have to be both mother and father to you; it's my job to be informed."

"Yeah and why is that? Punk nigga doin' whateva while we sit here in this gutter hole, I hate his guts, and I hate this place!" he said angrily.

Liz shook her head, watching the heated emotions on her child's face. "Where is all this anger for your father coming from? Where is all this anger coming from period?"

"It's not about anger, Ma. I just need to do what I need to get us out of here!"

"Yeah and what's that? What do you feel you need to do?"

"Get us out of here, just like I said. I mean why we have to be scraping and other people living all good?" Chico asked hotly.

"Your father did send a check the other day, Sean. I don't always tell you when he does, but then again that's not for you to know or judge. You have no right to judge him. I know it's hard not getting to see him, but..."

"Yeah whateva, he still don't care nuttin'...*nothinggggg*, about me, about you, or Asha either for that matter." Chico let out a frustrated sigh. "Forget it. I don't care anyhow...it's all good. I don't want to see him anyhow."

"It's all good, huh? Yes, you do care. Because if you didn't you wouldn't be talking like you are. But that has nothing to do with you staying out for days at a time. See you trying to be slick and change the subject. But I mean it, Sean. I don't like it, not one tiny bit. Your father being absent doesn't mean you have an excuse for yourself, nor an excuse for getting mixed up with what you know to be wrong."

"I'm not doing anything wrong," he insisted.

"Listen," Liz cut in, "Sean, you reap what you sow always."

"Well, I ain't sowing nothing, so I ain't reaping nothing..." he replied.

The stubborn look on her son's face told her she wasn't getting through to him. She could see it in the golden flicks of his eyes the anger, the pain aimed solely at his father. She had met the kids' father while working at Miller and Rhodes over seventeen years ago. There seemed to be an instant attraction, despite the racial differences. It was an attraction that both of them fought hard to ignore, especially Liz. She knew that her family and friends would see it as a crazy phase and totally forbidden, yet that was nothing in comparison to how his family saw it. When they found out she was pregnant they moved him to California. She didn't hear from him again until the twins were four years old. She still remembered how upset Robert, their father, had been when he reached out to pick Sean up and Sean had run behind the sofa clinging to her legs in fear. Since then his visits and even his support checks were few and far between. His lack of interest seemed to affect Sean moreso then Asha. This was not so difficult to understand, seeing he was a boy. And boys, well...boys needed their daddies. And even though he would die before admitting it she knew that Sean needed his, too.

"Okay...have it your way. I'm not going to say another word to you about it," she said as she got up from the bed. She slowly made her way to the door, then looked back after a moment. "Sean?"

"Yea?" Chico looked up at his mother.

"I don't want to see you on the news. I don't want to see you in a body bag. I don't want to bury you." Liz waited to see if her words had registered to him, then slowly shut the door.

CHAPTER SEVEN:
JUST ANOTHER DAY AROUND DA WAY...

Summer break left as it came, with a bang. Hanging at the playground and shooting hoops was the natural way to kill time in Highland Park. The courts were crowded with neighborhood wannabe Michael Jordans, struggling to better their game. For most of the male children raised by single mothers, balling was the only escape they had to get from behind the invisible bars trapping them in their insane ghetto world. If you saw a park or playground it would always be filled with dreaming superstars. Further down Brooklyn Park Boulevard could be seen the more fortunate kids in the neighborhood could be seen rolling around, showing off their rides. Then there were the young, single mothers strolling alongside the loud woofer-laced vehicles, rolling their baby strollers.

Asha Grayson laxed back on the park bench, bobbing her head to the slow jam, "Differences" by Ginuwine that was poppin' on her mobile CD player. She smiled as she watched the tall, sexy moves of the Highland Park brothas, always having preferred this side of town over Church Hill. The guys were oh so fine. Tall, dark and juicy is the way she would describe them to her cousin Jenene, who lived right off Groveland Avenue.

"Oh, gurl, this is my song," she hummed, bobbing her head and shoulders. "Ginuwine is fine, too."

"Naw," Jenene said. "He a lil too pretty for me; I like ruff-riders, ghetto-looking brothas like..."

"Pleazzzzzze, don't say Malcolm!" Asha exclaimed. "That Negro don't look like no ruff rider. He looks like a fool, chile!"

Jenene giggled. "Well, he's cute to me. And I know you ain't talking wit' that old Peanut head you messin' wit'."

"Well, Peanut is good at other thangs." Asha winked.

"What–ev–errrrr..."

Asha snickered, looked around at the ball players again and took a sip of her Nehi grape soda. She particularly noticed the brotha who seemed to be making all the baskets. "Ummmm...Who is that sexy Grant Hill-looking bruth...aaa, Jenene?" she asked, licking her lips.

"Who?"

"Right...*there*," Asha moaned.

"You mean Orlando?"

"Oh, is that his name? Mmm...he fine as hell." Noting the hysterical laughter of her cousin, Asha stared at her blankly and said, "What?"

"Oh, my gawd no, chile. That's Poochie's man visiting her from D.C. So unless you wanna rumble with her, you best to step back!"

"D.C., huh?" Asha said with a smirk. "I can do dat. How long he down here for?"

"Don't matter how long. Peanut is gonna kick your ass if you don't keep your eyes in your head."

"Ha!" Asha snorted. "I ain't thinking 'bout Peanut. That Negro don't own me. The only thing he can do is kiss and lick this ass..."

"Ewww, I know you joking."

"Look, I told you before, Peanut be all up in da mix, gurl," she said salaciously. "That shit be so good my toes be *curlingggggg!*"

"Hmm," Jenene hummed. "I wonder..."

"Don't just wonder, chile; get you a brotha who ain't scurred of da kat, that's all."

"Well, Malcolm ain't scared of it, but he ain't all nasty like that funky Peanut." Jenene smiled. Asha put her hand up in a "talk to the hand" fashion, and rolled her neck.

"Man, learn how to dribble a damn ball, aight?!" a voice screamed.

Both girls eyed the guy in question, dunking basket after basket. His smooth brown skin seemed to sparkle in the sun, complementing his young muscular physique perfectly. Suddenly the ball rolled near their bench, and the guy that Jenene had called Orlando was running over to grab it. As he bent down to pick up the ball, his eyes slowly worked their way up two pairs of feminine legs, a pair of mocha-brown ones, and a pair of light-toffee ones. As he moved up further, his eyes meshed with Asha's.

"Hey there, sexy," she said, smiling seductively at him.

"Sup," Orlando crooned back, as he looked her up and down.

Jenene cleared her throat, trying to grab Asha's attention. She could see there was *trouble* brewing if her cousin continued in her "steal your man" attitude.

"Well, we need to go, Asha. Remember we're supposed to meet Chico and Malcolm at Whataburger at three," she reminded her.

The mention of Chico and Malcolm seemed to wake Orlando up from his seemingly fascination with the sultry sistah in front of him. His eyes moved toward Jenene, in question.

"You mean Chico Grayson?"

"Yeah, why?"

"So you know him?"

"Know him? That's my cousin, and her twin," Jenene said, nodding her head over at Asha.

"Whoa! I've been trying to hook up wit' that nicca all day! So where's he at right now?"

Asha's expression suddenly changed to one of caution. "Excuse me, but do you mind telling me why you want him?"

"Oh, so brotherman answers to his sister?" Noting the look on Asha's face, he laughed and said, "Okay, listen. He knows me. We've talked on the phone and made plans to get up this weekend to do some business, aight?"

"So let me get this straight. You made plans and talked on the phone, and yet you don't know where he is? No address? Nada? Hmm..." she said, scratching her head. "Something don't sound right, my brothaaaa."

Orlando looked at Asha appreciatively. She flushed at the look in his eyes.

"Baby, believe me I'm not out here to hurt your brother. He gave me an address. 5607 Q Street is where he said he would be. I stopped by there earlier, but there wasn't anyone there. So...I bounced on over here to kick a few baskets. Which was smart seeing that I ran into a fine ass sistah like you." He winked at her.

Asha blushed, then looked toward her cousin. Jenene's eyes slowly read: *playa, playa*. They both looked back at Orlando.

"Hold up," Jenene said, taking Asha aside for a private word.

"Gurl, what you think?" she whispered.

"I don't know, I mean he seems okay. You did say he was that girl Poochy's man?" asked Asha. "I'm gonna call Chico on his celly and see if he knows him."

Jenene gave Asha the evil eye.

"What?"

"Hmph!" she said. "I'm just wondering what that bad news bear brother of yours is up to for you to be feeling like you have to check to make sure people are who they say they are. It just don't sound right to me."

Just then a dark blue SUV pulled up with Chico behind the wheel, and Malcolm in the passenger seat. Both had huge grins on their faces.

"Yo! Whut up, shawty?" Malcolm hollered out to Jenene.

She looked down, having a hard time keeping the smile from breaking out on her face.

The music from the SUV drowned out the sounds of Asha's Sanyo CD player. Sounds of Ja Rule and J.Lo were so loud, the ground felt as though it was shimmering.

Chico leaned over to the left window. "Bling! Bling!"

"Oh, my, gosh! Where'd you get this ride, Chico?" Asha screamed, circling around to view the back.

"That's right," Chico said, smiling as he hopped out. "It's all mine, in da clear, bab-bee!"

A look of disbelief coated Asha's face. "You are lying! Who did y'all jack this off of? Mama's gonna kick your ass."

"Jack shit, girl. This is mine. Bought and paid for. See, I handle my biz. A 2001 Ford Escape," he said with a cocky grin. "Come on, get in. I'll show you the inside, then we can go for a spin."

Asha giggled as she quickly jumped inside the vehicle.

Malcolm, who had spotted Jenene's smiling face, jumped out the car and landed quickly beside her. "So wassup, baby?" he whispered in her ear.

"If you don't stop! Ain't nuttin' up with you," she said sassily, rolling her neck and pushing his hands aside.

"Yea, okay." Malcolm laughed and slapped her on the behind. "Let's go. I got sumpin' for your lil ass."

"Hey," a voice cut in.

Nobody seemed to notice Orlando standing quietly in the background. He cleared his throat to get a notice, and all eyes turned toward him.

"Yo, what can I do for you, man?" asked Chico. The past few weeks working with Marco had taught him to be careful of everyone.

"You're Chico, right? We hollered on the phone earlier. I'm Big O," he said, reaching out for quick daps.

Both Chico's and Malcolm's faces lit up a bit when they recognized the brotha better known as Big O giving him a smile of recognition. "D.C. in da house! Hell yeah, we straight then. Wassup, dawg?"

"Man, just looking for you all over the place."

Chico and Malcolm gave Orlando daps, then walked off with him in private convo.

Asha caught Jenene's eye and shook her hair slightly. Jenene sighed in silent agreement. Each felt an odd, impending feeling of danger, from this new character known as Big O.

"So who is this guy?" Asha asked Chico, as they pulled into a set of Northside town homes.

"I told you. I'm doing some jobs for him."

"And what kind of jobs, Chico? Especially that would pay the money for a whip like this!" She pointed to his SUV.

"Stop buggin', girl," Chico said as he jumped out.

Asha followed suit, still sighing, and then trailed him to the front door.

"It was easy finding this joint," Orlando said.

He had followed them over from the park. Jenene and Malcolm had decided to lazy around at her place. Asha could only imagine what that lazying around would be all about.

The music screamed from the windows and door of the townhouse. Asha walked inside slowly, keep a close eye on her brother who was busy giving daps and high-fives to other unknowns. After about an hour of this, and listening to meaningless convo, she made her way to the kitchen for another wine cooler. She thought that she would give Chico twenty more minutes, then demand that he take her home.

"Malcolm!" Asha screamed as the front door opened wide.

Not able to get an audible word in edgewise over the loud, screaming rap tunes, Asha walked over and yanked on Malcolm's jersey urgently.

"Where's Jenene?" she asked him.

"Sorry, boo, she said she didn't feel like coming. But she told me to tell you to give her a ring."

"Ugh! I'm gonna kill her! I would neva have come over here with you guys if I knew she wasn't coming!"

"Well, I don't know," Malcolm said, shrugging his shoulders.

Asha looked around her. There were mostly guys, and a couple of hoochie mamas in da house, but she was straight up ready to go, and quickly walked over to her brother to let him know it.

"Chico, I wanna go home."

Chico turned around, looking at his twin through beer-dazed eyes. "Aight, I'll take you in a short."

"No, now!" Asha huffed.

"Look, girl, we just got here, okay?"

"Hey, Chico, I'll take your sister home if you want."

Both Asha and Chico looked up. Orlando smiled down at Asha, then moved his eyebrows up and down slowly.

"You sure, man? Cuz I wanna hang around here for a while," Chico said.

"Yeah I can take her, as long as she ain't scurred of me."

"I'm not scared of nobody," Asha hummed, giving him a challenging look.

Both he and Chico laughed.

"Okay, let's go then."

Ten minutes later as they rode down Laburnum Avenue, Asha fought hard not to appear fidgety or uncomfortable around Orlando. It was funny. Around Jenene, flirting at the park things had been fine and dandy, but alone with him she couldn't find a thing to say. She jumped at the sudden lightning streak that flashed in the sky.

"Whoa!" Orlando exclaimed. "Looks like we're gonna have a storm."

"Yea…"

Pausing at the light, Orlando's eyes rested softly on Asha, catching her own. She was about to look away before he reached out and took her hand in his.

"So as fine as you are, you have to have a nicca out here claiming you, right?" he said.

"I'm not claimable," Asha said confidently.

"Oh, is that right?"

"Yep."

She thought about Peanut, then looked again into Orlando's oh so deep eyes, and quickly dismissed her guilty thoughts as they continued on to her place.

Lightning flashed again as she opened the door to Orlando's car. Her heart lurched. One thing Asha hated was being alone at home in a thunderstorm, and Chico didn't look like he was coming home anytime soon. She knew her mom hadn't long gone off to her second job. She was surprised to feel Orlando walking up behind her. She looked up at him questioningly.

"Just making sure you're safe and sound," he said.

Orlando caught her eye and smiled.

"Um...thanks."

Asha looked up at him again, at his cute smiling face, then fiddled with her keys to open the door. Just as she got it open she felt Orlando's lips moving sensually against the back of her neck, causing goose pimples to break out all over her body. His hands encircled her waist as he pressed against her backside. Thunder meshed with lightning caused her to jump again, or maybe it was Orlando's hot tongue.

"Can I come in?" he whispered in her ear.

Asha knew she should have said no, but instead she said nothing at all. She simply walked inside with Orlando following close behind. She inched her way away from him slightly, and swallowed. Orlando swung her around and covered her mouth with his all in one step. Asha moaned as his tongue filled her mouth, stroking the roof of it.

"We shouldn't even be doin' this," she said, gasping when she could finally catch her breath.

Orlando pulled her tight against him and started grinding hard and squeezing her full behind. She moaned again.

"I don't even know you," she said weakly.

"You know me enough to know you want this. Come on, you know you feeling it, boo..."

Asha couldn't even muster up enough strength to respond. She was in a sexual daze as Orlando pulled her down to the rug-covered floor, inched her short skirt up over her hips; dazed as he started pulling her panties down with his teeth; dazed even more as his light kisses between her legs became deep, and slurping and devouring. Her mind slipped as he slipped inside her, not even thinking about the fact that this was a guy she didn't know, that she had just met, and that he didn't wear a condom.

CHAPTER EIGHT:
MONEY, DOUBT AND CIRCUMSTANCE...

"Damn, what took you so long, bruh?" Chico asked, as Orlando drifted into the room.

"I got lost, yo. I don't get to Richmond much. I know you was worried about your ride, right?" he said, laughing.

"Hell yeah!" Chico laughed back.

"That's all good and well," Marco cut in, "but we have things to discuss."

He walked slowly into the den, dressed to the max as always.

Chico felt a slight dizziness come over him. He had downed more beer and rum and Cokes than he realized. The blunts he had smoked hadn't helped any either. But he was happy for a lot of reasons, one being the tight-ass Escape Marco had gotten for him. (He had said it was a gift for a job well done.)

The party Marco had hosted started to fade out. Everyone was having their fill of food, drink and hot hoochies stripping on the kitchen table. Marco had ushered Chico, Malcolm, Junnie and finally Big O into his bedroom to discuss their planned trip to D.C.—what would be the guy's first out-of-town weapons sale. His clique, the Black Angels, who controlled much of the Southeast side of D.C., had sent Orlando to pan out a deal with Marco.

"So," Marco said, addressing Big O, "explain to me why the BA clique felt it necessary to send you all the way down here just to have my boys have to drive all the way back to D.C. instead of you bringing the money with you?"

"You know how it is, man. They wanted me to make sure everything was on the up and up."

"Oh, so what you saying is that they feel I can't be trusted?"

Big O opened his arms wide, and shook his head. "I don't know much about that, Marco. They sent me here, told me to get things set up, meet your boys and bring them back for the exchange. Now if you want me to contact them and let them know you aren't happy about how things are going down, I can do that, yo." He waved toward Chico and Malcolm. "We got along fine though, at least I think so. Right, Chico?"

Chico nodded in agreement. He was right in one thing that so far there didn't seem to be any reason to think that the deal had anything fishy behind it.

Marco was quiet for a moment, looking at Big O somberly. "Okay then," he finally said. "This is what we're gonna do." He walked around his waterbed and flopped down on the edge of it. "You guys take that drive tomorrow with Orlando, and call me as soon as y'all got the money." He looked toward Orlando again. "You give your peeps a message for me though. You tell them, intense love, don't creep in the shadows."

"Whas' that suppose to mean?" Big O asked.

"They'll understand what I'm saying. Just tell 'em that."

"Aight, man, no problem," Big O responded.

Marco then brought his beer can up in a toast. "Here's to a long and prosperous working relationship with the Black Angels."

"Long and prosperous," they all echoed.

"Well, I don't care, Chico, if you going, I'm going!"

"Damn!" Chico growled, looking at Candy in frustration. "Why you trippin' like this, girl?"

"Because I miss you, Chico," she moaned.

Chico looked behind him toward his SUV where Malcolm and Big O sat waiting. He had decided to stop by Candy's house before they headed to D.C. since he knew she was upset about their canceled date the night before—upset with him period, about what she described as his off-the-wall behavior for the past few weeks.

"Don't you miss me?" she asked pleadingly.

Chico could tell from the grin on their faces that his boys had heard what she had said. He looked away from them, nodding slightly at Candy.

"So what does that mean? Either you miss me, or you don't," she said, pouting.

"I do, Candy. Come on now don't be like this!"

"Then let me come with you."

Chico sighed. "I can't. I have so much to do. It wouldn't be any fun for you anyhow."

"Hey, Chico," Big O hollered from the car. Both Chico and Candy looked in his direction. "Let her come, man. What we have to do will only take a while. Then y'all can tour D.C. or something."

"See!" Candy exclaimed.

"Okay," Chico relented. "Go and get your things. We'll be waiting for you."

Candy smiled one of her famous cheesy grins and skitted back into the house. Chico looked toward her and sighed, then walked over to his vehicle.

"I don't want my girl finding out my business, O. So how are we s'pose to do all this with her around?"

"All I'm saying is that I know how it is with women. I have women here and in D.C., man. The best way to keep 'em happy is to avoid any unnecessary static. It won't take us any time to do what we need to do, and then you can show her around town or something. I'm just looking around your welfare, my man," he said, slapping Chico on the back.

"Yeah, right," Chico said, smiling. "But I feel what you saying, yo."

As Candy scrambled back out the door, she winked at Chico when she slipped into the car. He couldn't help but think that maybe Big O was right. A brotha had to do what was needed to keep the little lady happy.

Candy yapped non–stop as they headed north on 95 toward D.C. Traffic seemed to be moving at a snail's pace. Even though he was always glad to make Candy smile, Chico still felt uncomfortable about having her come along with them. She had no idea of what was really going on, and that worried him. He didn't want her to know anything about his business. Chico had always been a sucker for his boo. He'd been feeling his Puerto Rican baby, Miss Candy Rosas, since sixth grade. Shy smiles and note-passing had been all he had the balls to do back then. A few years passed with Chico thinking she was way out of his league, so he was surprised when he was finally able to grab her attention almost a year ago. They had been going strong ever since.

Something else was shaking in Chico's mind. He thought about the heated discussion that he had had with his mom a couple of days back while trying to explain how he got the vehicle he was now driving. He knew she wasn't too happy with his answers, nor with what she imagined he had to do to get it. But she had left it alone like he knew she would. Chico sometimes felt guilty of taking advantage of her weariness. His mom's weariness sometimes gave him the advantage of her just dropping the battles between them rather than worrying herself to death with what he was up to. It helped for him to think that this would, in the long run, make life better for them all. In fact, his having a vehicle already did; she didn't have to catch a cab or the bus everywhere she went.

"What you thinking about so hard over there, cutie pie?" Candy whispered.

Chico blushed slightly. "Nothing, just meditating. You know how I am."

"Well, you should be meditating on me," she said as she tucked herself up close to his side.

Chico buried his face into her neck, breathed her in and tightened his arm around her. He was glad that Malcolm had agreed to drive. It gave him the space he needed to think. Somehow Chico had managed to bury the Chamberlayne Avenue incident deep inside his mind and focus more on making money. Marco had been right that it wasn't something he had deliberately done. But even if it had been, he had crossed that line of right and wrong when he had decided to work for him. So there was no turning back now nor any need to cry over shit like a lil punk. Right now they had other things to think about, namely, the weapons deal with Big O, and the Black Angels.

The back of his Escape had been packed tight with rows and rows of .38-caliber semiautomatics—enough for a mini Civil War, Big O had joked. The Black Angels knew where business was good, and had been looking all over for cheaper prices. They knew the South was where it was at, since everything there cost less, from white bread to Spaghetti-O's to 9-milli Uzis.

"Man, them niggas tried to seriously jip us in PA," Big O said. He gave an *I'm sorry* look when Malcolm nodded toward Candy, reminding him that she was with them.

Big O cleared his throat and spoke again. "So, do all three of you graduate this year?"

"Yep," Candy responded. "Fun, prom; head chiefs in charge at school; the works. What about you? Is this your year, Orlando?"

"Naw, I dropped out over two years ago. I'm a self-educated man," he said laughing.

Looking over at Candy, Chico could already see the wheels turning around in her head. She was a sucker for education with her dad being an English professor at J. Sergeant Reynolds Community College, and her mom an economics teacher at Henrico High School. Someone dropping out of school equaled *B.U.M.* to her.

"Umm…you know you could get your GED with no problem. Even maybe go to night school. Two years is not so long ago that you would have forgotten too much. It's really important that our black men be educated and knowledge-able so that they can uplift and motivate the children." She took a breath before asking, "So, why did you drop out?"

Instead of getting the answer she sought, Candy instead heard hoots and howls of masculine laughter as if they were all sharing a private male gender only joke.

"Uh-huh, and what's so funny?" she asked indignantly, looking around at the laughing faces surrounding her.

"Nuttin', baby. We just trippin wit' you." Chico laughed.

"Yeah," Malcolm said teasingly. "Yo, check this out. We black men gots to get educated for da children now; yea we gots to support and uplift da black race." He then gave both Chico and Big O a high-five, swerving slightly on the road as he did so.

Candy gave the trio a disgusted look and rolled her eyes as she said, "Y'all are just too *stoopid*, ignorant and dumb; that's a shame, *soooo...niggerish.*" She shook her head and glanced back out the window. Laughter still rang out in the dark-green Ford Escape.

After the moment of cheer wore off, Chico focused on the cars rolling speedily alongside them. They were almost to D.C., and a lot of things were starting to look more familiar to Chico. It had been a long while since he had been in the District, but he knew he still had aunts from his father's side in Silver Spring, Maryland, which wasn't too far from D.C. Chico and Asha had only been to visit that aunt three times. But even those memories weren't the best ones. He still remembered the last time they had stayed the weekend. They couldn't have been more than eight at the time. Their father, even though he hadn't been able to come around much, or either didn't want to, had come up with this grand idea for them to spend more time with his family so that they could get to know their cousins, he had said. Reluctantly their mom had agreed to those visits. One time they stayed with their Aunt Jillian. Thing is, the family on their father's side are white. Where they came from, the neighborhood, the culture, the whole atmosphere was totally different from what Chico and Asha had known in Richmond. Their Aunt Jillian always had a way of reminding them that they weren't white, and not quite right—that they were indeed black, as if they didn't know that. She had resented her brother getting involved with a black woman, and had always shown a quiet disdain in her nice nasty way for them while they were there. Especially for Chico who had been hyper as a kid, (still was actually) and had always managed to stay in some kind of trouble.

During one of their visits, she had sent both him and Asha and their cousins on the front screened-in porch to play. While out there he had found a toolbox, and being a curious kid, had gone in the bag and pulled out one of the screwdrivers and started taking some of the screws out of the porch siding. It was already coming loose a bit, but when his aunt saw what he had done, she grabbed him by the ear and whipped him with a curtain rod so intensely that it left dark bruises across his back and legs. When they got back to Virginia and his mom saw the bruises, she went off. She called their Aunt Jillian. And there ensued a verbal world war three. That had been the last visit. Somehow, it never really mattered to him. He had never felt a part of that side of the family or of his father's life—period.

Now here he was, a teenage murderer. The thoughts and guilt about what had happened in that Chamberlayne apartment hadn't left his mind. He still felt the need to scrub extra hard every time he took a shower as if that could somehow wash away the blood guilt. But then again, like Marco had said, guilt was for punks; a man got to do what a man got to do. And his deed had won him the respect of Marco and his crew, and had also earned him the Ford Escape they were now riding in. Yeah, Marco took care of his own. But he also never forgot an enemy. Chico, Malcolm and Junnie had come to realize that since dealing with him for the past four weeks. Marco saw smoking a double-crosser as just part of the business, and had let them know and witness what would happen when someone he trusted crossed him.

"Oh, shit! Turn that joint up!" hollered Big O, waking Chico from his trip down memory lane.

The sounds of Ja Rule and Case's "Livin' it Up" rang throughout as they pulled up at an apartment complex in East D.C. Candy went to open her door only to be stilled by Chico's voice. "Hey, Malcolm and O have to take his stuff up, so we can just wait in here, okay?"

"Well, why can't we go? I'd like to see your place, Orlando," Candy said.

"It's kinda messed up right now. Not fit for your pretty eyes," Big O joked. "We won't be but a minute.

Hurriedly the two guys got the suitcases and packages out of the back and made their way up the walk to his apartment.

"Hmph, that's weird. Come all this way and have to sit in the car!" Candy protested.

"But hey, look who you get to sit with." Chico kissed her behind the ear.

"Don't be trying to sweet-talk me, lil boy." Candy giggled, then puckered her lips upward to meet his, both becoming oblivious to their surroundings.

CHAPTER NINE:
STAND UP, STAND TALL, BE STRONG...

Remembering back to yesterday while just a young black boy...
Back in the days of GI Joes and wind-up little toys...
Back when we'd walk a block or two to this candy store called Granders...
Then couldn't quite make up our minds about grape or lime Nowlaters...
And every summer it never failed the crab man ruled the corner...
Get a dozen crabs for $10.75 and a big boss with your order...
But you know what I best recall uniquely most of all...
Is the voice that taught me right from wrong...
Stand up, stand tall...be strong...
Her strong voice followed everywhere my hyper feet would walk...
Down Broad Street, 24th and 3rd for our son and mother talks...
So many times when things got rough and the streets would seem to mold me...
She'd snatch me up and get real tough while giving me what I would need...
She made up ten-fold best she could for that absentee called Dad.
When it came to teaching the birds and bees my mom gave all she had...
Now the love in her voice blows in the wind follows me as a man...
"Don't ever let them get you down, son, be the best you can"...
And whenever things get really hard and trials seem extra long...
I think back to those model words...
Stand up, stand tall...be strong...

Tears streamed down Liz Grayson's eyes as she read her son's latest words in his poetry notebook. She knew he'd never share it, so whenever she got an opportunity she would look in it. Somehow it gave her a glimpse inside of his head and heart. Here lately he had changed so much. Not that he had ever been open and free with his feelings, but now she felt like she was invading his privacy just by asking where he was going. Maybe he was growing up; she wasn't sure, but he seemed to be holding more in now than he ever had before.

Wiping her eyes with the back of her hand, Liz slowly turned to the next page.

Can't you see it's so hard for me to mirror to you the feelings,
tears and fears within? No, these won't let me be free...
Do you have those ugly, horrific dreams like me? The totality of your reality?
Can you see inside of me?
See most people live through life and don't experience such things. Most people
haven't felt the evil, sensed the bloody pain. Most people haven't buried most of their
best friends. Most people don't feel crazy, or don't feel half insane.
Have you seen the insides, the soul of your closest friends?
Have you seen it etched on their faces that fear before their end?
Have you watched a blameless child, curled up in pain? Did you tell them it
was not your fault, that it was just a misaim?
No, most people flowing through life haven't experienced such things. Most
people haven't looked in the mirror, and seen in their reflection society's stain.
Do you sleep good at night, is slumberland your friend?
Do you see that Krueger dude if you close your eyes again?
Can you hear him laughing; do you see his evil grin?
Or is that just your so-called friend, with a chainsaw in his hand...
Walking around, you front through life; you act like you're okay.
No one can ever know the things you did the other day.
No they don't know you popped two guys just walking down the street, and they
don't know you make-believe with everyone you meet.
They didn't see the horrific things you did the night before. They wouldn't
understand why you had to laugh at homeboy curled up on the floor.
See most people flowing through life don't experience such things.
Most people don't feel crazy, or don't feel half insane.
You want to know me; you want to see the world that makes me tick?
Just triple play the worse of scenes in the latest gangsta flick.
Then tell me if you think it's all good, it's easy, it's okay, when all
I've known is backstabbers, yea they taught me how to play...

Liz dropped the spiral notepad, and covered her mouth with a gasp of disbelief, shaking her head. There was no way she felt her son could possibly be involved in anything as dark and violent as his poem seemed to portray. She got up from the bed, laughing nervously. "This is crazy. I must be having severe PMS this month," she voiced aloud to herself.

"Who you talking to, Mama?" Her daughter's hazel eyes peered into hers from the door. "And what you doing all in Chico's stuff? He's gonna be mad."

"I was cleaning up this filthy room. Besides, what is he gonna be mad about? I'm the momma!" Liz declared jokingly, trying to hide her slight guilty feeling brought on by her snooping.

Both mother and daughter giggled naughtily and started a mock search through Chico's things. After a few minutes of this, Liz Grayson stopped. Sitting on the edge of the unmade bed, she gave Asha a serious stare.

"Asha, your brother is not in any trouble, is he?"

"What kind of trouble?" Asha asked. She pretended to be plucking lint off the bed covers.

Liz sighed. "Come on now. I know that you know everything that goes on with him, just like he knows everything that goes on with you. I'm not asking you to be a tattletale or anything like that. But I'm honestly concerned, Asha." She watched Asha, still quiet, biting her lower lip. "Do you ever read his poetry notebook?"

"Yeah, I've read it."

"And?"

"And what?" Asha asked innocently.

"Well, have you read this one here?" Liz showed her the poem that had caused her concern.

Asha read the words over carefully, swallowing continuously as she did. Her face showed that she knew what her mother was talking about. She knew a lot more than she was willing to relate.

"Chico is always writing something, Ma..." Asha looked down at the poem again. "I think it's rather good, actually."

Frustrated, Liz said, "It is good, Asha. That's not what I'm talking about and you know it. I'm wondering why he has been so distant lately and why did he suddenly want to go see your cousins in Silver Spring when he has never wanted to before? Especially I'm wondering where he's been getting all this money. And that Jeep? How did he come about that?"

"It's not a Jeep. It's actually one of those new Escapes," Asha blurted.

"I don't give a darn what it is, Asha. The only kind of people around these parts who be driving stuff like that are drug dealers!"

"You talk as if it's my fault, and I don't have anything to do with it. Chico told me the same thing he told you about his car—that it was a gift on loan from a friend." Asha crossed her fingers behind her back at that lie. "That's all I know. Plus, it beats walking, doesn't it?"

Liz looked hard at her daughter, trying to read her thoughts. She knew Asha was hiding things from her. She hadn't lived thirty-eight years just to end up blind and stupid. "Okay, Asha. Let's leave it at that and you can come help me with dinner."

Even though her words made it seem as though she was giving up, that idea couldn't be further from the truth. Secretly in her mind she knew that she would have to figure out what was up with her baby, with or without Asha's help. Somehow...

◆◆◆

The room seemed to have eyes all around it. Even though Malcolm hadn't known the two guys Big O had introduced him to for more than fifteen minutes, he could tell right away that something wasn't right about them. Now he was kinda sorry he had told Chico that he'd go in alone to make the trade so that he could stay out in the car with Candy. He and Big O had made the transfer of weapons for cash before they left Richmond. That had made Chico question why Marco needed them to ride Big O back to D.C. since the deal was already done. He had explained that there was a package that he also needed them to pick up while they were there.

Fifteen minutes later, both Malcolm and Big O sat quietly as the money that was exchanged for the weapons was counted, then the weapons themselves.

"It's all there," Big O retorted.

One of the guys, a tall, Latino brotha with big poppy eyes, looked at him, smirking slightly. "I'm sure it is, papi, but just to make sure, I count. Ya heard me?"

"Yeah, it's cool," O responded.

Malcolm watched quietly. After all, he was just a quiet spectator. The real deal had been between Big O and Marco. Besides that, he didn't know these D.C. brothas, and to be honest he was sure he didn't want to know them either.

After about fifteen more minutes of watching these guys counting product and capital, Malcolm looked at his watch. He sighed impatiently. He knew that Chico and Candy would be wondering what was taking him so long. The brotha who seemed to be in charge spoke up.

"So wassup? You in a hurry?" he asked.

"Naw, it ain't like that. It's just that my nicca and his lady, they wanted to go check out some of the D.C. sights before we headed back to Virginia. You know what I'm sayin'? But it's cool, man." Malcolm laughed slightly, noting the no-nonsense look on this bruh's face.

Big O cleared his throat slightly, and started cracking his knuckles. It was pretty obvious that he was nervous; about what was hard to pinpoint. After it appeared that the D.C. fellas had counted the money for the third time, they turned toward Big O and smiled oddly. The Latino guy spoke up.

"So, O, where's the suitcase that Barkley gave you?"

Malcolm was curious as to who Barkley was, but said nothing.

"He didn't give it to me; told me he would take care of it himself later," Big O responded, speaking rapidly.

"You sure about that?"

"Yeah, for real, man, that's what he told me." O laughed nervously.

"Yeah, okay," the Latino guy said. He turned toward Malcolm, then handed him a heavily taped box. "Let Marco know that I'll call him later, aight? We have some shit we need to get straight. He'll know what I mean."

Malcolm grabbed the box, figuring out this was the package that Marco had mentioned for them to pick up. He headed toward the door, glad to be leaving the tension-filled apartment. As he walked down the stairway he heard again, a frightening sound in Big O's voice. "So what's wrong, man?"

"Not sure, but we'll find out," came the reply of the Latino guy. The door slammed, quietening Malcolm's ability to eavesdrop. He was tempted to head back up the stairs so that he could listen in again, but a quiet premonition warned him as he headed to Chico and Candy.

Just as he was getting in the car, Big O came out of the project building.

"Listen, Malcolm, meet me back here in about three hours, aight? I'll show you guys around Chocolate City." He smiled slightly.

"Is everything cool in there?" Malcolm whispered to him. Chico looked at them both questionably.

"Yeah, there's not a problem. I know these dudes; they straight," Big O said, confidently. He looked over his shoulder slightly and laughed uncomfortably. "So, meet me back here in three hours then."

"Orlando, we got business, pa," a voice called out from the apartment window. Big O looked up toward the window, then back at Malcolm, Chico and Candy.

"Three hours, y'all; no later!"

CHAPTER TEN:
CHOCOLATE CITY BLUES...

"Girl, that is too funny; I can't believe you messed around on Peanut."

Asha frowned. It wasn't very funny to her. She had hesitated before to tell Jenene about what had happened with Orlando, but she couldn't keep nothing back from her first ace, cousin, and best friend in the whole world. Now she wasn't so sure about it, being that Jenene's face had a gloating expression.

"It wasn't like that," Asha finally said. "I didn't even think of it as messing around, because it wasn't planned."

Jenene leaned forward, still grinning. "But ya did it; that's the point."

"That's not the point!"

"Oh, girl, puhlease. He looks *wayyyy* better than Peanut, plus he would probably treat you betta."

Asha looked at Jenene in astonishment. "Now you saying he'll treat me better; now you pushing me to get up with him, when before you were screaming about his girl Poochie and all that shit. Make up your mind, chile."

Jenene smacked her lips before popping her Popsicle back into her mouth. She looked over at the television set.

"I'm sick of some of these characters," she said, commenting on their favorite show, *The Young and the Restless.* "As old as Victor is, and they have that fool still acting like he a playa."

"What does that have to do with what we're talking about?" Asha asked in frustration.

"I'm just saying. Anyhow, you already went there with Orlando. When I told you that you shouldn't you wouldn't listen. So since you didn't, you may as well go with the flow that you started. Naa mean?"

The phone rang before Asha could respond to Jenene's senseless reasoning. Both girls jumped up to answer, with Jenene beating her to the punch.

"Ha, ha," she teased, as she picked up the receiver. "Helloooooo?"

"Asha?" a male voice said.

Jenene looked at her cousin. "No...this is Jenene."

"Let me speak to Asha," he whispered.

Jenene handed the phone over to Asha, mouthing to her silently, "It's Orlando."
Asha grabbed the phone. "Yeah?"

"Asha, I need Chico's cell phone number, like now," he whispered.

"Orlando? Why are you whispering?"

"I don't have time to talk to you, girl. Give me the number; I'm in trouble."

"What kind of trouble? Is Chico in trouble? What's going on, Orlando?"
Asha began to panick.

"No, he's not, but I am. Come on, Asha, I don't have time for this!"

"What you doing in there, O?!" Asha heard a voice scream over the phone.
"Don't make me come in there and get yo ass!"

Asha's heart started beating fast. "Oh, my God...who is that?"

"Oh shit!" Orlando exclaimed. "Listen, call Chico and Malcolm. Tell them to
come back to the crib like ASAP! Call 'em, Asha!"

The phone went dead.

Funny thing about big cities, everything was always moving in fast motion,
and the farther north you went, the faster life seemed to become. Richmond
always seemed so city to Chico. It actually was, but in comparison to the
Northern ones, and even ones that weren't really north like D.C. and
Baltimore, Richmond didn't seem quite so city at all. It made more sense now
that the Northern brothas were always calling them country.

D.C. was especially fast-paced. Traffic was bamming, back-to-back conflict.
After making their exchange at Big O's apartment, Chico, Malcolm and Candy
took the "Chocolate City" tour. They had gone to a lot of museums, checked
out the African-American Arts museum. They also checked out some major
tour sites, the Monument and places like that. Candy had insisted on visiting
the Holocaust Museum, too, but was upset when they got there and was told
there were no more tickets available for the tours that day. So after viewing the
section that you could look at without tickets, they decide to check out the
National Zoo, which sat much better with Chico and Malcolm. That is until
they got there, and realized they weren't visiting the most nose friendly place
in the world.

"I can't believe I let y'all mofos talk me into coming to this shithole,"
Malcolm complained. "This joint ain't even fit for the monkeys."

"Well, I love the zoo. Thanks for bringing me, boobie," said Candy, kissing
Chico on the cheek.

"Ugg, y'all sickening with that boobie shit. That shit sounds gay."

"Everything sounds gay to you, Malcolm," Candy spat. "There's nothing
wrong with affection." She looked at him sideways, then pulled his pick out of
the back of his hair. "Of course you wouldn't know that since don't nobody like
your goofy ass."

Malcolm snatched back his comb. "Well, they don't need to like me. All a
bitch needs to do for me is like this..."

"Don't even say it," Candy warned.

"Dang, y'all a trip." Chico laughed.

"No, Malcolm is the trip. He's so nasty, and always calling women bitches. I hope you don't talk like him when I'm not around, Chico."

"Of course he does. He just fronts with you cuz you one of them proper shawties," Malcolm said, smiling.

"Look, keep me out of y'all fights, aight?" Chico said, shaking his head.

"Whateva! If you boys excuse me, have to go to the little girls room."

"Well, there's a lil shit hut over there by them birds." Malcolm was still picking.

"Oh, you're so helpful," Candy remarked sarcastically as she made her way over to the bathroom. "Be right back, boo." She gave Chico a special wink as he smiled back at her.

After giving Candy time to disappear behind the wooden bathroom fixture, Chico turn to Malcolm and asked him solemnly, "What went down at O's place?"

"Yo, I'm telling you, I have no idea. Those mofos up in that joint was like some serious-looking niccas." Malcolm stretched out his legs on the park bench, then looked down at his watch. "We need to be back up there in a lil while though. I just hope ain't nuttin' up."

"Yeah, me, too," Chico agreed.

He paused for a second, thinking about how uncomfortable the whole trip felt, yet at the same time, how cool it had been to just chill with Malcolm and Candy for the couple of hours that they had. His mind had been mass confusion ever since they had started working for Marco. But he had to admit the money was good. They were supposed to get a grand each just for riding the product up to D.C. Not bad for a day's work, minus having to deal with hostile ass niccas all the time.

"Hey, Chico, you think Candy would trip if she knew the real reason we're here?"

"Hell yeah, she'd trip. You know she don't get down like that."

"Hmm…" Malcolm hummed.

Chico yawned as he leaned back against a large wooden gate, which jailed the ever-famous Black Panther. The Panther gave a frightening roar, causing Chico to shriek as he jumped up from the gate.

"What the hell!"

Malcolm burst out laughing. "Damn, bruh, that cat is locked up; it's ain't gon' get cha."

"Yeah right, fuck dat." Chico huffed.

Malcolm laughed again. "Aight, we better get outta here. What's taking that girl so long?" He looked toward the restroom entrance.

"Here she is now," Chico responded, as Candy came into their view.

◆◆◆

On the ride across town toward Southwest, Chico thought about the day's activities. They had told Marco that they would be back in Virginia with the cash from the weapons sale by at least eleven or midnight. And Marco, he'd be watching the clock. Right now they were meeting Big O over at Kenilworth Gardens. He had said he wanted to square some other things out with them and get a last word on their next visit and exchange.

Turning the corner in the direction of the project housing, it was noticeably quiet for the time of day, or either it just seemed that way to Chico.

"It's mighty eerie around here," Candy noted.

Chico looked cautiously in her direction. He was about to say that he thought the same thing. Just as Malcolm parked the car, Chico's cell phone rang.

"Hold up," he said as Malcolm opened the door. He pressed the "on" button on his cell. "Hello?"

"Chico!" his sister Asha screamed. "I've been calling you for the past hour and a half. Why didn't you answer?"

"That's because we went to the zoo and I left my phone in the car. What you trippin' about? Is Mama okay?"

"Yeah, she's fine; it's not about Mama. Orlando called about a couple of hours ago. Said he wanted you to come back to his place right away. And, Chico, it sounded like something was wrong."

"Wrong like what?" Chico paused. "Hold up a minute."

Malcolm and Candy had already made their way out of the SUV, and were starting up the sidewalk when the doors to the project apartment building burst open. Big O flew out the door, rolling down the hard stone stairway.

"Who da fuck do you think you are, nicca! Who you think you fuckin' with?" a Latino brotha shouted, coming out the door behind him.

Big O got to his feet, and turned around to look at Malcolm, Candy and Chico. His fear-coated eyes bore into Malcolm's.

"Oh, shit!" Chico exclaimed, as he quickly caught up with Malcolm and Candy.

"What's going on, Chico!" Asha was still screaming over the phone.

Another dark-skinned brotha wearing the typical black-starred gray rag that all the Black Angels wore came out of the building holding a semi. Actually it looked like one of those Malcolm and Chico had just sold them that morning.

"Oh, God!" Candy cried as she covered her mouth with her hands. All of them stared helplessly as the dude with the rag pulled the trigger, catching Big O in the back. He screamed, then turned around to the guy who had shot him only to receive another spray of bullets, leaving his face an unrecognizable mask of blood.

Candy screamed again, as did many other females who had been sitting on their porches witnessing the execution. The tall Latino brotha who had pushed Big O down the stairs glanced at him and smiled slightly. Candy's screams then brought his attention toward her.

"Shut the fuck up, bitch!" he screamed.

He looked over at Malcolm and Chico. "What the hell y'all niccas looking at? We finished our business, so shut that ho up and get the fuck out of here before one of y'all be next!"

"Aight, man. Be cool," answered Malcolm, as he backed slowly away. "Come on," he then said to Chico and Candy, "let's get outta here."

As the three of them made their way back inside the SUV, Chico held Candy's mouth, muffling the screams that were still flowing uncontrollably.

"Oh, my God, Chico! Oh, my God!" she cried as they slid into the backseat. Chico motioned for Malcolm to drive. Candy trembled, rocking back and forth in the seat as Malcolm pulled off.

"Man, get our asses back to Richmond!"

Candy's voice quivered. "We...we have to go to the police."

"Police?!" Chico shouted.

Both guys looked at Candy with incredulous expressions as if she was speaking Latin.

"Yes, that guy shot Orlando. Shouldn't we go to the police? Tell somebody?"

"Girl, we ain't telling nobody nuttin', you hear me? We can't be ratting to Five-O. Not unless you wanna be ghost yourself. These brothas will hunt us down! This ain't no game, Candy."

Candy looked at Chico, feeling confused. "What are you saying? What is this, Chico? What are you two into?" She looked from him to Malcolm.

"Fuck, girl!" Chico screamed, grabbing her by the shoulders. "You keep your mouth shut about this, do you hear me! It never happened..."

Fear and disbelief filled Candy's eyes as she looked into the hazel ones staring back at her. The face of her adoration and affection seemed to be that of a stranger now. "You're hurting me..." she whispered tearfully.

"Man, let her go; she ain't gonna tell nobody," Malcolm said quietly.

"It *never* happened," Chico repeated, shaking her shoulders again. "Say it!"

"I won't say anything," came her hoarse reply. "It never happened..."

"Ever..."

"I won't say anything, ever."

Candy then turned her eyes away from the guys, closing them to block out the ugly visions that rested forever in her memory. She looked out of the window as they cruised down I-95 South. But even with her fighting hard to wash it from her mind, all she could see was Orlando's bloodied face. And all she could taste were her own salty tears...

CHAPTER ELEVEN:
MYSTIC WORDS OF WISDOM...

Fall quarter...Senior year...

Asha exhaled happily as she got off the yellow schoolbus. This was week three of her senior year. Her last year of prison in the Richmond Public School system. As for what she would do in the future, that didn't matter much now. The fact that she had no true direction didn't either. She simply couldn't wait to be free.

She smiled as she saw Candy hopping over toward her, then walked up to meet her.

"Hey, sis, you get that Government paper finished yet?" she asked her.

Candy gave Asha a suspicious grin. "Why do you ask? You wanna copy mine or something?" She laughed.

"Girl, please," Asha said, rolling her neck. "I don't want your wrong answers. I'm a genius, you know."

"Oh yeah? So spell genius." Candy smirked.

"It's A.S.H.A; a bad ass sista from Creighton Court!"

Both girls laughed.

"Anyhow, where's that brother of mine? You didn't ride with him today either?"

"No," Candy said, shaking her head. "He went to pick up Junnie, said they had something to take care of early this morning."

Asha's eyebrow rose. "Something like what? He did say he was coming, right?"

Candy sighed in frustration. She pulled her knapsack onto her back, tightening the shoulder straps before finally looking back at Asha. "Asha, I have no idea what Chico is gonna do. He's so different now, you know that. And at this point when it comes to what he's gonna do or what he's up to, I don't even ask him anymore."

Asha looked at Candy. She noted the worried lines that marred her olive complexion. Even though she didn't know exactly what had happened in D.C. a few weeks back, she did know that Candy had been acting differently ever since. She didn't dare ask Chico again, not after the way he had barked at her when she had tried to bring it up the day after they returned. But whatever had happened, she knew from all of their non-responses, it couldn't be good.

The second bell rang.

"All right, girl, we're gonna be late," Candy said. "I'll holla at you later."

Making their way into the school building, both girls had their minds occupied on not only school work but what dangerous activity Chico could be up to next.

"Why is my verse so barren of new pride?
So far from variation or quick change?
Why with the time do I not glance aside?
To new-found methods and to compounds strange?
Why write I still all one, ever the same,
And keep invention in a noted weed,
That every word doth almost tell my name,
Showing their birth and where they did proceed?
O, know, sweet love, I always write of you,
And you and love are still my argument;
So all my best is dressing old words new,
Spending again what is already spent:
For as the sun is daily new and old,
So is my love still telling what is told."
—*Shakespeare*

The room was so quiet you could hear a pin drop as Mrs. Mayes finished her quotation of the William Shakespearean sonnet. School had been up and going for over a week, and being that this was senior year, the teachers weren't cutting any slack. English Lit was Chico's favorite class. Of course he couldn't let anybody know that. Writing was for sissies, his boys would say. English was only a requirement. A real brotha wasn't supposed to like that shit.

"So," Mrs. Mayes said as she breathed a deep sigh of emotion, "can anyone tell me what they think Shakespeare was trying to say? Remember words have power, emotion, feeling and passion. They can start wars, heal sicknesses, cause pain and pleasure alike. So what emotion do we sense him feeling here with his words? What was he trying to say to us with his mystic words of wisdom?" She looked around the classroom, noting the blank stares. "Anybody?"

You could hear throats being cleared. Everyone in the class seemed suddenly still, praying that Mrs. Mayes would call on anyone but them.

Suddenly Chico spoke up and said, "Aight, I'll give it a shot." Mrs. Mayes' eyes brightened.

"I think in modern English, homeboy was saying this." He looked down at the poem in the book. "When he said, *Why is my verse so barren of new pride, so far from variation or quick change,* he meant what he was kickin' in his then note-book seemed to be the same words over and over again, nothing new. You know what I'm saying? And then," Chico looked down at the next few verses, "like

60

right here he says, *Why with the time do I not glance aside to new-found methods and to compounds strange?* He meant that he was tired of the same old game, same old words that had the same old feeling. He wanted a new flavor."

A giggle from the back of the room caused Mrs. Mayes to put up her hand in silence. "Go on, Sean."

"Well, I can kinda feel what dude is saying. Because I've felt like that before when writing my own shi...I mean my own stuff. Like you want new ideas, but it's like everybody has their own style and flavor. Sometimes it's hard to get out of your self mold. At least that has been my experience."

James, a speckled-face dude Chico had known and been irked by since sixth grade, laughed. "Go 'head, Shakespeare! Man, all you know how to write are your ABCs."

"Nicca, shut up! I know what I do. You don't know nuttin' 'bout me!"

"All right, gentlemen. Do we need to act like children? And by the way, the word *nigger* is not an acceptable word for this classroom," Mrs. Mayes reprimanded with raised eyebrows while "ohs," "ahs" and giggles floated throughout the room.

"Mrs. Mayes, actually Chico said 'nicca,' not 'nigger,'" Keisha, another student in the class, said.

Mrs. Mayes gave Keisha a pointed stare. "And is that supposed to make a difference?" Everyone chuckled again.

Mrs. Mayes looked back at Chico. "What else do you see in this sonnet?" she asked.

"Well," Chico said, clearing his throat and giving James the evil eye, "like when he says, *why write I still all one, ever the same,* then he pops us with, *that every word doth almost tell my name.* It's pretty obvious that the brotha is tired of writing the love stuff, like peeps don't even have to see the name on his writings to know it's him. *So all my best is dressing old words new; spending again what is already spent.* So you see there you go! Homie needs a new attitude, and something else to write about," Chico said with a smug smile.

Mrs. Mayes made a circular tour around her desk, nibbling on the end of her pencil as if in deep thought. "Interesting observation, Sean, and you are exactly right in your dissecting of this particular *homeboys* feeling, as you so eloquently put it. You see, people, even the best of writers get bored with their own material, and as you all know, Shakespeare was one of the best poets and writers who ever lived. But how would you say what he said, meaning, how would you describe your feelings about your work?

"With this in mind, your assignment today is to write your own sonnet, about the same thing that Shakespeare wrote—that is, expressing yourself as if you are a writer who has become bored with his or her material. But write it as Shakespeare did, the old English style. I want it at least ten lines long, and you have," she looked down at her watch, "thirty minutes, so get busy."

Moans of protest could be heard throughout the classroom, but after a minute or two all was quiet. Chico put on his thinking cap, trying hard to block out the events of the past two weeks, and focus on this love of his.

Digging deep inside my mind, trying eagerly to find...
That other vessel within myself, that other idiom...
That expression of variety, the diverseness of words...
Have I become reiterate in my thoughts?
My winsome words of love have become a mere echo...
Eagerly I seek fresh mystic words of wisdom...
My thoughts sometimes become as a tripod...
A multiple facade of repetition, looking for an out...
My poetic ghetto utterance of love...
I now feel the need to baptize in new waters...
So that the oneness of me may mutate...

The sound of the ticking clock alerted Chico from his assignment. He looked around as he finished his last sentence, and hurried his paper up to Mrs. Mayes' desk. After settling back at his own, he thought back to what had happened in D.C., and about Big O's murder. After they had gotten back, Marco already knew what had gone down. He said that Big O had copped a package worth over two grand of cocaine. He was to deliver it to his gang family. Marco had called before they arrived in D.C. to make sure that Big O had delivered it. When he hadn't, the Black Anges knew right away what was up. It hadn't been the first time he had stolen from them, Marco had said. So basically, the whole thing had been a test, and Big O, well, he had obviously failed this one, with deadly consequences.

Even though Candy had kept things quiet about the murder, the whole episode had changed things between her and Chico, as if she didn't quite trust him. That bothered Chico, but he couldn't let that get to him too much. He had a lot to do to be worried about her issues. Chico's biggest concern was helping her to see that she couldn't, for any reason, tell anyone what they had seen. The whole situation had bothered him though. Orlando had been an all-right bruh. That's the operative word, had been. But that was something else that he couldn't keep his mind too much on. Worrying about things like that would only cause him to make mistakes. There was no room for stressing about other people's fuck-ups.

Now school had started back and the summer's activities had created a new person in Sean Grayson. Even the after-school activities were different. Yeah, they were making mad loot, but it seemed like Marco was requiring more and more of them. He seemed to have so many enemies, and acted like they were his personal bodyguards. Marco saw himself as the coolest, baddest cat walking. He sometimes reminded Chico of the Shonuff character in this movie he once saw called *The Last Dragon*. The difference was that Marco never did any of his own dirty business, and didn't know kung fu.

Chico sat back in his chair and looked around when he felt a familiar stare. Alisha Johnston was eyeballing him. She was always looking at him, always telling him she thought he was fine and shit like that. She still had that phat, tangerine booty, of course. But no matter how phat her ass, he wished he had never fucked around with her. She was like a damn leech. Like he needed some Morton's salt to get rid of her clingy ass. The only good thing about her was that she had done things Candy never would, like giving him head. The girl was good, but she'd had lots of practice not only with Chico, but with half the juniors and seniors at John F. Kennedy High School. In a word, Chico thought she was a ho ho. But he had to admit to himself that he had never ever asked Candy for head, so maybe he was doing her a disservice by thinking that. As for Alisha, she could stare all she wanted to. As long as she never opened her mouth to Candy about their one-time tryst, she was cool with him. He looked over at her again catching her look as she wet her lips, flicking her tongue out at him and glancing down at his crotch, causing him to have an instant hard-on. Chico stirred uncomfortably in his chair, then looked the other way.

When the bell rang everyone else quickly passed their papers to the front of the class. Mrs. Mayes called out to Chico to stay back for a minute. He walked up to her desk, blushing slightly as Alisha brushed up against him as she passed by.

"Yeah?" he asked.

Mrs. Mayes smiled, looking up from the paper she had been reading. "This is really good—your sonnet, that is. What else have you written?"

"Oh, I mess around with it here and there, nothing to trip about though," he replied, trying to keep the huge grin off his face that seemed to come up automatically whenever someone gave him praise for his poetry.

"Well, I would like to see what else you have written. I am surprised to see that you have such a wide vocabulary."

Chico laughed uncomfortably. "What, you thought I couldn't talk, yo?"

"Well, you most certainly do your best to hide it, yo," she mocked back, smiling. "Listen, writing is a gift. It's not easy to just come up with poetic words, expressing what you feel. I know good poetry when I see it, and this is very good." She motioned toward his paper.

"I do have other stuff that I have written; I could hook you up."

"Then by all means hook me up, sweetie! There is so much you could do with this, Sean. Contests, scholarships even. So will you bring it in? Let me have a look at it? Share that gift, young man; don't just leave it buried in the sand," she rhymed.

Chico laughed.

"See, you thought you were the only poet in da house, right?"

"Dang, aight then."

"Dat's right, I'm hip, too. I have a cool son your age!" Mrs. Mayes giggled.

"I'm trippin'," Chico said in surprise. "Well, Mrs. M, I gotta bounce on outta here before I'm late for my next period. But thanks!"

"Okay, but remember what I said, and don't forget to bring me more of your poetry. Seriously, I would love to read it."

"Word. I'll do that." Chico walked quickly to his next class, still smiling as he thought about his hip English teacher.

After school that day, Chico thought a lot about Mrs. Mayes and his discussion. She was pretty cool for a teacher, but he still wasn't quite sure how comfortable he was about letting her see his poetry. His writing had always been something he did as a pastime or when he was feeling down about something. It was easy to let words wash away your anger, pain or aggravation.

He got into his SUV and was just about to start the engine when he was suddenly startled.

"What's up, babyeeeee!" Junnie banged on the hood of Chico's car and jumped quickly inside the passenger side.

"Man, watch the paint, yo!"

"Nigga, shut up. Ain't nobody hurting your damn car," Junnie said, making a goofy face. "Let's bounce. Malcolm paged me a short while ago. You know he cut classes today? I called him back and he said we supposed to meet him in Northside on Delaware Avenue."

"What's going down in Northside?"

"Hell if I know. Guess we'll see when we get there."

Heading toward the Northside of town, Chico's thoughts of mystic words of wisdom were momentarily put aside.

CHAPTER TWELVE:
LOST ONES...

It was ladies night. Or maybe ladies night to study was the better way to put it. Candy was feeling more and more depressed about her and Chico's relationship. It wasn't that she didn't want to be with Chico anymore. That was impossible to comprehend. She loved him, totally and completely, with an all-consuming love. It didn't matter how young they were, she knew that it was real. At least for her it was. With Chico she had to honestly admit that at this point she didn't know what he felt about her, or anything else. She fought to get her mind on more positive things as she lay across the soft, pink granny quilt that her aunt had given her for her birthday the previous year. She and her girlfriend Keisha had so much to talk about. They gabbed about the latest going-ons at school, home, and of course, boyfriends.

"So I only have half a day since I have so many credits. Basically all I need to graduate is Government and English 12," Candy said as she sucked down a blueberry Slurpee.

"I thought you were in Mr. Fietts' computer programming class?"

"Well, I am. That's my only elective. But I'm working in the library downtown stocking books and stuff. I get credits for that, too."

"You getting paid?" Keisha asked with a smirk.

"Of course I'm getting paid, girl. Believe me, I'm no fool."

"Well you go, gurl!"

Keisha paused for a moment, then looked at Candy from beneath her hood that covered her eyelids. "From what I've *heard*, you ain't the only one getting paid. That's a tight ride your man's been sportin' lately."

A funny look came over Candy's face. "He got that on loan from a friend of his. Chico's been working all summer at this garage after school so he can help his mom out with the bills." She wasn't sure if she believed her own words, even as she spoke them.

"Oh, puhleaseeee! Candy, you really believe that? You are not that naïve. He is rolling with them New York brothas that moved up this way, I'm telling you."

"How do you know that?"

Keisha rolled her eyes. "How do I know? Everybody knows. It's no secret, girl. You can't tell me you are that much in the dark with your man."

"Well, I don't know about all that, but I do know for a fact that Chico would never hurt anybody. He's not like that, Keisha. You have a bad attitude about all guys just because yours turned out to be a dog."

Candy sat up on the bed, sticking a big wad of Bubble Yum bubble gum in her mouth. She thought back to what had happened during their visit to D.C. She had read in *The Washington Post* about Orlando's murder, and the papers had stated that it had been gang-related. That very fact bothered her, especially after Chico's reaction to her telling anyone what they had witnessed. She kinda wondered the real reason they had gone to D.C. She recalled how Orlando hadn't wanted her to go inside of his apartment when they first got there. It didn't then and still didn't even now seem all on the up and up, and she still could not get the picture out of her head of Orlando's half blown off blood covered face. She hadn't felt so upset since the death of Tupac Shakur. Maybe it wasn't quite the same thing, but the physical and emotional effects for her were the same.

"So then, where do you think he's getting all the money to buy all these lil gifts for you, and taking you shopping? And what about that Jeep?"

"It's an Escape," Candy spat.

"Yeah, aight, but don't even try to tell me it was a loan, Candy, cuz you know better than that."

Keisha got up and made her way over to Candy's bureau, looking through her jewelry. She pulled out a gold chain necklace with a heart-shaped diamond at the end.

"Look at this. Where do you think he got the funds to pay for stuff like this? Working at a garage? Get real, girl!"

Candy jumped up and grabbed her necklace angrily. "Get outta my stuff! You don't even know where I got this! And what's your point anyway? If he was into something illegal, why would that be your business?"

She felt herself getting more and more upset as she placed her treasured necklace back inside her jewelry case. The truth was that Chico had not given her this specific necklace, although he had indeed been buying her a lot of pretty things lately. Jewelry, clothes, shoes, the works. But this necklace was a gift from her grandmother who had passed a year earlier, and she didn't appreciate Keisha touching it.

"Well, don't get all mad with me. I'm just trying to help you see that you need to be more informed about your man. But...he is fine with his lil gansta ass." Keisha laughed.

Candy frowned back at her, unimpressed.

"Listen, Candy, I know something else you may not know about."

Candy sighed. "And what's that?"

"Well, I've heard that someone else has her eye on him," she said, pausing at Candy's irked expression. "Okay, I'll leave it alone. But just don't say I didn't warn you, aight?"

"Nun-uh, you aren't getting out that easily. What you talking about now, Keisha?" Candy knew that Keisha was just trying to get her mad, but she couldn't let her get away after making a statement like that. "Who's been scoping Chico out?"

"Hmm...well, you've seen her. You know Alisha? She's cheering on varsity this year? She's been telling everybody that she sucked him off at Lisa Christian's party this summer. Remember she had that party after Summer Jam? Remember you was whining cuz Jakim was there and you was sick?" Keisha whispered.

"What the hell you whispering for? And that's a damn lie, Keisha! Alisha is ugly as hell, so why would Chico want her when he has me? She is ugly as hell!"

Keisha stood up, smacking her lips again. "Ugly don't have nuttin' to do with it—not when it comes to Negroes who like to get their thangs sucked, and Alisha is nasty like that!"

Candy stood up abruptly. "You know what? I don't even wanna hear any more of this. People just can't stand to see Chico and me happy together. People at school just talk too much with their nasty, jealous rumors!" She paused, catching her breath. She could feel her heart beating rapidly. Candy felt sick at the mental picture of Alisha's nasty mouth on her man.

"Candy, I said I heard the rumor, but I didn't start it. And I'm not saying it's true, okay? So don't be getting mad at me. I'm your friend, girl..."

"Let's just start our homework," Candy stated with a sigh, doing what she always did when she didn't want to face something—simply refuse to think about it any further...

◆◆◆

A harsh curse flew out of Chico's mouth as the paper trashcan bottomed out. The garbage fell to the ground in a heap.

"Aww damn!" he said to himself.

Looking to his left, he noticed nosey Mrs. Warren from the building next door looking at him with a snarl across her old dried-up face.

"Now you know you got to get all that up," she demanded.

"I'm getting it up now," Chico spat back. "Mind you own damn business, dried-up old bitch," he whispered under his breath.

The old hag didn't have a life. Always spent her time sitting on the porch trying to see what everybody else was up to in theirs. When they were younger she was the snoop who made it her business to inform their mama of everything they did, and everything they didn't do, too. To pay her back they used to throw bags of oatmeal into her yard. Oatmeal was some nasty shit, all slimy and stank. And when it's cold and old it becomes like rocks Chico found himself grinning, thinking about the look on her face when she realized that they were the ones torturing her with the oatmeal rocks.

Busy cleaning up the last of the wasted garbage, Chico barely heard his mom when she called out to him. "Sean?" she said quietly.

"Yeah, yeah, I know; and I'm getting it all up now. I'll run water over the stain so it won't draw bugs," Chico replied. He knew right away what his mother was gonna say, but she surprised him when instead she said… "No, that's not why I'm calling you. The telephone is for you. It's your father."

Chico looked at his mom, shaking his head rapidly.

"Come on, sweetie, give him a chance. Don't be like this."

Chico sighed and finally gave in. He sat the trash bag down and walked slowly into the house. He passed by his mom and gave her a reluctant frown. He wasn't in any hurry, just like his dad never seemed to be in a hurry to talk to him. Years ago it was different. He could remember when he would give anything for just a drop of attention from the old man—just a nod from him that told him he knew his son was alive. Now they talked even less since his dad would only call when he would suddenly get hit with this paternal virus and want to flex his fatherhood muscles. As far as Chico was concerned he didn't give a shit if the man never called. At least that's what he always tried to convince himself.

He slowly made his way into the kitchen and picked the phone up from the counter.

"Yep," Chico quipped.

"How are you, son?" his father asked, obviously choosing to ignore Chico's flippant tone.

Son? When the hell did I become his son? Please take that bullshit to someone who'll buy it, Chico thought to himself. "Same as I was last time, man. I'm straight," he said dryly.

"Sorry, it's been a while since I last called, but things have been so busy here, and I've been getting more and more cramped for time with work and all. But listen, I'm going to try to come and see you guys at Christmas. I really miss you, son. So I was also thinking you could come here for Thanksgiving. What do you think about that?" his father asked cheerfully.

Chico was quiet. He took a couple of deep breaths, trying to calm himself before he spoke. He always felt heated whenever he talked to his father, but he felt relieved when Asha walked up behind him, and whispered for him to let her talk to their dad.

"Listen, Asha wants to talk to you," he finally said to him.

"Yeah, but, Sean, I asked you a question."

"Yeah, you did, and the answer is no. I got business here. I'm working now, and Mama needs my help around the house. Maybe Asha will come there."

"It's only for a weekend, Sean."

The disappointment was quite evident in his father's voice. *As if he had a right to be disappointed*, Chico thought.

"Look, ah…Asha is here and she wants to holla at cha, aight? Peace…"

He handed the phone over to his sister and hurried away, making an abrupt exit for his bedroom door.

Chico knew his mom was right behind him. She was always the comforter, always the one trying to make things better. Well, nothing could make it better when it came to his sorry ass dad. Nothing! Grabbing his keys and wallet, Chico decided he would go out, get air, and clear his head by chillin' with his boys.

"He did tell me he was going to try to make more of an effort, Sean. Maybe you could give him a chance?" Chico's mom said, laying a hand against his forearm as he tried to make his way out the door.

Chico coughed, fighting hard to hold in the explosion. He felt like a ticking bomb. Memories started to surface, and all the old shit suddenly came racing back. He felt cheated! And it was all the fault of that bastard on the phone for making Asha and him the bastards, and not even giving a damn about them.

He jerked violently away from his mother; tears of rage coursed down his face. "A chance for what? *We are doing just fine!* Like we need him? I'm taking care of business, right? I'm bringing in the dollars. I'm the man! He sitting around talking like we some poor souls needing his attention! He talking like he doing us a favor, like we lost and shit. But we ain't lost; he is! And I'm tired, Mama. I'm tired of listening to that muthafucca play the concerned daddy when the mood hits him. I'm the man here, and we don't need him. We don't need him!" Chico screamed. He then ran through the house with his jacket, pen and pad that he had gotten from his room. He slammed the door hard behind him with an angry bang.

The smoky lair of evil…embodying in my world…
A city full of crimson deeds of boys and little girls…
A neighborhood of madness, society diseased…
A childhood without candy canes or joyful memories…
Are these the pitied lost ones? Entrapped in horror's maze?
Are these the ones still left behind with the puzzled defeated gaze?
A rose without the petals…a dog without a bone…
A home where fear and tepidity is all they've ever known…
A king without a kingdom…a queen without a throne…
A swing set that won't breathe a laugh…only a bitter moan…
Are these the pitied lost ones? Dead bones without a hope?
Are these the ones still left behind in darkness there to grope?

CHAPTER THIRTEEN:
GOTTA MAKE THE SONG CRY...

Asha felt as if her heart was embedded deep within her throat as she listened to Peanut and his cousin Lionel's boy talk. She kept quiet. Not because they didn't want her in their conversation but because she honestly didn't have anything to say.

"Yeah, they messed that brotha up," Lionel said, shaking his head. "See, that's why I don't go to D.C. no more. Them niccas up that way will kill you quick!"

Peanut was nodding his head in agreement, then looked at Asha. "What did Chico tell you happened, Asha?"

Asha cleared her throat. "He didn't tell me nuttin' about it. This is the first time I've heard that Orlando was dead." She put a fry in her mouth and focused on the sign at the McDonald's restaurant that said "Now hiring."

"Yeah, right. That's your twin wit' his tired ass. He had to tell you sumpin'."

Looking over at Peanut, Asha felt defensive. He knew Chico didn't like him, so why would he even ask her things about her brother? Deciding she would just ignore his question, she took a big bite from her double cheeseburger.

"Come on, girl, wassup? Did he tell you what happened up there?" he asked again.

"No, Peanut, he didn't, okay? Besides, that was weeks ago." Stuffing the last of her fries in her mouth, she said, "Stop asking me about stupid stuff. If you wanna know things about Chico, you can just ask him yourself."

Lionel laughed. "Ouch! I guess she told you, dawg." He looked down at his watch. "I'm outta here."

"Aight, I'll talk to you later, Lionel," Peanut said.

Lionel gave Peanut dabs and Asha a wink, then left.

Both Asha and Peanut were quiet as they cleaned their lunch space up to leave. They walked out to the car. As she went to open her door, Peanut grabbed Asha by the arm.

"You're moving too slow. I got shit to do, girl," he said harshly.

"Dang, okay. Let me go," she said, frowning.

She quickly got into the car, buckled her seat belt, then took a deep breath as Peanut buckled his. She could feel his mood, and really wanted him to hurry up and take her home. Dealing with his issues was one thing she was not in the mood to deal with that day.

"You thought you was being cute, didn't you?" Peanut suddenly said as he started the car.

"What are you talking about, Peanut?"

She felt a sharp ache boom in her head as he pulled her braid.

"Ouch!" she cried.

"Fuck a ouch, bitch. Don't you ever disrespect me like that again!"

"What are you talking about?" she cried. "How did I disrespect you?"

"The way you were talking to me just now in front of Lionel. You thought I was gonna just let you get away wit' dat shit? Hell da fuck naw!"

Asha closed her eyes and counted to ten before she spoke.

"Peanut, you need to stop calling me a bitch. I'm getting so tired of that. You're the one who's always disrespecting me. Besides, if I don't know nuttin' about Chico's business, then how am I s'pose to tell you, huh?"

He looked at her for a second, then pushed her away, hard, causing her head to bump up against the passenger door window.

"Keep it to ya self then. You just as stupid as your brother." Pulling out of the McDonald's parking lot, he kept fussing. "Black hoes always gotta be getting smart and shit. I need me a white bitch, a tame bitch."

Swallowing back tears, Asha was determined not to let him see them. Her common sense spanked her once again, but not hard enough.

Maybe someday it would wake her up...

The radio was singing out slow jams. Jay-Z's cut "Song Cry" crooned, setting the mood as Chico moaned behind it.

He closed his eyes as Candy bit softly on his nipple, then traced her lips down to his stomach, nipping at his skin. He held his breath as she went lower, kissing at his hipbone. As she moved back up and smiled into his eyes, he fought hard not to show his disappointment that she didn't go even *lower.*

"Want me to put it in, boo?" she cooed.

"Yeah, do that." He moaned. "Ride that pinga."

Candy laughed. "Umm-hmm...I'll ride it all right." She slid down slowly, rising again, then working an up and down rhythm that soon had both of them crying out just like Jay-Z's rap. Chico moved his hands up her sweaty back, struggling to hold back his nut. One final swivel of her hips killed that struggle, and had him moaning as he came.

"Ugg, Chico, wait...wait, cuz I'm not there yet!" Candy moaned before jerking against him as she joined him.

"Mmmmmmmmm..." they both said in unison.

The room got quiet. Chico had almost started breathing normally as Candy suddenly giggled against his ear.

"Wassup?" he said, smiling at her.

"You always coming too quick," she teased.

"Cuz you good like that." He smacked her butt.

Candy pulled away slightly, throwing her hands out in happiness as she looked around the fancy hotel room.

"I can't believe this. You don' hooked a sista up!" She leaned back toward him and traced her tongue around his ear. "I've never stayed at Marriott before."

"You better not have," he said, giving her a little squeeze. "Cuz that would mean some other brotha brought you here, and then I'd have to cap his ass." He laughed at Candy's shocked expression. "That was a joke!"

"Oh, I know. I'm just happy to be here with you is all."

They had been messing around since the morning, enjoying a carefree Saturday in a hotel, pretending they were somewhere else besides Richmond, and only twenty minutes from home.

"It's cool, ain't it?" Chico said. "We're gonna have to collect on a few towels for keepsakes. Oh, yeah and let's not forget this nice blanket here." He lifted the plush blanket up over Candy's back.

"Lawd, you crazy, boy!" She giggled. "Oh, and don't forget to stuff the King James Bible in your bag."

"Damn straight, we gotta read and repent for all this sinful fornication" was his cocky reply.

"Fornication?"

Chico gave Candy a sexy smile and whispered in her ear, "It's when I slipped my Ball Park frank deep inside your punanny and your rotisserie oven rolled around and around until my weiner went 'pop'! And all the juices just dripped and stained the inside of your carnal oven."

"My carnal oven, huh? You full of do-do, boy." She giggled again.

They lay there for a while, both in their own happy thoughts before Candy leaned up on Chico's chest.

"Chico, can I ask you something?"

"Yea, shoot."

Candy thought carefully before she spoke, wanting the words to come out just right. Her mind had been racing ever since her conversation with Keisha the week before. But she and Chico had been getting along so well lately that she was feeling like maybe now was the right time to ask him about some of the things Keisha had said.

"Well, you know my girl Keisha?"

"That crazy girl in my English class?"

"Yeah." Candy nodded. "Well, she was telling me last week that there are some dudes up here from Brooklyn who are like bad news, and have been hanging around Church Hill and that you and Malcolm have been rolling with them." Candy let out a big breath as she finished her sentence, waiting for his reply.

"So your question is...?"

"Come on, baby, I'm just asking if it's true," she said nervously as she sat up so she could see his eyes. You could always test truth in the eyes, her mother always said. The question was, did she really want the truth?

"I haven't..." she paused. "I haven't asked you about that stuff with Orlando, and I won't, I promise. But..."

Chico's playful expression suddenly changed to a guarded one. "Well, I guess you done already decided in your mind whas' true, right? So tell me, what else did Miss Nosy Ass Keisha tell you?"

"Now don't even start blaming her."

"I'm not blaming nobody. It just ain't none of her business. If you want to know something, you can ask me yourself. It ain't her place to be noising in my damn business talkin' 'bout what *I* do. She best be worrying about her own problems and that ugly-ass weave she keeps getting."

"But what about Orlando?"

"We ain't talking 'bout Orlando!" Chico screamed, sitting up abruptly. Candy froze. "Okay, let's just forget it..."

"Yea, let's *forget* it," was his sarcastic response. "Shit...we need to bounce on outta here anyhow. I told Malcolm I would meet him to help him pick out his new ride." Chico got up and made his way to the bathroom door.

Candy stared at the closing door. "I guess our conversation is over..." she said to herself.

The ride to Candy's house was a quiet one. Pulling up to the curve, Chico put his Escape into park and took Candy's hand in his.

"It's hard, you know? I mean, it's easy for you Candy; you got all this," he said, motioning toward her house.

Candy's dog, Snowflake, came running from behind the back. Water sprinklers gave off an evening mist for the lush, green grass that covered the lawn.

"I have nothing; we have nothing, my family and me. So yea, I've been doing a lil sumpin' to bring money to the table. I do what I have to do. You know me. I can't just sit back and watch my mom kill herself, even if that means doing something not completely legit."

"But you're smart, baby. You can use your brains to get ahead, not get lost in the streets. I don't want to see that happen to you. You could end up getting killed or something," she cried. "You did say that Ms. Mayes was entering some of your poetry in a city competition, right?"

"Damn, Candy, that's just poetry; that shit is just sumpin' to do. But some lil contest ain't gonna help pay bills. I'm talking about now, baby, now...today! Look...ain't nuttin' gonna happen to me. I'm not stupid, aight? And no, I don't expect you to see it. Your life is different than mine. Everything you got is what I'm trying to get...I don't expect you to under..."

"I do understand!" Candy cried, cutting him off. "Life isn't as easy for me as you think it, Chico..."

She took his face in her hands and began to kiss him deeply, slowly exploring his mouth with her tongue. After long moments, both pulled away, and dark brown eyes delved into bright hazel ones.

"I love you, Sean Grayson. I don't want anything to happen to you like what happened to Orlando. Think about what I'm saying, please?" Candy implored earnestly. "Just share with me. Don't leave me in the dark, boo..."

Chico sighed and looked away. He thought about the things Candy didn't know. She didn't know about that time he had cheated on her, *still felt guilty about that*. She didn't know the real reason they had gone to D.C. She didn't know how deeply involved he was in this business with Marco, and she definitely didn't know about the hit that took place on Chamberlayne, or that he himself had been the one to take Wesley out. Would she still be talking about loving him if she knew who and what he really had become?

"Look, just think about what I've said, okay? Okay?" she pressed.

"Yeah..."

Candy smiled tearfully as she jumped from the SUV. "I love you, Chico."

"I love you, too," Chico whispered, almost to himself.

CHAPTER FOURTEEN:
ME AGAINST THE WORLD...

Rims never had shined so brightly as the ones on Malcolm's spanking brand-new Acura Legend. The boys' activities were pretty obvious by this time. Their material prosperity was reflected by the toys they had bought. Chico pulled up in his vehicle, smiling as he spotted Junnie and Malcolm dancing around Malcolm's new car.

"Check out Malcolm's ride!" Junnie exclaimed. "I told him this joint is hard. All the honnies gonna holla wit' us riding in that!"

Chico smiled as he hopped out of his SUV. He and Junnie gave each other quick daps before going over to holla at Malcolm who was standing beside Marco as they signed ownership papers. Marco was in good with everybody it seemed, and this particular Honda car dealer was no exception. Marco looked over at Junnie.

"Come on, Junnie. You need to sign these papers after me. We'll be hooking you up with something sweet tomorrow," Marco said.

"Oh, yeah. Sounds good to me!" Junnie exclaimed as he bounced quickly over to Marco. Malcolm laughed, shaking his head at the two of them, and then walked up to Chico.

"What up, playa?" he said. He rubbed the hood of his car. Its shining body gleamed at them. "So what do you think?"

"She's tight, man. Those 20s are like da shit of shit! A muthafuccin' Acura Legend? You went all out, holmes!"

"Well, what you expect? I had to keep up wit' your high-rolling ass," Malcolm said, punching Chico playfully on the arm. "The sky is the limit. We like the Jeffersons these days; we moving on up!"

Malcolm and Chico took a few minutes to check out the inside of the vehicle. It was black with gold trim. Soft black leather clothed the bucket seats inside, and it had one of the new type of set-ups where there was a CD player along with a tape player.

As Marco walked toward them, with Junnie following close behind, he tossed the car keys to Malcolm. "Okay, she's all yours. Y'all meet me at my place. We got a few things to talk about." Looking over at Junnie, he said, "You riding with me, Junnie?"

"Naw, man, I wanna kick it wit' Malcolm and see how this baby purrs."

"Aight then, I see y'all in a short." He held up one finger, then got in his own car and pulled off.

Later on relaxing at Marco's apartments they found out just why Marco was being so generous with them, and why he had helped Malcolm to purchase the Acura Legend. Marco wanted some more weapons transported up farther north to York, Pennsylvania. Thing was, Five-O had really started cracking down on illegal weapons sales in PA, and being that Chico, Malcolm and Junnie were minors, Marco felt it was safer sending them to do the job. Except for the job in D.C. where Big O had lost his life, Marco had mostly been using them for small street sales in Church Hill, Southside and Highland Park. But the big money, he explained, was up North, being that they were willing to pay more for 9millis than the Southern bruhs were. Also, there was so much gang activity up North that weapons of the quality that Marco was pushing were in great demand. He was gonna put a lot of responsibility in their hands this time, and a lot of money, too.

"So when do you want us to leave?" Malcolm asked.

"Well, I have some people I want you to meet first. This job is a bit different than the other ones you have done. It's not just my money we talking, or my product. I'm investing trust in you guys, putting my reputation on the line. Some of my fellas from N.C. wanna meet with you boys, too."

"What do they wanna meet us for?" Junnie asked.

Marco leaned forward, handing Malcolm a lit blunt. "I told you why. This job here is an enterprise thing. We put our dollars together to make even bigger dollars. They wanna see who they're entrusting their money to."

"Hmm…" Chico hummed. "So they're coming here to Richmond?"

"Yep. They're on their way over here now as a matter of fact," said Marco. "So y'all can meet 'em, and then we'll get everything straight, the ins and outs and what's gonna go down once you all get there in York. It should be pretty easy. The only thing is that we got a lot of competition in York. Those North-Clique brothas, we owe them a favor. They got beef with these niccas in York that they want us to take care of."

"Why do we owe them a favor? I ain't neva met these brothas," Chico said.

Marco laughed. "Well, *I* owe them a favor, and if I owe 'em, y'all my niccas right?" He looked from Chico to Malcolm to Junnie. "Right?"

Malcolm spoke up. "Most definite, man."

Junnie was quiet, but Chico said, "So what kind of beef we talking about here?"

Before the question could be answered, the front door opened. It was two guys, who must have been the ones that Marco had mentioned since he didn't trip about them walking in without knocking.

"Wassup, my brothas," Marco said, greeting them. He stood up and gave both of them daps, and then introduced them to his boys.

After everyone had settled back down, the North-Clique guys started explaining to them what they needed done.

"These boys we need y'all to get at, they ain't new in the game. They know we coming at 'em, but they just don't know when. So you need to catch 'em unaware," one of the guys said.

Another one of the guys, who had introduced himself as Eazy, asked them the ultimate question. "I hope you boys see what we need y'all to do here. Don't want no misunderstanding or nothing."

"They understand," Marco said.

The room got quiet. Yeah, they understood. They had to run a hit.

They understood, totally...

Later after the meeting with the Charlotte brothas and Marco, Chico and Junnie rode quietly back to Church Hill. Chico couldn't help but notice how quiet his boy was, and wondered what was going through his mind. Even though he could kinda guess.

"So, what do you think about this York thing?" Chico asked.

"What do you think?"

"Nicca, I asked you." Chico laughed.

Junnie scratched his head, and then pulled his cigarettes out of his pocket.

"Come on, Junnie, tell me what's on you mind, bruh."

Junnie took a long drawl off his cigarette, swallowed, then blew out through his nose. He gave Chico a serious look. "Chico, don't you think this shit is getting whack? Like...like they got us pinned like we lil killers or sumpin'."

"You have never taken anybody out, Junnie. And that dude Wes, that wasn't a hit; that was an accident, and you know it."

"Yeah, but how come every time they want somebody wasted, they calling on us?"

"Like when?" Chico asked.

"Like now!"

Chico sighed. "I don't know. I don't like how this sounds either; Imma be real wit' you. But what else are we s'pose to do?"

"We can tell them no. N-O."

Chico pulled alongside the curve, stopping to look at Junnie. "Oh, so you gon' tell Marco that?" he said.

Junnie looked in the direction of the moving cars racing past them and was silent.

"Look, Junnie, I don't wanna be doing this shit forever either, and I don't trust Marco, and that's real. But right now, it's paying off, man. I mean you getting your ride tomorrow, right? You telling me you don't want that? Yeah, we having to do some dirty shit, but we're getting what we want, too. I don't like this killing stuff. But we won't be always doing this. Marco said it's just this one time, then we back to our regular business. I don't like going after niccas that ain't done shit to me, but I hate being broke even more. I want respect, and with all this, at least we're getting some of that."

Junnie breathed a loud sigh of frustration. "Damn," he said, looking out the window. "We still involved, Chico. I ain't never thought I would be doing no shit like this. We're gonna end up on the fuccin' *America's Most Wanted* or sumpin'!"

"So is that it? You're scared?"

"Oh, hell naw! I'm not scared of nothing. And I ain't trying to be no saint either. You know I take care of those who fuck wit' me. But it's like you said, Chico, we don't know these dudes."

"Then walk, man. Just don't do it. 'Cuz ain't nobody forcing you to do a damn thing. If you ain't in the game, then don't play it. As for me, I'm gonna do what I gotta do, you hear what I'm saying? Why do we gotta be living in shitland while other people living the American dream? Fuck America! It's me against the world. If society don't want me to take what I need then they should make it an on da real equal opportunity, and not just in the reach for some."

"Now you sound like 2Pac or somebody with that 'me against the world' shit." Junnie laughed.

"And I mean it, man. Hell, just like he said, ain't nobody worrying about poor black folks living in the hood; ain't no missionaries cruising these streets trying to save a soul with their hell and damnation bullshit. So we got to take what we need. You think I wanna be doing this? If I had it my way, I'd be heading to college. But it ain't like that. That's some other bruh's reality; this is mine."

"Come on. It ain't all that serious, right?" Junnie said.

Chico knew that. No, he didn't. He knew that it was serious and so did Junnie. But what was even more serious was the fact that both of them knew that regardless of their doubts and bravado speech, they were in too deep.

Chico swallowed back his hyped talk. Looking at Junnie, he asked, "So, are you down? Are you with us for PA?"

Junnie didn't respond, but he didn't need to. There was no backing out now.

After dropping Junnie off, Chico pulled up to his own crib, and slowly made his way inside. He felt slow, druggish. Maybe it was because the next day was coming a bit too quickly for him.

As he walked past Asha's bedroom, he stopped when he saw her lying on her bed listening to her portable CD player, head bobbing. "What up?" he asked her.

"Ain't nuttin' up. Wassup wit' you?" Asha asked as she removed her headphones.

"Ahh...not much." Chico swallowed, and looked around in Asha's room. He seemed mentally preoccupied.

"What's wrong with you, boy?"

"I need you to do something for me. I got some biz to take care of tomorrow, so I want you to drop my essay off to Ms. Mayes' class, okay? Just cover for me a lil bit?"

Asha sat up at full attention at his words. "What do you mean cover for you? You cutting classes, Chico?"

Chico jiggled his keys as he headed out the door. "Girl, just do it."

"This is senior year. You can't be just cutting classes whenever you feel like it. You don' gone just plain crazy, boy. What in the world has gotten into you?"

"Aint nuttin' got into me. My grades are fine. So just do it, aight? I need to get this essay grade," he said as he walked away toward his own room.

"Ugg...whateva!" Asha hollered back. She ran to her door. "Chico, this is your ass. I'm not gonna keep covering for you!"

She watched as he ignored her, then closed his door quietly behind himself.

CHAPTER FIFTEEN:
STREET REALITY...

The following day as they rode to York, Pennsylvania, no one seemed in much of a mood to talk but Malcolm. They had tossed a coin to see who would drive, and which two of the three would be the shooters for the hit. Knowing how doubtful Junnie was feeling about the whole thing, Chico secretly hoped he would end up being the driver, but unfortunately Malcolm had won the toss.

Malcolm's eyes were red as sausages, so Chico pretty much knew that he had smoked from the peace pipe before they left, just like he was smoking from it now.

"You need to chill with the weed, Malcolm. Those trees starting to take you over," Chico noted.

"Yeah, well, haven't you heard that green veggies were good for you?" He handed the pipe to Junnie. "Enjoy, brotha," he said, laughing.

Chico shook his head as Junnie inhaled right along with Malcolm.

"We're here," Malcolm said as he pulled to a duplex that had the address they were given. They got out of Chico's ride, making sure they locked the doors behind them. His Escape was packed with twelve 9-millis and seven 38s and seven 322s that were their sell items. The plan was to make the sell for Marco, pick up a dude named Lockette, then drive over to the Eastside and take care of their North-Clique's little friends. After that they were to head straight back down South to let Marco know it was done.

Unlike before when Candy had gone with them to D.C., Chico went inside with Malcolm and Junnie. They decided for safety's sake not to take any weapons inside until they had checked things out. They also were sure to be strapped themselves. They definitely didn't want a repeat of the Big O situation.

After ringing the doorbell that hung halfway off the grayed door that probably used to be white, they were greeted by a white dude who was styling some dreadlocks that looked better than how some brothas wore them. Behind him was a dude that sort of reminded Chico of a chubby Kobe Bryant.

"So, y'all got the goods?" asked the white dude.

"I'm Malcolm," Malcolm said, then pointed to Chico and Junnie, "and this is Chico, and that's Junnie."

"Aight, cool. Y'all got the goods?"

Chico looked at him warily. "Yeah we got it. You got the green?"

The guy smirked, then opened the ripped screen door. "Step into my office."

They went inside and all sat down on a black leather sectional. Chico was amazed at how hooked the dude had it inside, considering how nasty the outside was. He guessed it was a good way of hiding what you had.

"I'm Lockette," the white guy said, "and this here is Mick." All the guys gave each other a nod. "I got your money right here," Lockette continued. He patted a fat briefcase that sat on the coffee table in front of him.

"We were told to count it beforehand. You know how that is," Malcolm said.

Lockette threw up his hands and smiled. "Have it your way, dawg. Let's count."

The money for the weapons was more cash in hand than the guys had ever dealt with at one time. But there still was a big difference in Chico's mind from what Marco had originally said was the actual amount of weapons and money to be exchanged. It seemed more and more like this trip was mainly to run the hit than it was to sell some weapons.

Junnie, Malcolm and the Kobe Bryant look-alike went outside to get the guns while Chico and Lockette talked about what was next.

"So, you and your boys know wassup, right?" Lockette asked.

"Meaning?"

Lockette laughed. Seemed like this mofo had been laughing from the moment he opened the door, Chico thought.

The other guys came in and placed the weapons in heaps on the dining room table, then walked over and took a seat to join in the conversation.

"What I mean," Lockette said as he leaned forward, "you boys know what we have to do now. We have to make a run to east York. Just making sure y'all aware of this shit."

"Yeah, we're aware," Malcolm acknowledged.

"Good. Y'all need to get totally strapped." Lockette looked over at Mick. "Mick got one of my boys to check up on it. They ballin' at Raleigh Park, so let's roll."

Chico swallowed. Junnie bit his lip and lit a cigarette, and Malcolm grinned. They gathered the ammo they would need, and then along with Lockette and Mick they headed out the door.

"Don't y'all wonder why Lockette and Mick can't take care of this?" Junnie stated as they rolled down the street. "These niccas living right here in York and they have to have us come all the way down to do this?"

"What you trying to say?" Chico asked.

"Nothing, I'm just thinking out loud, that's all..."

Malcolm grinned. "Well, you think too much, nicca. Double-check those Uzis, make sure that shit don't backfire on ya ass."

Junnie gave him a dirty look, then continued checking the barrels. After removing their safety latches, he announced, "Okay, ready."

It didn't take them long before they were close to their destination. Lockette and Mick were driving ahead of them, since they not only were supposed to show them where Raleigh Park was but were also to point out the two guys they were supposed to take out.

Malcolm was driving Chico's SUV. He pointed toward a beige duffel bag on the floor. "We got some cool ass masks; those joints look like what Queen Latifah, Jada Pinkett and them was wearing in that movie *Set It Off*," he said. His eyes were blood red from the weed.

Chico looked at him, and then pulled out the masks. The grayish, clear faces on them looked almost eerie. He threw Malcolm and Junnie theirs, then put his own on. The rubber band on the back puckered at the back of his neck. His eyes blurred, he tried to focus on the road ahead; he tried to keep his eyes on Lockette's car. But he could feel his heart pounding. What they were about to do was so extremely foul that he had to work hard to block out the conscious his mama had trained. He had to bury it somewhere deep; he had to focus. His ears were ringing but he could hear Ja Rule and J.Lo music somewhere in the deep recesses of his mind.

"Turn it up!" he said to Malcolm, not even sure why he said it.

Malcolm turned up the speakers. "You need to get ready. You, too, Junnie."

They pulled up to Raleigh Avenue and spotted Raleigh Park. It was early evening, so the courts were mad busy. Lockette signaled as he had said he would, flashing his park lights twice. He then parked his car. Passing his car slowly, Malcolm stopped right in front of Lockette. The guys watched as Lockette's friend Mick got out and looked at the tire on the car as if it were threatening to flat.

He didn't look at them, but said, "Green jersey, number thirty-four. The other dude, cut-off jeans, red scarf wrapped around his head. Get thirty-four first." He then got back into Lockette's car.

Chico pulled out two Uzis and placed them in his lap. He held on tight to the handles, waiting...

Everything was moving in slow motion.

"Now," Malcolm shouted, "do it now!"

On cue, Chico leaned his whole torso out of the window and pointed, when suddenly he heard Junnie, who also was leaning out the back window scream, "Kids! They got kids on the court, man! Oh shit!"

"Do it," Malcolm screamed again.

Chico pulled out both Uzis, one in each hand, and began firing. Both he and Junnie aimed at number thirty-four, spraying a round of bullets his way. Screams could suddenly be heard everywhere as the guy fell to the ground in a puddle of blood, along with two other guys who were not the intended targets. The other guy, red scarf, cut off jeans, seemed to have guessed what was going down and started running. Malcolm swung the car around, chasing him. The guy just about ran into the SUV, halfway flipping over the hood before rolling over and jumping right back to his feet. He looked in all directions trying to get away.

"Man, that nicca crazy!" Malcolm cried, as Chico and Junnie both fired simultaneously. Still running, the dude's body all of a sudden stilled and shook as bullets ripped through him. He then fell, face forward into the street.

"Let's go, Malcolm!" Chico demanded. Drivers were honking horns at the violent transaction; female screams were deafening. "Hurry up! We need to get outta here!"

Even though he was steadily giving orders, Chico could feel himself getting sick, just as he did after what happened on Chamberlayne Avenue. Hot nausea bit at his stomach, causing him to feel like he had just taken a deep drop on a roller coaster ride.

After about fifteen minutes of driving, Malcolm looked in the back seat at Junnie. He had been mysteriously quiet the whole time, and Chico, noticing the directions of Malcolm's eyes, looked back at him, too. Junnie still had his mask on.

"Yo, you need to take that off before the cops see you and wonder wassup with it," Chico said.

Junnie removed his mask slowly, but continued looking straight ahead as if in a daze. He was still holding on tight to his Uzi.

"What the hell is wrong with you, Junnie?"

"Nothing." Junnie blinked.

Suddenly Malcolm yelled, "Shit! I'm pulling over." He pulled roughly to the side road on I-95.

"You act this same whiny-ass way every time something goes down. I'm not going to jail for ya ass, so you need to put that piece away and calm the fuck down!"

"I'm calm!" Junnie exclaimed. He quickly removed his mask, dropping his Uzi in the process. His hands were shaking. Chico stared at him. He knew what Junnie was feeling. But it was over now. At least for the moment, it was.

Asha jumped off the bus, holding her CVS bag tightly. As she turned the corner onto Groveland Avenue, she prayed silently that Jenene was home. She was at Jenene's door within two minutes flat.

"Did you get it?" Jenene asked as she opened the door.

Asha walked inside, slipping off her Nikes and jacket. "I'm going to the bathroom. Your mom's not home, is she?"

"No. What kind of test did you get? EPT?"

Asha nodded, then made her way into the bathroom, shutting the door. After peeing on the little white stick that was in the box, she set it on the counter, leaned against the wall, closed her eyes and waited.

Jenene knocked quietly on the door.

"Asha?" There was silence. Feeling concerned, Jenene knocked again. "Asha, what did it say?"

Finally after still not getting a response from her cousin, she opened the door slowly. Asha was stooped down against the wall with her head bowed. She looked up as Jenene walked through the door. Tears reddened her face as her lips trembled.

"Oh, girl, it's positive?" Jenene exclaimed.

"Yes…"

Jenene sat down beside her, grabbing the EPT stick. The plus sign was visible and blue. She sighed as she saw it.

"So what you gonna do, sis?"

"I don't know," Asha cried. Her shoulders shook as she cried softly against Jenene's shoulder with Jenene squeezing her tightly. After a few minutes, she looked at Jenene. "I have to tell Peanut, I guess."

"And what you think he's gonna say?"

"Who can know when it comes to him?" Asha shrugged.

"Asha, what if…what if it's not his?"

Jenene didn't have to put that question in Asha's mind. It had already been there, deep and embedded ever since she realized she had missed her period. The crazy thing was, when she and Peanut had sex they always used protection except for a couple of times. But she couldn't forget that she had kicked it with Orlando the day before he got killed. Had kicked it hard on her mama's floor, and hadn't used condom the first.

For some reason, at that time, she wasn't very worried about it. But she knew she couldn't block it out now. She had a baby in her stomach and she needed a baby daddy. Orlando was dead and gone, so all she had left was Peanut.

"It is his," she insisted to Jenene.

"I know, but what if it's not? What if it's Big O's baby?"

Asha jumped up, threw the EPT tester in the garbage and stepped to the sink to wash her face. After that she stood up straight, flattening her shirt against her belly as if to test and see if it was getting bigger.

"You're gonna just tell Peanut it's his baby?" Jenene asked.

Asha didn't answer her.

"Asha, what if he wants a blood test?"

"He won't."

"But what if he does?"

Asha looked at her and wiped her tears off her face. Firmly, she said, "He won't."

CHAPTER SIXTEEN:
TO THE POWERS THAT BE...

What are the powers that be?
Controlling mine...controlling my destiny...
Determining my fate...
My reality...some are positive
Others are filled with negativity...
What are the powers that be?
Pulling backward and forward taking charge of me...
Like a heavenly force, strong as gravity...
One part of me seeks the goodness the fair...
The other part seeks what's evil and vile...
So for me, what are the powers that be?
How do I postpone the inevitability?
What future will these bring in?
Or what will suspend the payback for my sins?
And yet again I ask...
What are the powers that be?
And just what does it say...about me?

Liz Grayson smiled as she spotted Aileen Mayes sitting quietly at Friendly's restaurant. They had been talking on the phone a lot lately. Talking about Sean's future, and also his present. For some reason she felt comfortable with Aileen. They had even gone to the point of talking on first-name basis. What was more a first for Liz was that she actually felt that Sean's teacher cared. A caring teacher was a rarity in this area. Most were so busy trying to keep their classrooms quiet enough to avoid constant headaches that they didn't have time to see their students as individuals or worry about their home life. There was so much darkness where Liz was raising her children. Even though she sought a beacon of light for them, she had a hard time keeping it lit even for herself.

"Liz, I'm so glad you could make it," Aileen said.

"Well, I'm sorry I'm late."

Aileen sat down, then hailed the waitress to bring Liz coffee. "Oh, don't worry about it. I thought I would be late myself. There was a horrible situation at the school today. I had a hard time getting away, although I had already made plans to leave early."

"What happened?" Liz asked.

"Oh, it was awful." She sighed. "One of our teachers, Viva McNeal, she just transferred to us actually from L.A., she had a problem with one of her students this morning. The girl came in late; she is habitually tardy, even for my class. So this morning when she did it again, popping in twenty minutes late, Viva reprimanded her and wrote her up for CBI, in school suspension. Jacqueline, the student we're talking about, went off. Basically she attacked Ms. McNeal."

"Oh no!" Liz exclaimed. She quieted when the waitress came with coffee, then took their orders. After she walked away, Liz asked, "So what happened? Was the girl suspended?"

Aileen scooted her chair closer to the table, leaning in as she whispered, "Liz, it went further than that, much further. Jacqueline got Viva McNeal in a chokehold. She was choking her, and Viva...well, she bit her."

"Bit her!"

"Yes," she said, nodding, "in the face."

"That's awful, Aileen! What's going to happen to Ms. McNeal?"

"I don't know. But the police came. And right now it's up in the air. But listen, the real reason we got together today was to talk about Sean. How is he?"

Liz ran her hands over her face. "He's very quiet these days. It's hard to know really. But I do think he's in trouble. I can always tell when my kids are in trouble." She took a sip of her coffee.

"And you think it's the area you live in of course..." Aileen whispered.

"I know that has something to do with it. I just don't know what to do about it."

They quieted when the waitress walked up, serving Aileen her club sandwich, and Liz her chicken salad club. Both ate silently for a while, each caught up in their own thoughts.

After a while Liz swallowed a chunk of her sandwich and said, "I'm thinking about sending Sean away."

"No!" Aileen exclaimed. "Liz, I know he's your son, but there is so much that Sean can do here. He is a wonderful writer. And I'm not just talking about his poetry. I'm speaking on his short stories also. I think I could really talk him into applying to some colleges." Her hand went up. "I know you told me before that money is a problem, but that's why I think it's so important that he stays here. I've submitted him into several scholarship programs, and I really think he has a chance, Liz."

"Are you serious?" Liz asked, feeling hopeful.

"Yes!"

Liz smiled to herself, imagining her son, the writer, and the wonderful future he could have if it worked out for him that way. She frowned as another thought hit her. Nodding, she said, "But see, I've been thinking that he has been doing something illegal. If he stays in Richmond, he'll still have all of those negative influences around him."

"That's true," Aileen agreed.

"My sister and I have been talking about her son Kenny coming down and spending some time with Sean. Perhaps talking to him and helping him to think more about his future. Kenny is a fantastic example, and he and Sean have always been so close."

"So then if that works, maybe he won't have to move away?" Aileen asked. "I'm not trying to press, but I really enjoy teaching your children. I want to see them excel."

"I'm not even sure I could get him to leave even if I decided that was the best thing to do. Sean is his own man now. He really doesn't listen to me at all." She shook her head in confusion. "I really don't know who he listens to now, except for maybe his so-called boys."

Aileen reached her hand out to Liz, squeezing it tightly. Both black women looked at each other with mutual understanding. Both knew that the problems they spoke of were not necessarily unique to them or theirs, but to all black women—to all impoverished women struggling daily to save their children.

Liz only hoped and prayed she could save her son before it was too late.

An early winter chill was in the air. The green, orange and yellow kaleidoscope of colors which clothed the trees all fall was slowly dying off, leaving pointed naked branches waiting for snow time. Everything seemed to be coming early for the year, and time seemed to be passing by too quickly. Chico feared that the early cold was a warning from the man upstairs of his wrath, which was also coming quickly. He wasn't worried about Hell. To him, Hellfire fables were just like tricks, which were for kids. But he did fear that all his whack deeds would come back on him. That fear was also in the air, and no matter how hard he tried to squash the morbid thoughts, they played on his mind like a bad movie.

He had set some time aside to spend with Candy, but she seemed to be in one of her "tell me everything that's on your mind" moods. His shawty sure as hell didn't want to know what was on his mind. Although they were supposed to be studying together, Candy seemed to be more preoccupied with staring him down as if she were ready to rumble. He ignored her best he could until she jumped up, placed her hands on her hips and shouted his name.

"Chico!"

He looked up from his notebook. "What?"

"I don't know why you're playing me like this. Why you're trying to act like nothing's wrong, and you know damn well there's a hella lot wrong!"

"What are you talking about?" asked Chico as he looked at her blankly.

Candy growled. "What am I talking about? What am I talking about! Chico, look at you, you have barely said two words since you got here. Normally I can never shut you up. I mean are you upset with me for some reason? Is there something going on with you that you haven't told me? Is there another girl?"

"Lawd...Where is this shit coming from? Now it's another girl, huh?" He shut his notebook.

"It's coming from my heart, and you ain't hearing my heart no more, Chico." She gave him a pleading look. "That's one of the things I used to love so much about you. You saw me, heard me. Now you don't even seem to wanna be with me no more."

"How you figure that?"

"Chico, we are never...together...anymore! You're always too busy. You always have something better to do. So what else am I to think but that there's another girl? Outside of all the stuff I've been hearing about you. You're always in Highland Park and never with me. So who you messin' with, huh?" Candy asked accusingly.

Chico looked in Candy's eyes for a minute, saying nothing. He then got up and slowly began putting his Nikes on, grabbed his books and keys and headed for the door.

"Where are you going?!" cried Candy.

"I'm getting outta here. I'm not gonna sit and listen to this bullshit. Listen, if you don't trust me we don't have any reason to be together I got enough on my mind without adding this, too. Maybe we just need to give it a break for a while..."

"No!" Candy moaned in protest, jumping up to grab him by the arm. "Why you gotta act like that?! You know I love you, Sean! I just want you to *talk* to me. Talk to me!" she cried, holding tight against his chest.

"Why you always gotta be talking about what somebody don' told you, Candy? You got some nosy ass friends; I told you this before. So they tell you some silly shit and here you come at me with it. Baby, I got mad shit on my mind. I'm not about hearing all that! You can't understand that!"

"Okay, I'm sorry. Please...I love you." Thick tears streamed down her lovely face as she spoke. "I just want us to be as close as we were before..."

Candy looked pleadingly into Chico's eyes "We used to talk to each other about everything. I used to feel you and thought you felt me, too. It's like you're so far away from me now. I just want to know what's wrong, what's changing. Please?"

What was wrong? What had changed? If only she knew. How could he possibly explain the person he was now to her, to his mother, to himself, to anyone?

All he had wanted was a chance to get out of the hood madness. And now his conscience was starting to eat him alive, and there was no way he could fix it or make his mind believe that it was just *business* as Marco called it. That the two innocent guys that were killed and the fourteen-year-old girl that was shot in the crossfire last weekend in York, not to mention the two guys they actually meant to hit, was something they could just put in the back of their minds. Maybe others could but Chico hadn't cleansed himself of it since the moment he found out what the casualties of their *out-of-town job* actually amounted to. Maybe *he* was the punk Malcolm was constantly calling Junnie, but all he knew is that standing there looking into Candy's eyes, he would give anything to be the person he had been months before. He needed her warmth, her touch, something to make him forget.

With his eyes never leaving her tear glazed ones, Chico locked the door, fell to his knees in front of her, and buried his face against her belly. He stifled a cry as he inched her skirt up…slowly. For the moment, at least, he was able to forget, in her arms…

There was silence on the other end of the phone; a deafening silence. Asha didn't know what she was supposed to say to her cousin who for the past few weeks had been hounding her unmercifully about her pregnancy.

"I know you hear me, girl, so don't act like you don't," Jenene sassed.

Asha said nothing, just continued to wipe at her salty wet face. Jenene was really getting on her nerves. She had enough to deal with than having to cope with her cousin's controlling ways. Even though deep inside she knew that Jenene loved her and was really just showing her concern, it was still hard. She needed time to think—time to decide what *she* wanted to do, not what someone else thought she should do.

Finally getting fed up with Jenene's obsessive chirping, Asha said, "What do you want me to do, Jenene?"

"It's not what I want you to do. It's what you *should* do."

Asha held her breath. "And what is that?" *As if she didn't already know.*

"You can't have that baby."

"I'm not killing my baby, Jenene…"

"If you have it you're gonna be stuck with Peanut, and then what? Huh?"

"Well, he is my boyfriend. You talk as if he's some strange Negro or something." Asha paused, closing her eyes for a moment so she could gather her thoughts. "Jenene, I love him, okay? I don't even want to think about this not being his baby, because I know it's his, and I know that once I tell him he's gonna be happy about it."

"Who gives a fuck if he's happy? I can't stand his ass!"

"Well, I love him," Asha said defensively. She had said those words, *I love him*, so often, that she had convinced herself of its truth.

"Love him? Girl, he ain't even cute! I don't see the attraction, for real! Now you're gonna have a baby by a watermelon-head, broke-ass woman-beater. I don't know who needs help the most, you or him!"

Jenene's screaming and rants and raves didn't alter. She had never made it a secret of her dislike for Asha's boyfriend Peanut. She didn't like the way he talked to her. She didn't like the fact that he had hit her more then once. She had always said that sistas who got their ass beat could blame nobody but themselves, and if any man ever put their hands on her she would cook up a nice pan of grits, even salt it up for them, wait until they weren't looking, and then feed them the pan, on da house! If there was one thing about Jenene, she did not play. Asha knew that she wanted her to have the same diva attitude. Maybe it would've saved her a couple of slaps across the face, and getting knocked up by the certified punk ass that she was gonna have to deal with now.

"You know you need to stop, Jenene; I don't need that stress," cried Asha.

"No, you don't need that stress. He's the stress! I don't blame Chico and Malcolm for kicking that ass, 'cuz he ain't shit, he ain't never been shit, he ain't never gonna be shit, and if you have his baby you just gonna be loaded down with his shit for at least eighteen years!" Jenene's rambling left her breathless, hardly noticing Asha's whimpering cries on the other end of the phone.

"Oh, baby girl, I'm so sorry!"

"Now you sitting there, calling my baby shit." Asha sniffled. "Look, I'm gonna go. I'll talk to you lata."

"Ashaaaaaa!"

She hung up the phone.

CHAPTER SEVENTEEN:
AND THE WINDS OF WAR CALMED...

A month came and went. Things appeared to quiet down for the VA troop. Marco wasn't calling on them as much. He said he wanted to keep things a bit on the DL since the situation in York had caused such a media stir. He also said that it had somehow gotten out that the hits were done by out-of-town gangbangers. Chico cracked up on that. Like how did they know it was out-of-towners unless Lockette and his fat friend put it out in the street? He tried not to think about it though, and took time to focus on his writing and making things up with Candy. He was starting to realize that he had let go of some of the good things in his life while trying to reach for better things. Was it worth it? He wasn't sure. But the happiness he had thought would come from more material goods hadn't yet arrived. Maybe it never would.

Another thing that was cool to him was that his cousin Kenny from Charlottesville had come up to visit for a couple weeks. They had hung out all the time when they were little kids. Charlottesville was like the vacation spot for him and Asha, although there wasn't shit to see there other than the Thomas Jefferson sites, the places he used to bone Sally Hemings. Another hot spot was *"The Mall."* That place was funny as hell. Everybody in Charlottesville talked about *"The Mall"* as if it was like the bomb-diggity of Harlem or sumpin'. Thing about it was that *"The Mall"* was an outdoor marketplace type of thing, looked more like a flea market with an outdoor BBQ joint in the middle of it. It was wack, but it was also the landmark of Charlottesville, Virginia.

Chico washed his ride 'til it shined like glass, then sprayed his tires with Armor All. Even though it was cold out he wasn't one to drive around with dirty wheels. The cold was bearable since the sun had come out of hiatus. He could feel warmth beaming down on his neck. A slight chilly breeze offset it, but he didn't care. His main man was coming to town and he was gonna enjoy his week; cool weather be damned.

Just as he wiped the last of the moisture from his SUV, he looked around to see a cab pulling up. He saw Kenny's wide, picture-taking grin peeping from the passenger window.

"Oh shit!" Chico exclaimed. "Man, get ya ass over here!"

Kenny jumped from the cab and met Chico for a tight brotha-to-brotha hug. "Wassup, cuz? Man, I've missed the hell outta you!"

"Of course you have. I mean just look at me," Kenny said. Both guys laughed, looking at each other.

"I'm glad you could come, Kenny," Chico said. "It's been too wild around here."

"Why is that? I heard you need me to come set you straight." Kenny punched Chico playfully on the arm.

"You need to pay me and get your bags, brotha!" the cab driver shouted.

Kenny eyed the cabby, looked over at Chico and laughed. "Come on, help me with my bags. And oh…" He punched Chico on the arm. "Pay the man!"

A couple of hours later they were chillin'. Both were starved as they chowed down burgers and homemade fries. Chico was always amazed at how Kenny could lift his mood. This time was no different. Chico looked over at his cousin as he was stuffing another humongous quarter of his sandwich in his mouth. Looks-wise they were very similar, except for their coloring. Kenny was a light-brown complexion, styling a low-cut fade, thin mustache and goatee. He was a year Chico's senior, but that slight age difference never affected their unique closeness. One thing that was different about them was the way they grew up. Chico always would tease Kenny about being a hick, but in reality, he envied him more than anything else. Even though both of them were raised by single mothers, Kenny's father had always been active in his life, and he saw him on a regular basis.

"So, how are things in Charlottesville?" Chico asked.

"How do you think?"

Chico smirked. He knew Kenny was bored at home. It certainly didn't take much persuading to get him to come to Richmond. Although it was Chico's mom's idea, he didn't have to guess why she was so eager to get the two of them together. Usually she'd be complaining about Kenny's smoking, and the noise he and Chico made whenever they were together. Yet the truth was, she figured that Kenny could talk to Chico and get him straightened out.

Chico looked up to see Kenny staring at him as if he was waiting for him to say something.

"What?"

"Chico, what kind of work are you doing now?" Kenny asked.

Chico shrugged. "You know me, anything to earn a dollar."

"Anything?" Kenny's eyes went wide.

"Aight, what's your point, nicca?" Chico laughed uncomfortably.

Just as Kenny was about to tell him exactly what his point was, the door to Chico's bedroom opened. It was Liz Grayson, beaming down on them with her "you're in trouble" look.

"Why are you two eating in here? I told you before, Chico, no eating outside of the kitchen!"

Chico and Kenny looked at each other and laughed. It was good having old times spin back for a while, even with the growling of Liz Grayson.

◆◆◆

Asha's heart was pounding. She couldn't understand Peanut's response to her announcement that she was pregnant. His response was actually none at all. She didn't know what she had expected. Screaming, hollering, maybe a couple of slaps and "how could you let this happen" statements. What she got though was complete calm.

"Peanut, did you hear what I said?" she asked him.

"Yeah, shawty, I heard ya."

Asha sat back further on the couch. She watched Peanut in amazement as he opened an Icehouse beer, and took a long swig of it.

"Ahhhh..." He blew out a sigh at the refreshing taste, and then sat down beside her.

"Peanut!"

"Let's not talk about that right now, aight?" He pulled at the hem of her skirt. "What you got under there?" he asked, giving her a sexy smirk. He wanted sex.

"I don't know, Peanut..."

Sucking his teeth as he watched her slowly, Peanut whispered out, "You gonna give me sum?"

"No, Lionel might walk in any minute now," she protested.

Ignoring her, Peanut pushed her skirt up higher, steadily rubbing her thigh. He moved his lips to the base of her neck and started nibbling at it. Oddly enough, Asha didn't feel moved. This was a first for her when it came to Peanut. The realization of that, of the numb feeling that she felt, amazed her. Before she realized it, her skirt and blouse were just about off and Peanut was feverishly feeling her up.

"Come on," she hissed, pushing him away. "Peanut, I don't wanna do this right now. Stop it!"

Peanut pushed her back, hard. "Fuck is this? Why you trippin' all of a sudden?"

"I'm not, I just...I'm just tired and I told you I don't feel like having sex, but you haven't heard anything I've said all night, so I shouldn't be surprised!"

Asha wasn't sure why she did it, but she sometimes felt as if she instigated fights with Peanut, as if she already knew how he was going to react, and yet she couldn't seem to stop herself. She held her body rigid after her last words, expecting him to squeeze her jaw or pinch her maybe. But as she waited for his volatile response with closed eyes, she instead got nothing. Opening her eyes, she looked up to see Peanut had slid over, and was lighting a cigarette.

"What are you doing?" she asked him.

"I'm leaving your ass alone, like you just told me to."

"I didn't say I wanted to be left alone!" Asha screamed in frustration. "But, Peanut, we need to talk about the baby."

Peanut laughed nastily. "We don't need to talk about shit. You're pregnant, cool, but I don't give a fuck what you do about that. You got a problem."

Asha looked at him in shock as he got up and walked from the room.

The week had been everything Chico had known it would be. He and Kenny had partied, talked, scoped out girls, talked, hung out with his boys, talked, talked, and talked some more. They had mostly chilled in Northside and Highland Park, although Kenny had complained about how Brooklyn Park Boulevard had become more like a ho strip, and he was right. There wasn't a corner that was ho-free, even with the cold, winter weather. They laughed about that. That still didn't stop their search for a good time. The shawties were sniffing around like moths to a flame. At least that's what Chico's and Kenny's cocky vanity had them bragging.

They spent Saturday night at a party in Central Gardens. The whole evening was cool. There were a lot of ladies showing love, lots of partying and drinks, and plenty of weed, although Kenny didn't indulge. But for Chico things seemed almost back to normal—the normal that existed before all the madness had started.

While the party was up and roaring, Chico and Kenny left to get some more junk food, chips, Doritos and stuff like that for Tarika, the shawty who was throwing the party. As they sat in his Escape the freeness of the evening had Chico coming out with some things Kenny hadn't been able to get out of him the whole week. The happenings that had been going down for the past six months. It was like a heavy weight was being lifted off his shoulders.

Somehow, to Chico's own amazement, the murderous events of York, Pennsylvania came out of his mouth. He waited for Kenny's reaction. The moments seemed to tick by slowly. Kenny was quiet as they turned the corner to Holly Street. The hiphop noise leading to Tarika's party was like a magnet. Chico pulled up and parked. He looked toward Kenny again, who at this time was staring hard at him.

"What?" he asked.

"Chico, you killed people?"

Chico sighed, and laid his head back against the leather upholstery. "I told you what happened."

"I know you did," Kenny argued. "I just don't see how you could have let yourself get wrapped up in some shit like this." He paused, then pulled out a new pack of cigarettes and started patting it on the bottom to push the tobacco back. "Does Aunt Liz know anything about it?"

"Hell naw! And she's not gonna find out either. Besides, I'm thinking about a change anyhow. It's not like I plan to make a career outta this shit."

"Okay." Kenny nodded his head. "So when is this change happening? Now right?"

"What do you mean now?"

A loud knock on Chico's window broke their conversation. Tangerine bootie Alisha stood there, smiling gingerly. She gestured for him to roll the window down.

"Wassup?" Chico asked.

"Somebody told me they had seen you here. I was wondering if you were coming back." She leaned a bit closer inside of the window, bringing her lips close to his. "So when we gonna get up close again, boo?" she whispered.

Chico squirmed uncomfortably in his seat, glancing over at Kenny who was laughing outright by this time. As he turned his head back toward Alisha, she met him with her lips pressed against his. He pulled away quickly with her laughing, then wiping her lipstick from the side of his lip.

"Alisha, it was a mistake what happened with us. You know I'm with Candy."

"Baby, what Miss Candace doesn't know won't hurt her. I kept our secret before, didn't I?"

"Alisha…"

She ignored his weak protest, whispering in his ear, "I know for a fact she don't do the things for you that I do. I'll be inside…"

Kenny and Chico watched her as she walked away, her hips moving in a sexy swing.

"Who the hell is that?" Kenny asked, laughing. Chico shook his head.

"Don't even ask. Let's get this stuff to Tarika and get outta here."

After they got back to Chico's place, he was hoping that Kenny's interrogation was over, but that's when he decided to bring back up the subject of York.

He asked all kinds of questions, things that Chico had thought about himself, kinda, but not in the way that Kenny was lashing it out.

"You need to think about something, Chico," he said.

"Something like what?" Chico asked as he took off his Timberland boots.

"Like the fact that you're doing the white man's job, killing your brothas. And the thing is the cops don't even care who smoked those peeps. Have they even been looking for y'all?"

"Shit, I hope they don't!"

"Of course you don't," Kenny lamented, "and I hope they don't start looking either. I don't wanna see my family in prison. But didn't whitie kill enough of us during the civil rights era? And now here we are thirty years later doing the job for them. If you think about it you would see how crazy that is."

"Aww shit, you plan on preaching to me all night or are you gonna let a brotha get some zzzz?" Chico put his pillow over his head and growled.

"Okay, fine," Kenny said, "but just think about some of what I've said."

The following morning Chico heard a loud roar. It sounded like thunder, roaring thunder blasting in his ear.

"Chico, wake up! Don't make no sense; you and Kenny out running the streets all night, then y'all thinking y'all can sleep all day. Get up! You, too, Kenny; don't make no sense I say!"

Sitting up slowly, Chico shook off the cobwebs to address his pissed-off mom. She was dressed in her work gear—white nursing pants and a pink and yellow flowered shirt. This specific job she was working liked their cooks to be what you would call "uniformed."

"What time is it? Chico asked, yawning.

"Time for y'all to get out of that bed is what. Now move!" his mother commanded as she walked out the door.

Kenny was already up and surfing around for his pack of Newports for a quick smoke.

"Yo, if my mom comes in here and sees you smoking, she's going the hell off on you."

"Aww, man, your mom won't say nuttin'," he replied, blowing out a puff of smoke. "So whas' the plans for today? You know it's my last weekend here and I ain't got no ass yet, boyee. I think you mofos been lying about them honnies. Nobody decent has come my way, and it sure ain't me, not as pretty as I am," he said with a laugh.

"Conceited ass; I taught you well, son! Listen up, we need to do some running for my mom. That's the main reason she getting us up in the first place. Then I'm gonna hook you up with this girl. Candy has this cousin, phat as hell! All you gotta do is throw a lil sumpin' sumpin' on her, that Grayson touch, ya know!"

"Well, what we waiting for?" Kenny put out his cigarette, making an exit for the door. "Better get in the shower before you do. You always calling me country yet y'all the ones with the water getting cold after a five-minute shower."

Chico chuckled as he watched Kenny make his way for the shower. Kenny had mentioned to him about maybe coming to Charlottesville to graduate. He had declined right away. But the more and more he thought about it, the more the idea didn't seem so bad anymore. A chance to start over, he had said.

Suddenly that idea didn't seem so bad...

CHAPTER EIGHTEEN:
SHADOWS OF DARKNESS...

Isn't he darling, isn't he cute...
That little male child in his birthday suit?
Got big plans for this little man...
Gonna watch him grow, help him learn all he can.
See this is my golden chile,
That dark cloud won't touch him.
That shadow of darkness is for people like them
You know "those" people, lost in that ghetto blind hood,
Whose trifling mentality holds them more captive than prison bars ever could.
Soon came his first birthday, his second, his third,
Such a happy, joyful innocent child...free-minded little bird.
That shadow of darkness can't touch him,
Not my beautiful little one.
See we live here in the suburbs
Protected from the dark setting of the sun.
That shadow of darkness is for people like them.
You know, "those" people, groping around in that ghetto blind hood,
Whose trifling mentality holds them more captive than prison bars ever could.
He's safe, raised right, see we didn't raise OUR boy to cuss or fight.
That horrific error is for "those" people,
You know, the ones groping around in that ghetto blind hood
Whose trifling mentality holds them more captive than prison bars ever could.
So why do I now see shadows?
Why are my hopes now blurred?
Could it be that we are no different than "those" people...
In that ghetto blind world?

Later during the day, they somehow managed to connect with Junnie and a few other guys for a quick basketball game. Their hunt for a girl for Kenny had come up empty. He had joked to Chico that it was a conspiracy. But even with their earlier plans altered, they were able to pull together a perfect final day of chilling. After about an hour or so of playing ball, Chico heard his two-way go off. He rushed over to the bleachers to answer it.

"Damn, Chico. Wassup?" Junnie shouted. "We have a good game going!"

"Just hold up. I'll be right back!"

Checking his pager, Chico saw that it was Asha, whom he quickly dialed back.

"What up?" he asked his twin.

"Guess who's here?" she sung out.

"Who?"

"Aunt Delores. She came to pick up Kenny."

"She came early? Dayum, I wonder why? I was supposed to take him back in the morning."

"Well...she's here. But I think she said she and Mama are gonna hang out for a bit first, go to the Piece Goods shop and all. But still they wanted me to page you so that you and he won't go too far. So I was thinking that maybe y'all can come by and get Maxine and me. You know she likes him, right? Jenene is over here, too. Maybe we can go to the mall and hang."

"What makes you think we wanna hang out with y'all," he joked.

"Whateva, we're waiting. Bye."

He hung up the phone, smiling slightly. He and Asha had never been mushy-mushy with each other. They had always had a quiet understanding that most people would say stemmed from the fact that they were twins. He knew that along with everyone else she was concerned about him, and he couldn't help but wonder what her reaction would be when she learned that he was going back to Charlottesville to finish his senior year. Outside of his own problems, he felt something was up with her. He couldn't put his finger on it, but he wondered if it could have something to with that knucklehead boyfriend of hers. Maybe it was a good thing he was leaving Richmond. He had done enough to kill his conscious for the rest of his life. But the more he thought about Peanut, the more he wanted to add one more X to his "bad" Chico rep list.

"Let's finish the game, Chico!" Kenny shouted.

"We can't," Chico replied. "Time to hit the mall!"

It was time to shop. Chico, Kenny, and Junnie, who had decided to come along once he heard the ladies would be present, spent the rest of the afternoon battling over who was buying the tightest pair of Timberlands—then adding Sean John oversized sweatshirts to the set. They were sure not to get anything matching. Junnie reminded them about what Malcolm would say to that. *That's gay, yo!*" They laughed, agreeing since all of them knew how homophobic Malcolm was.

"Where is Malcolm anyhow?" Jenene asked as she, Asha and Maxine shared tables with Chico and the guys at Virginia Center Commons mall.

"Don't know," Chico answered as he stuffed shrimp fried rice in his mouth. "I paged him a while ago. I'm sure he'll come around later to see Kenny off."

"I'm gonna miss you," Maxine purred to Kenny.

He looked at her and gave her a salacious wink. She was a short, thick, dark-skinned girl with humongous tits.

Chico gave Asha a crazed look as she jumped up all of a sudden, proclaiming that she had to make a bathroom run. She had been acting like she wanted to eat everything in the food court, and had been making bathroom stops ever since they had met up with the girls. He shook his head at her weirdness.

"We really will miss you, Kenny. You seem to calm our boys down whenever you come around," Jenene noted.

"Who says we need calming down?"

All eyes looked toward Chico, who had just spoken. They all burst out laughing.

"I don't need anybody to calm me down. I don't know about Junnie, but I'm straight. Now as for Malcolm…" He looked at Jenene, who looked ready to jump to defend Malcolm. "Somebody does need to curve his badass!"

"Well, if you ask me, it's all of you," Jenene barked.

"On that note, listen up, everybody," Kenny announced. He ignored Chico's kick of protest from under the table. "Chico is coming to Charlottesville to finish up school."

All eyes turned back to Chico. Asha stood beside Chico's chair, having just come back from the bathroom and catching the end of Kenny's statement.

"Are you serious?" she asked as she sat back down.

"You're joking!" shouted Junnie.

"Wow!" said Maxine. "I've heard that Charlottesville was *real* country."

"What's *real* country, Maxine?" Kenny asked, irritated.

Everyone laughed at his defensive 'tude. Junnie looked at Chico with questions in his eyes. "Are you really moving?"

That question made Chico pause. It was no joke to him that his life had turned haywire. He was tired of Richmond and tired of the killing and bullshit that he had gotten involved in. He needed this change, or he feared he would get stuck in a life he didn't want for his present or future. He thought about Candy and his mom and Asha. Then his mind flipped to his boys, Junnie and Malcolm. Yeah, he would miss them all, but Kenny was right about the one-way ticket to prison or the grave. Chico didn't want either to be his fate. He figured he would move to Charlottesville, take his SATs and see if he could get into a good college like Kenny was doing. Maybe try for some of those things that seemed so far out of his reach. Mrs. Mayes had been trying to encourage him to get his degree in journalism or English. And maybe, just maybe that's what he would do.

"That's the plan," he finally said. "But nothing is sure right now, plus I haven't talked to Mama yet."

"You sho haven't." Asha gave him a tsk-tsk look. Chico gave her back a hard stare, which basically ended that conversation.

Chico really didn't want to see Kenny leave, even though he knew he had no choice. After a couple of hours at the mall, they decided to go to Chico's place and talk to Kenny's mom about him and her staying overnight so that the crew could catch a movie. As they walked out of the mall, Kenny gave Chico a hard slap on the back.

"Here's my chance," he said.

"Chance for what?"

"To drive your Escape!" Kenny said, grinning broadly.

The girls laughed at Chico's sour expression. It wasn't that he didn't want his cousin to drive his whip. Okay, he didn't want him to drive his whip. But regardless, ever since he had gotten it he had only allowed Malcolm to drive it during the York hit, and if it hadn't been for that, nobody would have wheeled his baby.

"Come on, cuz, let me drive that Mack truck," Kenny pressed.

Chico hummed. He looked back and forth from his SUV to his cousin as if contemplating. "Okay, but remember she ain't a Mack truck, aight? You drive my baby as if you had Halle Berry sitting in the front seat with you."

"He has someone way finer than Halle Berry," Maxine bragged, giving Kenny a wink.

Kenny blushed at Maxine's words as he reached out to grab Chico's keys. Chico tugged back.

"Come on now, give it up!" Kenny laughed.

With Junnie leaning back against his own car, the girls looked at him as if daring, and Kenny's hand was still out, waiting for his keys.

Chico finally gave in. "Remember…" He nodded toward Maxine. "That's Halle Berry who's gonna be riding beside you there. And my ride is the coach that's gonna earn you an ass kicking if you don't treat her right."

"Yeah, yeah, yeah," Kenny mocked. He kissed the keys when they were finally in his hands, and made way for the Escape. "Come on, ladies; y'all in for the ride of your lives!"

After having relented, Chico decided to drive back to Creighton with Junnie. The girls rode with Kenny in the Escape. Junnie had a lot of questions, which was to be expected. Even though Chico and Kenny had discussed and decided that he would talk to his mom about moving to Charlottesville, it still hadn't been something that was totally worked out. Now that Kenny had let the dog out of the bag, Chico figured that he would make his decision more final in his own head. As he knew would be the case, Junnie completely understood.

"What made you decide to roll out like this, man?" he asked as they cruised down I-95.

"I would think that you more than anyone would know why."

Junnie nodded slowly. "Yeah, I do. I'm just surprised is all." He paused for a second. "What do you think Malcolm and Marco is gonna think about this?"

"Malcolm is gonna think it's stupid of course. Marco, who gives a fuck." He sniffed.

"True," Junnie responded, laughing. He drove solemnly for a while, then said, "I'm glad you're doing this, Chico, and that's real—from the heart, aight?"

They tapped fists together. At least one of them was getting out of the jungle.

Kenny was in his domain. With his cousin in the back seat, and Maxine in the front, they were having a field day seeing how loud they could get the woofers to blast. He turned up the volume another notch when Nelly's new rap came on, straight up blasting eardrums.

"I can't even hear myself think!" Asha complained.

"What you mean? You want me to turn it up louder, you say?" Kenny shouted, laughing as he finally turned down the sound. He laughed as Asha took a deep breath.

"Ugg, finally!" she said.

"Asha's just been buggin' lately; don't pay her no mind," Maxine commented. She looked at Kenny again, and winked. "So when are you gonna invite me to Charlottesville, Kenny? Oops, I forgot. When are you and Chico inviting me to Charlottesville? Actually I think it's a good thing for him to move down there with you, although we'll miss him."

"And of course you'll miss me." Kenny smirked.

He pulled up behind Chico and Junnie. Taking a look around, he noticed his mom's Ford Taurus station wagon parked on the other side of the project housing. He also noticed a car he had never seen parked behind hers. For some reason it gave him a funny feeling, like a sixth sense, as two guys got out the car and looked toward them.

Chico and Junnie failed to notice the car. As they pulled up they were too busy talking in depth about Chico's move to Charlottesville.

"Malcolm needs to make a move, too. It's like none of this shit even bothers him," Chico said.

"I told him that once before. He's starting to talk like Marco."

Chico shook his head. "Well, I'm not gonna worry about it. All I can do is think about taking care of myself, yo. That's wassup."

"Yeah," Junnie agreed as he turned off the ignition. "That's wassup."

"What about you?"

"Me?"

Chico nodded. "Yeah, you. What you gonna do?"

"I'm running for governor. I plan to be the next Doug Wilder!" Junnie joked.

"And that's supposed to be a good thing? I heard Wilder was a crook."

"Yeah, yeah. He was the first and only black governor so they would have to find a way to diss him. Besides, if a crook can get in office, then it shouldn't be a problem for a law abiding citizen like me!"

Chico shook his head at his boy's silliness, and then noticed that Junnie had stopped laughing.

Two guys walked past them, not even seeming to notice they were there and approached Chico's Escape. Junnie zeroed in on them like any eagle from the hood would, questioning it right away.

"Hey," he said in a low voice, "who's that walking up to your ride?"

Both he and Chico turned around to have a look.

"I don't know, but let's find out..." Chico said.

They got out of the car to check it out, and then things seemed to move in extra-slow motion.

"Who are they?" Asha queried as the two guys who had gotten out of a blue Jeep walked up to them. They tapped on the driver's side of the window. Kenny immediately rolled it down.

"Yeah, wassup?" he asked curiously.

"Nice ride," one of the guys said.

"You Grayson?" the shorter one who stood beside him asked.

Kenny nodded. "Yeah, why? Do I know you?" His eyes got big as he saw something silver coming out of the shorter guy's pocket.

Asha noticed it, too, as did Maxine and Jenene. The guy pointed the gun to Kenny's head, and a harsh, echoing pop filled the air. Kenny slumped over into Maxine's lap with blood pumping out of the hole in his temple like a faucet. The three girls screamed in unified horror.

"Ken-nnyyyy!"

CHAPTER NINETEEN:
A BROTHA'S WORLD...

"Man, he packing!!" Chico screamed.

He moved as fast as lightning when he saw the black and silver .38 shining in the sunlight. But it seemed that no matter how fast he moved, there was some weight dragging, tugging at his legs, slowing him down. Like a demon laughing, wanting this bad thing to happen, making sure that he didn't make it over to stop this nightmare in time. Screams radiated throughout the air. One of the guys dressed in all blue started running at top speed after firing inside Chico's SUV. His partner had appeared to run past them and jumped into the Plymouth within seconds, pulling up the car to get him. Chico wasn't even thinking much about them though; he was screaming even before he got to his vehicle. He didn't notice Junnie firing wildly at the guys who had done the shooting. One of Junnie's slugs hit the guy who was still running in the left thigh. He howled as the hot acid pain ripped through him. The driver of the Plymouth was struggling to drive and still trying to aim his gun at Junnie, but only managed to fire aimlessly in the air. He finally succeeded in pulling his wounded homeboy into the car.

Inside her project apartment, Elizabeth Grayson jumped when she heard the shots. She looked at her sister Delores in panic. Both of them moved at the same time to look out the window. Spotting Chico's car, Liz screamed, "The kids are out there!"

"Oh, my God...Jesus, no!" her sister cried.

They raced quickly out the door.

With bullets flying, the neighbors who had been walking carelessly down the street began running to escape the familiar poppin' sounds of gunfire in the projects.

Chico finally made it to his SUV. He yanked the door open to see Kenny slumped down over a screaming Maxine. Blood was trickling down Kenny's face, pooling his left eye that was wide open. Noticing the hole in his head, Chico grabbed his cousin out of the car. He fell to the ground from the weight of him and pulled him into his arms.

"Aww naw!" he cried as he rocked him. His eyes were blinded with tears. "Naw, Kenny, naw!"

Chico looked at Kenny. He was hardly able to see as Asha, Jenene and a bloodstained Maxine circled around him.

"What da hell y'all looking at?"

He wiped at the blood that still raced down Kenny's face, and then looked back up at the girls in a daze, his voice shaking. "Stop...fuckin'...looking...at him! Call the ambulance!"

"He's gone, Chico," Asha cried. "Kenny is gone!"

"Shuddup!"

Asha got on her knees to hug her brother as he instead, buried his face against Kenny's, crying bitterly.

"What happened?!" their mother exclaimed. "What happened, Asha? Who did this?!"

Delores came running behind Liz a split second later. Her eyes bugged in disbelief as she saw her child bloodied and stilled in Chico's arms. A slow moan poured from her mouth. She fell to her knees and rocked back and forth, wrapping her arms around herself while still moaning and looking toward the heavens.

"Dee, Dee, honey..." Liz Grayson went over to grab her sister's quivering shoulders.

"*Jezuzzzzzzzzz! Jezuzzzzzzzz!*" Delores cried. She crawled over to her son, almost gagging in her grief.

The early evening became dark, almost as if the same cloud that gripped the angry heavens at Christ's crucifixion was bidding farewell to yet another of God's children. There was an ever-increasing circle of neighbors congregating around them, and the sounds of Richmond police cars coming closer to the scene. Chico was looking around as Junnie walked toward them, gun still in hand.

"They got away," he stated blankly.

But Chico didn't care. He felt a moan that almost echoed his Aunt Dee's building deep within him. Kenny was gone. He was the one person who didn't deserve it; the one person who had everything going for himself and had never hurt a soul; the one person who believed in him. He was everything that Chico ever wanted to be, and he was dead.

It seemed like as the sun set that evening it also set on Chico's world. A world where he was never allowed a moment...to exhale.

"It shouldn't be so hard...oh, Lord. As you lay our brother down to sleep, we know that he is now at peace, with you...

The spiritual sounds of the Mount Zion Baptist Church filled the room. A burgundy maple coffin surrounded by a multitude of flower arrangements housed Kenny. He was dressed up in street clothes of baggy FUBU jeans, and a tee shirt that he and Chico had gotten a week earlier, two days before his murder, with a picture of them on it and ONE LUV plastered on the bottom. His face was still and cold, a bit darkened by the embalming fluid. And one thing was certain as far as Chico was concerned. He did not look good like the old folks kept saying. He looked dead. Chico wore the same outfit that had been dressed on Kenny. He also wore one of the buttons that Asha and Jenene had had made for all his friends. It read...though he sleeps in death, he will rise in glory. It had a picture of him on it with RIP across the bottom of his chest.

You told us, never doubt or fear, for the spirit host, is near...so now the test is upon us, Lord, and we know...we know...we know...that he is now at peace with you...

Chico swallowed hard. This wasn't for Kenny; this was for Aunt Delores. The whole funeral deal was for her. He and Kenny had talked many times about funerals and what would happen if one of them were to die. And Chico knew for a fact that his cousin would not want to be put to rest with this holy-roller preachamatism surrounding him. Kenny had told Chico that if he ever went, he wanted to be cremated.

"Why waste good money just to put a box in the ground," he reasoned. "Shit, save that money to pay my mom's electric bill!"

The fact was, it was easy to talk about funerals and how they wanted to go when neither of them had any plans of going anywhere anytime soon. But if one of them were to kiss the night, Chico always thought it would be him first. That was right. He was the bad one, whereas Kenny...

"Yes! We are promised by our Lord, our loved ones are at peace," Reverend Winston shouted as the singing chorus paused, humming while the music played on. "Let us not mourn that we have lost our young Brother Kenneth Grayson; let us rejoice! Rejoice I say! That he is now tasting and enjoying that life. The real life, by Christ Jesus!"

"And what's the real life?" Chico mumbled to himself. He looked up to his mom's stern expression. One look was all it took. He knew she would light into him otherwise.

After the hymn was finished, and the preacher stopped blabbering, one by one, friends and family members of Kenneth Jamal Grayson came up to say their last words—Chico's mom, Asha, their other cousins, uncles and aunts. Everyone expressed his or her grief and loss. Chico sat and watched silently, having no words of his own to say. But then just as they were about to do the last prayer ending the service, he stood up and walked to the pulpit and gestured to the preacher to give him his say.

He stood quietly at the pulpit. Red eyes and lost expressions were everywhere. Everyone was waiting to see what he had to say. For a moment his thoughts were lost, and he wasn't sure himself what he could possibly express on behalf of Kenny. It suddenly hit him. All he had to do is open his mouth and let the words flow. Why stress over something that made absolutely no sense?

Chico cleared his throat and began to speak. "I don't know what I'm supposed to say. Everybody wants to know why this happened. They wanna know why someone as good as Kenny could be taken away like this. I guess the fact is there is no reason. There is no why, or any answers that make any sense."

Chico's eyes were dry. His face was solemn as he continued. "While I was sitting down there with you, listening to what was being said about Kenny, I wondered how I could say my goodbye to him; how I could apologize for the unforgivable. I can't seem to find anything; nothing that will make it all right or will make it better or will bring back Kenny."

Chico looked over at Kenny's casket and said, "Me and ace boon, we used to do a lot of crazy stuff together. We had a lot in common. And even though we are close in age he taught me a lot in his own cool way." He pulled out a piece of paper. "We both were into writing thoughts and feelings down on paper, and sometimes we would do some pieces together. We didn't get to finish this one, but I want to share this with you all and with him before we lay him to rest."

Nobody ever said it would be easy...
standing tall when I'm pinned as low...
Everyone slaps me as a disease to this world
hold me down as my wings start to grow...
When I do good...then I'm uppity...
When I do wrong...I'm a thug...
What must I do for you to see me for what I am,
a black man needing a hug...
I run when I see shadows...
I hide when I feel fear...
I sigh at all my fallen kin
wondering why I'm still here...
I laugh when I hear justice...
Available to all?
Conspiracies are what they are...
for black men to feel small...

The sounds of "yes, umm hmm..." flowed throughout the church as if he was singing a psalm or praying a prayer. The older ladies fanned themselves with closed eyes.

I've buried many brothas...
yet I can't even cry...
Black kings without their kingdoms...
like mother earth without the sky...

Prayed many prayers to Allah…
Cried silent tears to Jah…
So lost inside a brotha's world,
the sun can't reach my heart…

"Sleep in peace in our world, my brotha. The sun will shine for you…one day."

All were quiet as Chico finished the poem and walked back to sit down. He felt like Jay-Z. As if the only tears he could cry now were the ones in his heart, and the ones he would allow in his poem, his song.

The rest of the service went by unceremoniously. At the gravesite, the preacher kept going on and on about how Kenny was awaiting the resurrection and the archangel's call to rise to heaven. It tripped Chico out how at the church this same preacher had just said that Kenny was with the Lord. He started to ask him, which is it—is he with the Lord or is he waiting for the Lord to call him? But he knew his Aunt Dee was half in love with her preacher and all into the church thing, so he kept his feelings on the DL. That was one thing he could never get with, the mixed messages and confusion from church. As far as he was concerned it was all a bunch of bull anyhow, and just a chance to hear some good singing.

Everyone met at his Aunt Delores' house for the dinner. That was another thing that pissed him off. Why did the family have to feed all these mofos? As if this was some kind of circus show that peeps had done them some kind of favor by showing up for the funeral. So many things that he knew were just part of their culture as African Americans, but that irked the hell outta him.

Junnie was there, and Malcolm, calling him outside to the porch. Malcolm lit up a cigarette before Chico quickly let him know that Aunt Delores was gonna fry his ass if he didn't put it out. That was one thing that Chico's mom and his Aunt Dee had in common: no cigarette smoking in their house.

"This whole day sucks," Malcolm said as they sat on the porch.

Chico said nothing, just rocked back and forth in the porch chair.

"So what do you wanna do about this, Chico?" Malcolm asked. "How do you wanna handle this?"

"How are we supposed to handle it?"

"You already know the answer to that. Those niccas was after you, not Kenny."

Chico looked at Junnie to see what he was thinking. His eyes were hard.

"He's right, Chico. That was some ill shit. We can't let this one go, coz you know they could be after you still. Shit, us, too."

Chico sighed. He could still see Kenny, his eyes wide in death. His cousin bit the bullet for him. It was his fault, all of it. His heart grew heavy with remorse.

"Y'all know if I hadn't told Kenny it was cool to come hang with us for a minute, none of this shit would have happened." Chico looked at both his boys. "Y'all know that, right?"

"It ain't yo fault, yo," Malcolm replied.

"Straight up," Junnie agreed. "We just need to find out who did this, that's wassup."

A bird came and rested on the porch banner, and then flew up high into the evening sunset. A messenger bird. Maybe sending a message from Kenny? Chico looked at Malcolm and Junnie. All the positive thoughts of college and the changes he and Kenny and he had talked about quickly evaporated. The only thing that was on his mind now was revenge.

"Yeah," he finally said, "that's wassup."

CHAPTER TWENTY:
NO CRYSTAL STAIR...

Asha paused at the door. The small sign read: "The Pregnancy Crisis Center." She wasn't sure if this was the place she needed to be, but she needed someone to tell her where to go, what to do, and most importantly, how to do it. With all the commotion since Kenny's death and funeral, she hadn't talked to Jenene much about her pregnancy. She figured that with Jenene's stank attitude about Peanut, she should deal with it all by herself.

After she had looked up information about abortion in the telephone book, she found the address and number to the center and called. She asked the woman who had answered the phone if they were able to give information about abortion. As soon as the woman said yes, Asha was on her way there. She had to do this by herself, for herself, and that's exactly what she planned to do.

Taking a deep breath, Asha slowly entered the building. There was a heavy-set black woman sitting at a small desk, typing away. She looked up when she heard Asha walk in.

"Can I help you?" she asked.

Asha blinked rapidly.

"What can I help you with?" the lady asked again.

"I...I need to talk with a counselor."

The receptionist's eyes held a question in them, as if she was trying to make out what Asha's problem was. She stood up and beckoned her to come around to the side door.

"Stay right here," she said.

Asha waited patiently as the receptionist went to get a counselor. Asha began to have second thoughts, but somehow her feet would not move to go back out the door she came from.

"Did you call earlier?" a tall black woman asked as she walked into the room.

"Um...yes, I did."

The woman smiled, and then motioned for Asha to follow her. She then looked at the receptionist and thanked her.

Asha and the woman walked into her office.

"I'm Melody Robinson," she said, extending her hand out. "I'm really glad you called. What's your name?"

"Asha, Asha Grayson."

Melody Robinson smiled cordially. "How did you find us, Asha?"

Asha looked down and cleared her throat slightly. "Well, I found you in the telephone book. It said that you counsel and help young women who are pregnant and considering abortion."

"And is that what you feel you want to do? Have an abortion, that is."

"I'm…I'm not sure," Asha said, shaking her head. "But I believe it would be the right thing for me at this point. My mom doesn't know I'm pregnant. I want to finish school and I can't afford to be a mother. I can't have this baby."

"I do understand, sweetie. And please, feel comfortable talking to me. We are here to help you."

Asha looked at her hopefully. "Then can you help me get an abortion? I don't have a lot of money, and I'm only seventeen. But is there still a way for me to get one without my mother signing for it?"

The woman was silent for a moment. "Tell me how far along you are."

"I'm not sure, about three months I think, maybe four."

"You're pretty far along. Have you been to a doctor?"

"No…not yet."

Melody Robinson leaned forward. "Then that's the first thing you need to do. You know you may be too far along for an abortion, don't you?"

Asha teared up. "I was worried about that."

She sighed as the lady grabbed both her hands into hers. "Asha, you do know that there are other choices. No matter how many weeks you are. You don't have to think that abortion is the only answer. I know you feel that your mother wouldn't understand. But the first thing we need to do is find out how far along you are and then help you see the choices that you have."

"There are no choices," Asha said quietly.

"There are always choices. I'm here to help you see what they are." She handed Asha a folder with flyers and printouts for reading. "Take a look at this; I also have a movie, a very short one that I want you to look at, okay?"

After Melody Robinson left the room, Asha glanced through the folder, looking at different pamphlets about the formation of a fetus and its growth in the uterus. None of what she was looking at made her feel any better. In fact, it made her feel worse. It was as if this humanized the being that was growing inside her.

She was about to close it up until she came across what seemed to be a poem.

No one asked for my opinion, no one cared of what I thought
Even though I had my beginning when my tiny cells first began their course…
I started out as one small cell, too small for the eye to see.
Then slowly I began my trail to a temporary home made just for me.

Each moment, each day, each new week; the cells would increase and increase.
One week I had little buds, little arms, the next week, little feet.
As an ocean of life swirled over me, I felt safe and secure in her womb.
Who would have guessed that in her heart she felt it had happened too soon?

See, she didn't know that I could hear; that I knew Mama's voice…
She didn't know that when it came to life, there shouldn't be "a choice."
She didn't realize I was a life the second I began.
She had no clue that as I grew, I could have been her closest friend.
I kicked, I throttled in her womb: I AM HERE! I AM HERE! I AM HERE!
I felt her quiver as she lay on the table, I felt her shake with fear.
So unsure of her decision as my solemn end drew near…

No one asked for my opinion, no one cared of what I thought
Even though I had my beginning when my tiny cells first began their course…

Melody Robinson rushed into the room at the sound of heartbreaking crying.
"What's wrong, Asha?!" she exclaimed.
Asha flipped around when she heard her, throwing the folder to the floor.
"You know what's wrong! Why da hell did you give me that shit to read?"
"Asha," Melody Robinson said calmly, "we are here to help you."
"Well, I don't need *your* kind of help! I'm having a hard enough time dealing with this without your kind of help!"
Asha stormed out of Melody Robinson's office, and then made a beeline for the center's door. When she got to the cool air outside, she breathed in deeply, struggling to wipe the tears from her eyes.

Chico kicked at the chair at the end of his bed, causing it to twirl around and around in a circle. He pulled it with his ankles, bringing it to a stop when he heard Candy's voice on the other side of the phone. He couldn't believe she had finally answered. He hadn't gone to school for the past few days, so he hadn't seen Candy in all that time, but every time he called, her mother or father picked up and said she wasn't home; she was in the shower—any, every excuse.
"I'm surprised that you answered," he said to her.
"Hey, boobie!"
Chico made a face. "Hmm…so wassup?"
"Nothing; I just got in from a job interview. I've missed you!" Candy exclaimed. "When do you think you'll be back to school?"
"I'm going back Monday."
"And how are your mom, and Asha?"
"They're fine, Candy. Listen, where've you been all week? How come I haven't been able to get you?"

There was a short silence at the other end of the phone.

"Are you there?" Chico called.

"Yeah, I'm here," she replied in a whispery voice. "Chico, you know I wanted to be there for you—with you. But Mom didn't feel it was a good idea, and she said that she didn't want me riding to Charlottesville with all that going on..."

"All of what going on?" he said, as if he didn't know.

"Chico..."

"I guess your mom ain't diggin' me much these days, huh?" Chico gave a sarcastic laugh. "Oh, wait a minute. The question should be, has she ever thought much of El Chico, huh?"

He could hear Asha's deep breath intake.

"That's not true, baby! She just felt I should give your family their privacy. You know I wanted to be there for you, and with you."

As he lay on his bed on his cell phone, thoughts flew through Chico's mind. All the shitty remarks and sweet lil put-downs issued out by Candy's mom over the past year. But no matter how much sugar she added to her comments, they came out clear and even to him. Oh, she would never just come out and say anything. Sugarcoating was her prim and proper way of saying everything, but Chico wasn't blind or stupid. Hell, Candy's father, that bougie mofo just straight up ignored him, which was fine by Chico, just fine.

"Are you there?" Candy asked, cutting into his thoughts.

"Yeah, I'm here."

"Look...I know you think my family doesn't like you. And you're wrong."

"I never said that, Candy."

"Yeah, but I know you're thinking it. I mean yes, they are concerned about me, but that's only natural. Chico, Kenny was murdered right in front of your house—in your car." She paused for a moment. "I need to ask you something..."

"Like what?" Chico asked, as he again started his chair roll.

"Were they after you?" she whispered. "And if so, why, Chico?"

Chico sat up on his bed. Heat surfaced to his face. "Wha' da fuck? You think Kenny being dead is my fault, don't you?"

"Of course I don't! Chico, that's crazy!"

Glancing impatiently at his watch, Chico spurted, "Look, I need to go. I'll hook up witcha lata."

"Boo, that's not what I was saying! Let's talk. I miss you. I really do."

He had missed her, too. But Chico felt like he had been kicked in the stomach. Not so much by what Candy had asked him, but mostly because he felt guilty himself. He felt it was his fault, but he didn't need anyone reminding him.

"Yeah, but I'm out right now. Lata." He hung up the phone quickly.

He sat up on his bed and ran his hands over his face. He looked into the mirror of the old dresser that sat in front of his bed. Chico knew the truth, and even if he didn't, the eyes don't lie. His guilt was written all over his face. He knew those guys had been after him. He knew. Everyone knew.

"Kenny..." he whispered his cousin's name achingly.

Ever since it happened, the pain of Kenny's death had been like a volcano. Simmering quietly—waiting for an explosion, some kind of answer, some solution. Asha had told him that the guy who shot Kenny had asked if he was "Grayson." Of course Kenny's last name was Grayson. But no one in Richmond had known Kenny that well, so Chico knew that he had not been the Grayson they were looking to hit. It kinda unnerved him that someone wanted him dead, but it unnerved him even more knowing that Kenny had paid the ultimate price for him.

If onlies came to his mind over and over again. *If only* Kenny hadn't come to visit him. *If only* they hadn't come back home when they did. *If only* he hadn't let Kenny drive his SUV. *If only* he hadn't gotten involved with Marco and his crew in the first place. But like his mom always said, life didn't exist in a basket of ifs. There were consequences for every action. One thing was for sure, there would be consequences for what happened to Kenny. Chico would make sure of that.

Chico started to make his way out of his bedroom. He decided that he would take a quick shower and wash away his bad feelings. He had almost made it to the bathroom when he heard the front door crashing open.

"Damn, girl! Wassup with you?"

"Fuck you!" Asha screamed.

"Fuck me?"

"That's right!" She threw her purse on the couch. "Fuck you and all niccas!"

She stormed off to her bedroom, and almost got her door closed until Chico pushed back against it. Asha moved back, slumped to her bed and burst out crying.

"What's wrong with you, girl?" Chico asked, perplexed.

"Nuttin'." She sniffed.

"Then why you trippin'?"

Asha didn't respond as Chico looked at her quietly from across the room. "Ahem," he said, catching her attention.

Suddenly Asha looked up, wiped her eyes with the back of her hands and carefully avoided Chico's eyes.

"So…you got drama, huh?" He leaned back against her room door.

"I guess so. I'm pregnant, so, that's drama all right," Asha replied sarcastically.

"Like whoa!" Chico said in shock. "By Peanut?"

"Yes, by Peanut, I ain't no ho!"

Chico's eyes narrowed. "Oh shit! I outta kill that nicca!"

"Stop it, okay? You're always talking about killing somebody. And from where I sit, there has been enough of that to last me a lifetime."

Chico immediately felt bad about Kenny again. He didn't wanna think about that though, and this bit that Asha had laid on him was a big enough whopper to peel over.

"So now that you all pregnant up, whatcha gonna do? Is Peanut gonna do right by you?"

"He says I have a problem…" Asha sniffed, grabbing her pillow to her stomach.

"That lousy ass bitch! I oughta go fuck his shit up right now!"

Chico ran out of steam when he saw a silent Asha shaking, with her arms tight around herself. He sighed. "Who knows about this, Asha? And are you gonna tell Mama?"

"Jenene of course, Maxine, Candy and Peanut. Whatever good that does." She swallowed. "I haven't told Mama yet. But I'm gonna have to cuz my stomach is already getting big."

"Yeah, you gotta tell her or she'll trip even more for you taking so long to spit it."

Asha started taking her shoes off. After her run-in at the Pregnancy Crisis Center she was completely burnt. She fumbled with the elastic at her waist, touching the slight swell that had grown, almost it seemed, overnight.

"I can't believe Candy didn't tell me," Chico said. "But listen, you keep your head up, shawtygirl, aight? I mean, I know we don't do stuff together a lot like we used to when we was younger, but you still the only pain-in-da-ass sister I got. And I kinda love ya ass." He laughed, joking over what actually was a sweet thing to say. Asha wasn't letting him off that easily.

"Don't be acting like a loving brother. I won't know how to take you." She reached out and gave him a hug. "Thanks, Chico."

CHAPTER TWENTY-ONE:
THE DEPTHS AND THE SHADOWS...

"Ouch! You pulling too tight, girl!" Malcolm screamed, stretched out on the wood floor at Jenene's house.

"Well, if you want the braids to hold, Malcolm, they have to be tight. I thought you and Chico were getting twists anyhow?"

Malcolm winced at the sharp pull on his hair. Jenene was cornrowing it back in small even braids. He knew he would have a helluv a headache for the rest of the day.

"I told cha, girl, he got his done, but it took so long that I told shawtygirl that I'd hit her up another time." He smiled a crooked grin. "Besides, aren't you glad I came to you? You know you feenin for a brotha." He winked at her. Jenene in turn gave one of his braids a hard jerk, causing him to cry out.

"You best to stop trying to mack, Negro, and keep your head still," she said, laughing.

"Aight, aight!" Malcolm looked at her and winked.

Both then sat quietly while she finished up his hair. Malcolm watched through the window as some kids their age were riding up and down Groveland on bikes, heading for the playground that was just around the corner. Everyone in this area of Highland Park seemed to use Groveland as a side street for the courts. In the background, he could hear Jenene singing "Dilemma" along with Nelly and Kelly. Her self-involvement with trying to sing better than Kelly, which wasn't hard to do, gave him time to reminisce. Malcolm was born in Highland Park, but when his moms passed away, he moved to Church Hill, where he still lived. He still hung out in the Northside neighborhoods though. He had his boys in Church Hill, yet he still was able to form and keep connections with his dawgs in Highland Park. That was the best of both worlds to him. His pillar had always been his boys.

For some reason Malcolm still felt like he had to be hard around everyone. Never let 'em think you're weak, his older cousin used to always preach. He knew that the way he carried himself sometimes made him appear cold, and unfeeling, but the truth was he felt a lot of shit that he just chose to keep to himself. If anyone knew how he really felt; how scared he was; scared of life; scared of death; scared period, he'd be a goner. So he just kept that feeling wrapped tight within himself.

"What you thinking 'bout, boy?" Jenene asked him quietly. She then bent down and kissed his cheek. Malcolm looked up at her mocha brown face, her sweet smile encased with a set of deeply imbedded dimples.

"Gimme sum," he whispered, pulling her head down to mesh his lips with hers.

Jenene right away slipped her tongue inside of his mouth. She moaned softly as the sweet wetness of his mouth filled hers. They had always played and sexed a little, but Malcolm knew and had always known that Jenene's feelings for him ran deeper. It was moments like this that he couldn't help but wonder why he had never taken her seriously on the emotional tip.

Jenene pulled away, sighing as she ran her hand alongside his cheek, and looked deep into his eyes.

"Wassup?" he said.

"You're wassup, Malcolm."

"Yo, this is a trip. You trying to get all serious up in here." He blushed, and then looked away from Jenene's penetrating stare. She made him uncomfortable when she looked at him like that. As if she were trying to see inside of him, and that he could not have. Not from her, not from any girl.

"What's so bad about being serious once in a while?" Jenene said, in a half-question, half-statement sort of way. When Malcolm didn't respond, she quickly changed the subject. "Anyhow, when are you gonna get it together, boy?" She pushed at his shoulder.

"You done?"

"Yes, I'm done. But don't be trying to avoid my question. I see what you're doing."

She brushed the hair from Malcolm's shoulders, and then inserted her comb into her brush. Malcolm still wasn't talking, so Jenene then said, "I know you were close to Kenny, just as we were, Malcolm."

"Yeah, we were cool. I'm just sorry I didn't get to holla at him before all this went down."

Jenene turned his face toward hers. "Then you know why I am so worried about you, right? I mean I don't want to see the same thing happen to you, boo. I don't want you to go out like that."

"Ain't nobody after me, yo," Malcolm said, laughing.

Jenene frowned. "It's not funny, at all. Doesn't anything ever bother you, Malcolm? You always have to play the hard ass!"

Malcolm stood up and faced Jenene. "Look, I never said it didn't bother me. Hell yeah it does! It bothers me that Kenny got hit and he wasn't even in this situation. The whole thing is pure-dee fucked-up. You know what I'm saying? But I'm not gonna run around like some punk ass worrying about dying. When it's my time to go, it's my time. Shit, I'm gonna die young anyhow. I know that, I've always known it. But when it does happen I'm going out fighting like a muthafucca, that's fo sho!"

"God, Malcolm, you sound so stupid! You know damn well you're afraid of dying. You can front all you wanna, but I see you, and you don't have to die young!"

She stood up in front of Malcolm, poking him in the chest. "When are all you Black men gonna stop letting society and circumstances decide your fate? It's like you don't even care." Jenene poked him again, this time harder. "I'm sick...of burying y'all, and I'm sick of funerals. And if you die I'm not going to yours, you hear me?"

Jenene jumped up and rushed out of the house. The screen door slammed hard behind her.

"Dayum!" Malcolm said, cringing at the loud sound.

After a few seconds, he followed Jenene to the front porch, slipped his arms around her waist and started kissing the back of her neck softly. "You shouldn't be trippin' like this, baby girl; you know I'm just yappin'."

Jenene ran her lips alongside Malcolm's jaw, teasing his sparse goatee with her tongue tip. She looked him deep into his eyes. "You promise?"

"I promise, yo."

Jenene poked him again in the chest. "Hmm...witcha stoopid self."

Malcolm back away from her and pulled up his shirt to show his well-defined abs. "Shittttt, is this stupid?" They both laughed, then turned around when they heard a car pulling up.

It was Chico, honking and rolling down his window when he spotted them.

"Wassup, black peeps!" he hollered.

"Yo, dawg!" Malcolm hollered back. He looked at Jenene. "I gotta bounce. Me and Chico need to get his ride to the dealer cuz he's gonna trade it in." He kissed her on the cheek. "Lata, sexy. Thanks again for the braids. I'mma holla at you, aight?"

"Wait." Jenene reached up to kiss Malcolm one last time. Her eyes read doom, concern, worry. Malcolm gave her a crooked grin and hopped down the porch stairs.

◆◆◆

"Ma?"

Liz Grayson looked up from her sewing machine. Stress was an understatement to describe how she was feeling. Her bobbin was constantly getting hung in her machine, and she had to use black thread since she was out of blue, which was the color of the dress she was trying to finish up so that Asha could wear it to her chorus program later that evening.

Liz felt overwhelmed with the things that had been going on in her household lately. Her nephew had been murdered in cold blood right in front of her house. Her sister's grief knew no end, and Liz knew no way to comfort her. She was tired, tired of everything. She was tired of trying—tired of going it alone and getting nowhere for all her hard efforts. And as much as she loved her children she simply was tired of being both mother and father to them, and failing miserably at both.

"What is it, Asha?" Liz asked with a sigh, massaging her temples with closed eyes.

Asha walked cautiously into her mother's bedroom. She tried to swallow past the lump in her throat but was not succeeding. "Can I talk to you about something?" she asked.

Liz looked at Asha expectantly. But her daughter looked like she was having a hard time spitting out words.

"What is it, girl? Why are you just staring like that?" Liz asked impatiently.

"Maybe...maybe, I'll just come back another time when you aren't so busy."

"No, I don't think so. If you have something to say, just say. Now what is it?"

Asha sat down quietly in the old rocking chair sitting in front of her mother's bed. She appeared shaken, and was biting her lip between seconds of opening and closing her mouth.

"Asha!" came the demanding voice of her mother.

"I'm pregnant," Asha said in a low, timid voice. The room became silent for a moment. Just the sound of the ticking clock broke in with a ringing loudness.

Liz laughed. "You want to repeat yourself? Because I know you didn't just say what I thought you said. I know you didn't just tell me you are pregnant."

Asha didn't say anything; she just looked her mother, as if awaiting the storm.

Liz felt a sick feeling rolling around inside of her, which quickly gained momentum at Asha's silence.

"Mama..."

"No!" Liz's voice cracked. "You say that again, Miss Thang. You are *what?*"

"I'm sorry, okay?!" Asha screamed, tears gathering in her eyes. "I'm pregnant, and I felt you need to know, that's all..."

Liz was almost gasping in shock. "Oh, you felt I needed to know, huh? You felt?" She growled, and came charging at her daughter, grabbing her by the hair while crying and screaming. "How dare you! How dare you tell me this!"

"Mama, stop! I'm sorry! I'm so sorry!" Asha cried. She fought to cover her hair from her mother's blows.

"I'm sick of this shit! I'm sick of this disappointment! You and Sean. I'm sick of all the work with you two, and never getting back anything but pain in return!" She finally loosened her daughter, and fell to the end of the bed sobbing. "I give up," she said quietly, sniffing. "I simply give...up."

Both mother and daughter sat in tears. Both searched for an answer in the midst of pain where there were no answers. Liz felt as if time were repeating itself. No matter how hard she had tried to instill and get something better for her children, it had all been fruitless.

"How did you let this happen?" she finally asked. "Why, Asha?"

"I don't know. I thought I was being careful."

Liz fought hard to slow down the fast beat of her heart and to cool her anger somewhat. She took a deep breath. "Okay, okay... so how far along are you?"

"I don't know for sure, but I've missed my period for a few months," Asha mouthed quietly. "I told Peanut about it."

"And what did he say?"

"Nothing. He said I have a problem..."

"Uh, just like a no-good man!" Liz closed her eyes, trying her best to calm down so that she could address her daughter properly. She regretted now that she had gone off as she had. "Asha, if you've missed your period for a few months, didn't you realize that you were pregnant? Or was it just that you intentionally waited this long to tell me about it?"

Asha wrapped her arms around herself and looked into her mother's eyes. "Mama, I didn't know for a while, but when I did find out I was scared, so scared..."

"You were doing so well, Asha!" Liz said, as she sat down beside her. "Sean has become someone I don't even know these past few months, and this thing with Kenneth just proves that, but you..." Liz sighed.

Asha grabbed her mom's hand, holding it close to her heart. She looked as green and sick as Liz felt. Liz wasn't able to focus on that. All kinds of thoughts went through her head. How far along was she? How long had she been keeping it from her? How? When? Where?

"I wanna keep my baby, Mama, and raise it. I know it's gonna be hard, and I've thought about other things, like abortion, but I don't wanna kill my baby..."

Liz was quietly gathering her composure. She knew what she had to do. There was no other choice.

"You don't have to," Liz finally said. Asha reached out for her mother. They embraced in the ancient ritual of black womanhood—tears, pain and sweat, and the need of a mother's love.

CHAPTER TWENTY-TWO:
RAINBOW CHILD...

I was born a child of rainbowness of mixed united birth.
Welcomed by some, frowned on by many as my soul
Encompassed this earth...
As I opened my tiny infant eyes I saw two faces there,
One face was fair; one face was dark,
yet both shared a proudful stare...
I knew not of the oddity, that my existence brought.
I didn't know of massah and slave and the race wars that had been fought.
I knew not of such hurtful terms, mulatto, zebra, half-breed.
Or that to some people in this world
your worth was based on the color of the seed...
See a rainbow child is innocent of all these cryptic truths.
It is the skin he is in, that mixed-up blend, and not the good that he do...
But as he grows he sees the truth; he recognizes the facts,
that in this world of fake false peeps no one will have his back...
Was it his sin, his moms, his dads, that brought him to this place?
That told him he did not belong among the humanrace?
So before you turn your back upon that rainbow-coated child...
Remember in the rising sun the colors can be wild.
But through the brilliance of these colors shines a glorious smile.
Brings life and peace and happiness, just like a rainbow child.

Malcolm and Chico were oddly quiet for a while as they drove down Parham Road. Chico really hoped he wouldn't have any problem getting the trade in, although Marco had already called and they said all was cool. You never could tell what would be up once the dealer saw that he and Malcolm were teens.

Malcolm looked up at Chico and noted the tiny zig-zagged braids that blanketed his head. He smirked. "Jenene did a better job on me than Massie did on you."

"Yeah right!" Chico laughed. "Jealous nicca."

"Naw, for real, she hooked you up, man. Massie charges too much though."

"Hell yeah," Chico said, tugging at his braids. "She charged me a hundred twenty for this job. But she gave me the look I wanted, so it's all good." He honked at the busy traffic ahead. Chico couldn't wait to trade in his Escape. He had gotten the front seat shampooed. So there were no remaining signs of what had happened in it, yet there still remained what couldn't be shampooed away, that is, the memory of it for him.

"I'm surprised your hair can even hold braids, man. You got that Johnny blood in ya."

"What Johnny blood?"

"Ha ha. You know that white-boy blood. With them light eyes to prove it!" Malcolm hooted.

Chico shook his head. "Hateration is a mutha."

"Shittttt, I ain't hating. I love my chocolate ass, and so do da ladies!"

"Aight, nicca, I see you got jokes," Chico barked. "Jenene must've pulled them braids a bit too tight."

As they pulled into the car lot, Chico took a quick note of all the vehicles that were visible. He wanted to make sure that no matter what, he got this one off his hands before they left. He spotted a Ford Expedition, and wondered for a moment if it looked too much like his Escape. But since he had always had a weakness for SUVs he decided to get it. Since his ride was basically new and still under full warranty, the car salesman was all but happy to let him trade it in for a more expensive vehicle. Within an hour and a half, he and Malcolm were cruising back down Parham, with Chico feeling much better.

After they took Chico's new ride for a spin, and checked out all the extras that came with it, the hunger bell rung, and they decided to roll down Broad Street and hit Mickey Dees. They chowed down for a bit in silence before Malcolm let Chico in on some news he had gotten wind of.

"Listen," he said, "Marco got a handle on the guys who smoked Kenny."

The food in Chico's mouth suddenly turned sour.

"What did he say?" Chico asked.

"Well, he says the North Clique called it."

"North Clique? You mean these mofos who sent us to York?"

"Yep," Malcolm said, mumbling with a mouth full of fries. "The very ones. See, they knew, man; they knew that those guys who they sent us to York to smoke were from the 56th Clique. Those mofos are vicious in PA, and growing, too. Marco says even he wasn't aware of it, but North Clique, they knew. So it was a setup from the start. Put us in out there; get us to do their dirty work, then when 56 come for payback, it's skin off our asses. Now 56 got us in the spotlight, and Marco, too. See, that's how I know for sure that he didn't know what wassup."

"This is some fucked-up bullshit, man!" Chico stormed. "So why do you think they came after me first?"

"Lockette; remember him?"

"Lockette!"

"You remember him, don't you? The wigger with the dreads."

"Hell, yeah, I remember his ass! So he's a rat, huh?"

"Yep, and he paid for it, too."

Chico started smiling. "Marco took care of him?"

"Naw, man, 56 probably did it. If it was Marco, you know he would've let everyone know it."

Chico nodded in agreement.

"But they found dude's body behind a Hardee's somewhere in North York. A hole right between the eyes."

"Good for him!"

"Straight up; that nicca was a straight-up snitch," Malcolm spat. "I'm glad they got his ass."

Both Chico and Malcolm busied themselves with food for a while—lost in individual thoughts. Nothing seemed to be as easy as either of them had thought it would be months earlier.

Chico grabbed his trash together and placed it on the food tray. "I swear, Malcolm, this is so fucked-up, ain't it? I wish we had never met Marco. I wish we were still walking, carless, broke and complaining about not having shit. At least Kenny would still be alive, and we wouldn't have a bunch of crazy niccas on after us."

"I guess it's my fault for getting you involved in this," Malcolm said quietly.

"Naw, man!" Chico replied. "I was ready to roll just like you were. I don't blame you, dawg; you know this."

Their eyes met. As always they had that bond, good or bad, that united them. They bumped fists, neither of them having to say another word.

The following weeks were quiet ones. Even though they stayed on their toes, Chico and his boys tried to focus more on normal things. Marco had warned them to watch their backs. Chico figured he was more worried about watching his own. Marco was not Chico's worry though he had his own problems, Asha had her baby problems, and as for their mother, she was worried about both her twins.

By the end of the second week, Chico had moments when he almost forgot about the dangerous situation he was in. He had some exams, and oddly enough, Chico had always been worried about his grades, and used school to block out home and the streets.

He was packing up his knapsack in government class when Mrs. Mayes tapped on the door, causing all the students that were still in the room to look toward it. She motioned for Chico.

"Sean, come into my room for a minute, okay? I want to talk to you," Mrs. Mayes said.

"Oh, okay."

Chico wondered what she wanted to talk to him about. He made a quick trip to the bathroom before heading to her class.

After doing the toilet thing, Chico wandered over the sink to wash his hands. He paused briefly, and looked at his reflection in the mirror. He swallowed hard, seeing the same picture he had always seen. His hair was neatly rowed with tiny light brown plaits. He saw the same face, minus the sprinkle of freckles that usually visited him every summer. He also saw other things that looked the same, too. His eyes, the color of warm honey, which was a trademark of his Johnny blood as Malcolm called it. Even with all the familiarity in the mirror, there was someone new there that he didn't know at all. There was an emotion that he didn't care to acknowledge. Fear. He was scared. Scared of the way his life was turning out; scared of living in this hell; scared of dying and going to hell for all the hell he had caused on earth; scared of his reflection.

Chico shook his head, and his thoughts; finished drying his hands and headed for Mrs. Mayes' class. She looked up smiling as he walked in, gesturing for him to have a seat at the desk in front of hers.

"So how is my favorite young poet today?" she asked, smiling warmly.

"I'm aight," Chico responded.

"Well, I have news for you, Sean. Remember I told you about that International Library of Poetry contest? Remember the one for high school students that was offering a scholarship?"

"I think I remember. The one you wanted me to submit to?"

"Mmm...hmm, well, you were a bit slow moving on that." She looked at him with an evil eye. "So, I hope you don't mind me pushing ahead, but I haven't seen poetic talent like yours in a long, long time, Sean. I just knew you had a very good chance of winning that contest and getting that scholarship. So, I submitted one of the poems you gave me." Mrs. Mayes blurted everything out in one breath, smiling broadly.

"Whoa!" Chico was a bit more than speechless.

Mrs. Mayes had so much faith in him, and really believed he had a gift. That was almost funny. He had always loved writing, and if no one else knew that, she did. In school he had always been in trouble. He had made so many trips to the principal's office from kindergarten onward that the thought that someone actually considered him gifted was a hard pill to swallow. He had no idea why she believed in him so much, but he didn't know if it was because she was a sista and wanted to see black kids succeed, or if it was because she sincerely thought he had a chance of making something out of himself. Either way it made him feel like whoa.

Mrs. Mayes looked at him, raising her eyebrows and biting her bottom lip nervously. "I hope you don't mind what I did, but the good news, Sean? You are in the semi-finals."

"Straight up! Hell no, I don't mind! I mean heck," he said quickly, covering his mouth as Mrs. Mayes laughed. "Which one did you submit?" Chico was having a hard time keeping the smile and blush from his face.

"Well, you had so many excellent ones to pick from. But I really loved 'Rainbow Child.' I think it could be an anthem for biracial children. Now the finalists and then the winner will be picked in the next couple of weeks or so, so as soon I hear something you will too. Just keep your fingers crossed," she said, smiling proudly.

"There's just one thing, Sean, you still haven't signed up to take the SATs. Do you want me to set it up for you?"

"Aww, man, I don't know," Chico said, suddenly avoiding her eyes.

"Why don't you know?"

"I don't think the college thing is for me."

"I thought just a few weeks ago you were saying you wanted to go to college, and was feeling pretty positive about the SATs?"

Chico was quiet.

"Listen, hon, I just hate to see you waste your talent. You could be a published author, journalist, poet, who knows, the next Langston Hughes maybe."

She walked over to him, lifting his face to look into his eyes. "There are no limits to a dream if you really truly want it to be. And there are so many avenues you could take with this. So please don't try to tell me you are not interested. I see the light in your face when we are discussing literature in class, or whenever you sit down to pen out a poem or an essay."

"Just a lot has changed, you know? I'm not saying I don't want to go; I just don't know is all." Chico grabbed his books to take his leave.

Touching his arm tentatively, Mrs. Mayes said, "I know about your cousin. I know you have had troubles, Sean. And yes, I know things change. But your future is what you make it. From what I have been told by your mother, that young man had a very promising future that has been cut short. So maybe you should think of this as a way of extending his future with your own dreams. Make him proud; make your mother proud. And most of all make yourself proud. Not even to mention a certain English teacher of yours." She winked.

Chico laughed shyly. "Aight, I hear you. I'll think about it, okay?"

"That's all I'm asking."

Chico gave his favorite teacher a big hug and walked out the door, feeling a little bit better about himself and feeling like he was walking a little bit taller.

CHAPTER TWENTY-THREE:
THE OTHER SIDE OF THE FENCE...

Lucky happy hand of the draw,
living on the right-hand side of the law...
Born into sunlight, born within the rays...
Happy, shining luminous days...
Thus around the corner the other side of the fence...
stands the ghetto-chained child in darkness entrenched...
never given a choice of candy-coated domains...
chocolate castled dreams and sweet striped candy-canes...
Flipping the script to the silver-spooned tip, manicured lawns...
European vacation trips...
Blinded rose-colored middle-class eyes, lost in the matrix
white picket-fence lies
As opposed the poor yet clammer at that wall, fighting injustice
yet still standing tall...
Two ciphers separate and yet still the same, each holding down
shelter under the Lord's domain...
Man-made fences built on greed, blocking the unity
that would allow them to succeed.
Maybe one day these words will make sense...
the folly of having two separate sides of the fence...

Asha's heart hammered as she faced Peanut. She was on her way into the house minding her own business when he pulled up, and she didn't want to have this discussion with him. In fact, she had decided that she wouldn't talk to him about her pregnancy again period. But he had suddenly called her, demanding they talk about it for some odd reason. From the time she had discovered she was pregnant she had put it completely out her mind that it could be Orlando's baby. She almost hoped it was, but at this point, she supposed it didn't even matter.

"So why you ain't call me?!" Peanut shouted.

Asha looked at him, hardly able to stand the sight of him. "Please tell me what reason was there for me to call you, huh? You made it clear how you felt, Peanut. I was saving you and me the stress."

Instead of addressing what she said, Peanut decided to throw a curve ball. "Whatcha gonna do about that kid?" he asked, pointing to her already extended belly.

Asha looked him up and down as if he had gone half-crazy. "I'm tired, Peanut. I'm going in the house."

"Wait!"

She paused.

"I just wanna know what's going on, that's all," he said.

Asha looked him directly in his eyes and said, "I'm taking care of *my* problem, that's what. The problem that you let me know you wanted no part of."

She opened up the screen to her apartment door. Peanut grabbed her arm.

"Oh, so you're gonna hold that over my head forever?"

"I'm not holding anything over your head!" Asha screamed as she let the screen door slam again. "I'm not asking you to do anything for me, Peanut, or the baby!"

"Shit, girl! You telling me I'm 'bout to be a daddy; what you expect me to do?"

A cool wind blew. Asha pressed up against the door as if it had thrown her there. She felt mentally thrown as well. As strong and sure as she was talking to Peanut, she felt anything but. She had told herself that she wouldn't do this—wouldn't discuss the baby with him anymore, and wouldn't ask him for anything regarding it. She still didn't know for sure if it was his baby, even though she suspected it was when calculating the number of weeks. But regardless, she had somehow gained a new strength within herself. And with that strength and the help of her mama, she was gonna handle this. She was going to have her baby.

She mustered up her will, looked Peanut in the eyes and finally said, "I don't expect or want you to do anything. That's just it, Peanut. I don't think we should see each other anymore. I don't think we're good for each other…"

Peanut looked shocked. One thing he did not expect Asha to say, she had. She wanted him out of the picture, and out of her life.

"Oh, you don't? Well, fuck you then, stupid bitch," he snarled. "I don't want your ass no more anyhow."

"Good," Asha replied as she opened the door and walked inside.

"You ain't shit no how!"

"Good…"

"Good Lord, you can eat, boy!" Candy exclaimed as she watched Chico down his second mushroom burger.

"I was hungry," Chico mumbled, wiping his mouth with a napkin. "So…you plan on eating that?" He pointed to her half-eaten Chef's salad.

Candy laughed. "Help yourself, boo."

She watched his handsome features as he ate, smiling softly to herself. She loved him so much. Lately Chico had been acting more like the boy she had fallen in love with. More like the Sean Grayson she had known months before. Candy tried to pin down when exactly he had started changing. She remembered the incident in D.C., and noted that was the beginning of the new person that she couldn't recognize. It was understandable that after his cousin Kenny was killed Chico would have that mourning period, and she knew that he had that, and probably still was mourning. But in a way it seemed to have a positive effect on him.

She slowly got up and slipped on Chico's side of the booth, kissing him on the cheek.

"Wassup?" he asked, smiling.

"Can't I just wanna kiss you?" Candy said softly. She breathed in deeply, happily. "I just miss us doing stuff together like this. Just chillin', you know?"

"Yeah, I know what you mean."

Candy was a bit nervous as she admitted, "For a while there, I thought you wanted to break up with me."

"Now why would you think something like that? You know how I feel about you, Candy."

"You know why..."

Chico really didn't want to go where Candy was trying to go, so he decided to change the subject. "Guess what?" he said cheerfully. "Mrs. Mayes submitted a poem I wrote to this contest thingy. She says I'm in the semi-finals with it, and that the winner receives a scholarship! Ain't that some shit?"

"Oh, my God! You're gonna win, baby, for sure!"

Chico looked around the Friendly's ice-cream store, hailing down the waitress when she looked their way. He looked back toward Candy. "I don't know if I'm gonna win or not. But like I said, there's a scholarship connected with it, so I'll have to decide something about that, too. I may have to get a job or something. My mom needs money now, not four years from now."

"So, that means you're going to stop doing whatever you are doing?"

Chico's invisible guard came up. "Let's not get into that, Candy."

"Chico, I'm not trying to ruin our good day, but you know how worried I've been about you. When you start talking about money, I get worried. You had said for sure that you were going to college. That you would even try to get into Howard like me."

The waitress walked up before Chico could answer. She left the bill on the table, gave them a bright smile and asked if they needed anything else. Chico ordered a Coke and a peanut butter sundae. Candy shook her head when he asked her if she wanted anything. She knew she was putting a downer on things, but in her mind, she was seeing again, in rewind, Orlando's murder. She had known since that time that Chico was involved in bad things, but she didn't want to face it. She just kept her thoughts to herself, afraid of pressing him about it for fear she'd lose him. She thought about Kenny. Why would someone want to kill him? Or was Chico the target? The very thought made her grow cold, and caused Candy to wrap her sweater around herself a bit tighter. Chico looked calm. But then again, he didn't know that she was wondering what had happened to her sweet little cutie that wrote poetry to her, and had swore that he'd had a secret crush on her since forever, ever since their years at Woodville Elementary.

"I don't know about Howard," Chico suddenly blurted. "I'm surprised that your mom and dad are letting you go to such a ghetto school anyhow." He laughed.

The waitress brought Chico's sundae, which he immediately began to gobble down.

"What is that supposed to mean?"

"It means that you keep saying how much I've changed, but, Candy, me and you have always been different, from the jump." He noted her flawless, light brown skin, her curly hair and dark, Puerto Rican eyes. Everything about Candy screamed high maintenance. "I figured I'm just a high school thing with you. So whether I go to college or not, is it gonna affect your future? I don't think so."

Before Candy could respond, Chico continued, "Your parents don't even like me, girl. We're from different sides of the fence."

Candy was in quiet shock for a moment. "How could you even say that?" she whispered with pain in her eyes. "Do you really see me that way? Some snob? We both go to JFK, and that is not a snob school, mind you! No, I have never had a relative blown away in front of my house, but does that make me a snob? I'm there for you, Chico! I've tried to be there for you! I want you, only you. And there is no fence that separates us, only the one in your mind!"

She watched as Chico scraped the bottom of his sundae dish, not responding to her. Candy couldn't help but wonder if he had heard a word she'd said. It was so frustrating to her.

"Dammit, Chico, there is no more ice cream in that fuckin' dish!"

Chico swallowed with a gulp. "Don't be cussing like that, girl. Wassup with you?"

"What?" She looked at him in amazement. "That's a joke the way you be cussing all the time."

Chico looked up at her, finally putting his empty sundae dish on the table. "That's not what we're talking about. I'm talking about you trying to talk hoochie, and I don't like it. I like you the way you are."

"Trying to talk hoochie? Because I said fuck?"

Chico's eyes bulged. Candy almost laughed. She knew he was faking. "There you go again. Cut it out!" Maybe he wasn't…"If I wanted a filthy-mouth hoochie I could hook up with Letisha or Kiki or any of those tricks from school."

There he went. Candy couldn't help it. She had sworn never to think about it again, but Alisha instantly came to her mind, and that nasty little rumor about her and Chico. Candy cleared her thoughts.

"You are such a hypocrite with your attitude. So you can cuss but I can't? And, boy, you best not be getting with no trick from school!" *On the real he best not!* she thought.

Chico laughed at her vexed expression.

"Aight, Mama." Chico grinned. "We need to roll out. I have some things I need to take care of."

"Hey, are you planning on messing with that dude who shot Kenny?" Candy asked, off subject. There was a tense silence.

"We need to roll out," Chico responded finally with a guarded tone. Standing up suddenly and placing a tip on the table, his actions told Candy quite clearly that the subject was closed.

◆◆◆

They road in silence for a while. The ten o'clock hour of the "red light special" was purring from the 92.1 airwaves. As they got close to her street, Candy motioned for Chico to stop.

"Hey, pull up to that alleyway there for a minute. I have something for you." She smiled seductively at him.

"Something like what?" he asked, grinning at her as he quickly obeyed her request.

He pulled into the dark alleyway. Just as he was turning off the ignition, Candy slid him over away from the steering wheel, and moved into his lap in a face-forward position. She kissed him on the neck with a wet lick.

"Leave the radio on, boo. I love that old groove," she said, humming the tune of Mya's "My First Night with You" as the soft melody filled the air.

Chico watched Candy intensely as she unbuttoned her coat. She then loosened the buttons of her blouse, and pressed his face to her breast. Chico kissed between them for a few seconds before Candy pushed him away so that she could slide her panties off.

"Someone is gonna see us here," Chico said nervously.

Candy ignored his comment. She loosened his jeans, pulled out his manhood and giggled slightly as she then slid down on it. Chico gasped and threw his head back against the headrest.

"One magic moment, made one magic night. I fell in love with one look in your eyes…baby," Candy sung sweetly in his ear. She could hear Chico moaning as she moved up and down atop of him, squeezing him inside of her. "I love you, boo," she crooned, "I love you." She stifled her own moans as Chico slipped his tongue deep inside of her mouth, moaning as he kissed.

Chico could only think of how good she felt—how warm, wet and intense, just like the first time, even moreso. *Make me forget it all…make me forget…*he thought to himself as she continued to ride him, grind him, rolling, thrusting faster and faster against him. They were both sweating, even as the cool air filled his new Expedition.

"Ahh, Chico!" Candy screamed. Looking at her through pleasure-glazed eyes, Chico soaked in her pretty face, her flushed expression. The damp hair plastered against her cheeks as she convulsed again and again. Feeling tiny pin needles moving up his groin, he exploded inside of her.

After a few moments passed, Candy whispered against Chico's ear, "Do you love me? You love me don't you, boo?"

Chico didn't respond right away. He was having a major problem catching his breath as Candy slid off him to adjust her clothes, also giving him room to adjust his own.

"Chico!"

"What?" Chico looked into her eyes and saw what the problem was. "I'm sorry, babe. You have to give a brotha time after throwing that kind of loving on me." He looked at her and winked. "You know I love ya."

Candy kissed him on the cheek as he started the engine again. They were quiet as they headed down the couple of blocks to her house. Just as they pulled into the driveway, Candy's father came storming out the house.

"Candy, go in the house. I need to talk to Sean."

Chico rolled down the window, curious about what Candy's father could want to talk to him about. He also wondered if he could somehow sense what they had just been doing. Candy jumped out of the passenger-side door.

"What's going on?" she asked. "What do you need to talk to Chico about?"

Her father ignored her. "Listen, Sean. I don't want you coming around here no more. I don't want you seeing Candy."

"What?!" Candy screamed.

"You heard me. Your mother and I have talked about this and we feel it's for the best."

Chico couldn't completely make out Mr. Rosas' face, but he could feel the color draining from his own.

"You never seemed to have a problem with us seeing each other before," he said slowly.

"No, that's where you're wrong. I have always felt this way. You're too different. I just never said anything because her mother approved of you for some reason."

"So what's wrong now?" Chico asked. He could feel his head buzzing. It was getting louder and louder.

Candy was quiet. She watched her father as if she was seeing someone she didn't even know.

"I want something better for my daughter. You are too dangerous, Sean," he said pointing his finger in Chico's face. "I don't want her around gangster stuff, drive-bys, thugs and murders. I don't want her involved in any situations like the one that took place at your house a couple of weeks ago."

"I can see who I wanna see!" Candy shouted.

"She is *still* a minor!"

"And so am I," Chico responded. His face turned hot as Mr. Rosas went on.

"You put yourself in very dangerous situations—too dangerous to allow Candy to be involved with you any longer," Mr. Rosas said.

He doesn't think I'm good enough for his daughter, Chico thought.

"You're much older than her in many ways."

And I didn't have a choice in that, Chico thought.

"You two were raised differently."

Of course we were; I didn't have you, did I? he thought.

"This was a mistake from the start. And my decision, well, it's final. I'm sorry. Maybe if you get yourself together, we can reconsider this."

"Okay, cool," Chico said blandly. He quickly put up his protective shield— his " I don't give a fuck" shield.

"No! It is not cool!" Candy cried. Her face was red and streaked with tears. "You can't tell me who I can see, Daddy! I can't believe you're doing this when Chico and I have been together all this time. It's not fair!" She looked at Chico. "Baby, don't let him do this to us. Don't listen to him!"

"I told you to get in the house, young lady!"

"I will not! I won't!"

Chico took one final look at Candy. Her brown eyes met his hazel ones briefly. He tried to swallow the knot in his throat before putting his car in reverse and backing out. Candy was still screaming *"no"* as her father dragged her away.

"There is no fence? That's a joke," he spoke aloud to himself as he made his way back to *his* side—Creighton Court.

CHAPTER TWENTY-FOUR:
A MOTHER'S LOVE...

L iz looked out of the huge picture window. The bright sunshine masked the chill of the winter morning, yet nothing could mask the bone-chilling cold and pain of her heart as she sat having coffee with Aileen Mayes, whom she had of late, gotten really close with.

"I just don't know, Aileen, I don't know what to do. And sometimes I feel so resentful towards the children's father."

"Well, you should feel resentful, Liz. You've had to do everything for them by yourself while he keeps making promises about what he is going to do, yet he does nothing."

Liz sighed deeply. "Yes, but, I never wanted those resentful feelings to show to the kids, you know?" She paused momentarily. "Aileen, you remember I wanted to know what was up with Sean?" Aileen nodded. "Well, I found out."

Aileen put a comforting arm around Liz, knowing from the look on her face that whatever she had discovered it could not have been good. Elizabeth Grayson was one strong woman, and it was rare that she ever let anything get her down like this.

"So what did you find out?"

"Outside of the fact that Asha is pregnant?"

"Asha is pregnant?" Aileen gasped. "Oh no, Liz!"

Liz sat forward and got the coffee pot that sat on the table in front of them. She refreshed her cup, then Aileen's.

"Yes, she certainly is. That will put a damper on graduation for her, and her life in general. But she wants to keep the baby, and I'm going to do all I can to help her."

"She's lucky to have a mom like you. I wish all of my kids had parents that were as concerned and supportive, Liz."

Liz sighed deeply. "That's the least of it. Sean, I think he's selling drugs or something. I'm not completely sure what he's doing; Asha won't tell me much, but whatever it is he's in real deep, and has been traveling to do it, going everywhere, all these different states. It's so unbelievable. But the thing is? I feel partly responsible because I knew—I knew he couldn't have been making the kind of money he's been making working in a garage. But I went along, pretended it away; closed my eyes to it because we needed the money. And I feel like I peddled out my son for it. For a phone bill, an electric bill and all the other little things Sean have been taking care of for me for the last few months." Liz blew her nose hard on the tissue puffs she was holding, feeling almost breathless from stress and her stuffed-up nose.

Aileen laid a comforting hand on her. "Liz, any woman would want a bit of relief from the financial burden you've carried on your back. You shouldn't blame yourself! I pray to God that you're wrong, but Sean is responsible for his own actions, not you. Do you want me to talk to him?"

"Oh, goodness no! Sean would have a fit if he thought I had talked to you or anyone else about this."

"I understand." Aileen squeezed her arm again.

"But we made it this far without that kind of help, the drug kind of help. You may find this hard to believe, but Sean is a good boy, a good boy. No matter what others say. And he has never even been in trouble before. He's never been arrested, or given me any kind of serious trouble."

"I know he is, Liz..."

Liz could feel herself getting more and more upset as she spoke. "You don't understand though. My sister, she allowed her son Kenny to come to my house under my protection, and that allowance got him killed. I know she blames me; she won't say it, but I know it. It was all over her face at the funeral, and Kenny was all she had. Oh God, I blame me, too! I blame me, too!"

Aileen reached out, hugging Liz tightly. Tears flowed from her eyes at Liz's inconsolable grief. It was tears that only a mother living in this age when kids have lost their minds would understand.

Tears of a mother's love.

◆◆◆

It had been two days since Chico had heard from Candy. Even though he had said to himself that he would chill and let her dad have his way, it wasn't like he could get her out of his system that easily. He could kinda understand her father's reasoning. Chico knew better than anyone else how dangerous his life had become. Maybe it was best that Candy wasn't around him, being put into just as much danger as him. But none of that changed the fact that she was the one good thing going on in his life.

He breathed in deeply as he lay on the couch. Stress was straight up killing him. "I need to get a grip," he said to himself.

There was a loud knock at the door. Nobody was home but him, so automatically, Chico reached for the gun that he kept tucked in the front of his jeans. It was needed protection just in case someone was coming to finish the job on him that had failed.

Chico walked slowly to the door, holding his .38 close to his chest. There was no use looking out the peephole since when it was nighttime it was virtually impossible to see clearly.

"Who is it?" he called out. There was silence for a moment. "Aight, if you don't wanna say who it is you must not wanna get in."

"It's Peanut," a voice called out.

Chico opened the door fast. Peanut looked nervous.

"Uh, is Asha around?" he asked.

Chico leaned against the door. "Naw, muthafucca, she ain't here. What the hell you want with my sister?"

"Look, Chico, I don't have no beef with you, man."

"Punk nicca. Yeah, you got beef with me. I heard you don't wanna own up. Wassup with that?"

As far as Chico was concerned, Peanut was the worse type of brotha. If it wasn't for Asha, his ass would have been ghost a long ass time ago.

"When I first heard that Asha was pregnant it took me by surprise, yo. But I'm ready to do right by her now," Peanut said. "I wanna take care of my seed."

Peanut looked warily at Chico's chest. Chico's eyes followed in the direction of his. He laughed when he saw what the problem was. Peanut had spotted his piece. He brought it up to his face and ran it across his cheek, smiling.

"I'm being serious, Chico," Peanut stammered.

"And I am, too," Chico responded. "You gon' come at her correct, ya heard me? Or don't come at her at all."

Peanut backed away from the door. "That…" he pointed to the gun, "is not needed, man."

Chico laughed, and put it away. "I see you trippin', nicca."

"Look, I know we ain't never been boys, but it don't make no sense for us not to be now. It's like we already family, right?"

"Nicca, we will *never* be boys. It don't matter if you have a kid wit' my sister or not. Cuz see I don't even like your ass. You fuck around and make a wrong move where my sister's concerned? Imma cap yo ass. Recognize that." Chico gave Peanut one last penetrating stare. "Watch your step, nicca…"

He slammed the door shut.

An hour later, Chico had just gotten out of the shower and was changing his clothes when he heard the front door open. He buckled his belt, slipped on a wifebeater, and went to see who it was.

"Hey, Ma."

Liz Grayson stretched her back and yawned to show her tiredness. "I'm glad to see you home, Sean. I need to talk to you."

Chico felt an "oh Lawd" feeling come over him. He knew that it was gonna be one of those conversations.

"Um...I know you tired, Ma. Don't you wanna take a shower first?"

"No, I don't need to take a shower first. I need to talk to you now."

Chico sighed, flopped on the couch and felt it give way as his mom sat down beside him.

"I know what you've been doing," she said.

"What are you talking about?" he asked guardedly.

"Come on, Sean, what have I always told you? I know when things are not right with you. Okay, first let's start first with Kenny. Now I know it's painful," she said, seeing Chico's face cringe with pain, "but the subject of Kenny seems to be the best place to start to me. What was that? What happened and mostly, Sean, why?"

Chico was silent, trying to look past his mother. Why was the one thing he could not answer, the one thing she wanted to know? "I don't know why, Mama. It was some dudes that are pissed at me. That's all I know."

"And why are they pissed at you?"

Chico got up and wandered aimlessly around the living room as if he were looking for something. Glancing back toward his mother, he could tell from the look on her face that she was getting more and more impatient. He slipped a CD into the portable CD player sitting on the table.

"Will you cut that off please and answer me?" Liz Grayson insisted.

Chico sighed. "I don't know why they pissed...they just are. I mean everybody is not gonna like me, that's not how life is. I'm taking care of it though."

"Hold up," she said, swinging her hands animatedly. "You're trying to tell me how life works? And you, you're just a seventeen-year-old, still-wet-behind-the-ears lil boy. I'm the one showing you how life works, Sean, not the other way around. Don't you ever assume that you know more than your mother. You think because you know street stuff, because you know a bunch of thugs, and because you live that life yourself that I'm too blind to know what's going on? Come again, child." She put her hand up as Chico opened his mouth to protest.

"Don't even try to deny it, okay? I told you I know when something is going on. And where I may not know it all, I am not stupid by any means. And, Sean? You may or may not like this, but if you keep on this wild and rowdy road you're rolling on? I'll send you to your father."

"What!"

"Yes I will. Before I see you in a casket, I will see you with him."

Chico felt himself hyperventilating. "Oh, hell naw. I'm not living with that nicca!"

Liz paused in shock. "What did you just say to me?"

Chico rushed in his room, grabbing his shirt and slipping his Nikes on quickly. It was as if a heat wave hit him when his mom had mentioned his dad. Months would roll by without his dad contacting them, and yet his mom says she will send him to live with the asshole? Just the thought set a fire to him.

His mom was waiting as he rushed out the door.

"What is wrong with you?!" she screamed, grabbing him by the arm. He jerked away hard. Both Chico's and Liz's eyes got big when they saw what flew out of Chico's pocket and fell to the floor.

Liz shook her head slowly, unbelieving. She then looked up at Chico. "Who are you?" she asked, dazed. "Who are you?"

Chico bent down and picked up his gun that had fallen out. He slipped it back into his pocket. He couldn't look at his mom. Like what could he say anyhow? He needed to get away, fast.

CHAPTER TWENTY-FIVE:
WHEN THUGS CRY...

Saturday night was an all-girl sleepover. Asha, Jenene, Maxine and Candy had just finished gobbling down a huge pepperoni pizza. Now it was time to gossip, as only they knew how. Candy had wanted to be at her place this time though, since her father basically had her on lockdown. He was so worried that she would run off and meet Chico, which she probably would have.

"What kind of lip gloss is this?" Maxine asked Candy as she smeared it across her full lips.

"It's cotton candy flavor. I got it from CVS on sale. That stuff is nasty tasting, but it has mad shine, girl," Candy commented. She looked over at Asha. "Hey, have you talked to Chico yet?"

"I tried, boo. But when I mentioned you to him, he told me to mind my own damn business. You know how my brother is sometimes."

Candy swallowed the bitter taste in her mouth. It was a sick thing waiting and hoping a boy would call you. "It's just so unfair," she finally said. "I know he was upset over what my dad said, but it's almost like Chico is willing to just step back and let it happen instead of working with me to find a way for us to still see each other."

Asha gave Candy a pat on the ankle. "Girl, you know he got it like that for you. Just give him time."

"For real," Jenene agreed. "And keep your head still." She pretended to pop Candy upside the head with the comb.

Candy sighed again, watching as Asha rubbed her blossoming belly. She looked to be around four months pregnant. Candy couldn't help but secretly wish that she and Chico had gotten pregnant. At least she would have a part of him with her always. That wasn't something that was about to happen though, seeing that they had always used condoms. But then again the last time they had been together, condoms was the last thing on their minds. Maybe, just maybe...

"Asha, that belly is looking big, girl. You sure you aren't farther along?" Maxine suddenly said, echoing Candy's thoughts.

"I am big, ain't I?" Asha rubbed her belly some more.

Both Candy and Maxine suddenly screamed out at the same time, "What if you're pregnant with twins!"

"Oh, God, don't even say that!" Asha exclaimed, laughing. She sat quietly, halfway listening to her girls talking. But mostly thinking about her brother and how quiet he had become. Asha loved her twin. They were extremely close, but she figured he knew that it had been she who had told their mother some things about what he had been up to. Maybe he was pissed at her over that. She also knew that he wasn't taking Kenny's death well, or Candy's father's attitude toward him. It was odd, but to her she could always feel what he was going through, as if it was the fact they were twins that allowed them to share spirits. And if that was so, right now he was a troubled spirit indeed.

"Oh, turn that up! That's me and Chico's song..." came another sad reply from Candy, referring to Mya's "My First Night with You."

"Oh, Candy, will you stop! I mean call him, girl. Stop waiting for him to call you. Believe me my cousin is not all that!" Jenene declared. She sighed in frustration at her attempt to braid Candy's hair. "And you have got to keep your head still. You got that soft hair and yet you still want it cornrowed like the nappy stuff. Not an easy job, J.Lo."

"Okay, okay, just don't pull so hard!"

Asha and Maxine laughed as they listened to the exchange between their two other sisters-friends, what all of them liked to called one another. It always helped as far as they were concerned to have each other—no matter what other situation they were individually going through.

Later after all the other girls had drifted off to sleep, Candy decided to take Jenene's advice and call Chico instead of waiting for him to call her. She dialed his cell phone number. She didn't want to wake up his mother knowing that it was three in the morning. She held her breath as the phone rang.

"Hello?" Chico murmured sleepily.

"Hey, baby."

"Candy?"

"Yea..."

"Wassup?"

"You know what's up, Chico. I miss you," Candy said softly. There was silence on the other end. "Do you miss me?"

"You know I do."

Candy swallowed hard, closing her eyes as if that would mentally bring Chico to her, in her arms. "We need to meet; we need to talk. Don't you think?"

"What are we gonna talk about?" he replied. "I think your dad said it all the other night."

"I'm talking about us, not him."

"But what about him?"

Ignoring his question Candy continued. "Meet me at Maymount Park tomorrow. I have church all morning and afternoon because of revival. So make it around four, okay? I love you, Sean Grayson..."

After she hung up the phone, Candy offered up a silent prayer. She prayed that he would be there, and that they could somehow work things out.

◆◆◆

Marco was down for Marco. That's all Chico could think about as he waited impatiently in his vehicle in Blackwell as Malcolm and Junnie went in the project housing to do another of their sell gigs. It would be better Marco had said if Chico laid low for a while. But then here they were again doing the same old shit.

As he turned up the sound a bit on his CD player, Chico also thought about his situation with his mom. She wasn't happy with him, that was for sure. After he had walked out on her a couple of nights earlier, he spent the night with a friend who lived over in Southside. That night away gave him time to cool his temper somewhat, but it didn't help matters once he got back home the following day. He had expected his mom to be trippin' once he walked into the door, but instead, he'd gotten the silent treatment. At this point she still wasn't talking to him.

Chico sat up as he noticed Junnie and Malcolm coming out the apartment. Daryl, the guy who they were selling to, walked out with them and approached Chico's Expedition.

"What's going on, dawg?" he said.

Chico nodded to him. "Not much." He looked around as Junnie got into the front seat beside him and Malcolm got into the back. Both of them gave him a "be careful" look.

"I wanted to holla witcha," Daryl said. "I heard you had some drama around your way last month."

For one, Chico thought, he didn't know this nicca but in passing. For another, how did he know so much about his business?

He gave Daryl a straight face. "Drama is everywhere, man. But all is cool in my camp."

Daryl leaned against his ride, taking a cigarette from his pack and lighting it. "Cool, cool. Just watch your back, dawg. There's some shady niccas out here. You feel me?" He looked Chico dead in the eyes, unblinking.

"Chico, we need to go, man," Junnie whispered from beside him.

"Aight," Chico finally told Daryl, breaking his stare. "We gotta roll."

"Aight, word. Hang tight, nicca."

Daryl backed from the Expedition, putting up one finger and then aiming it in a point at Chico, as if saying, "pow."

As they pulled off, Junnie looked at Chico and asked, "What the hell do you think that was about?"

"Something's up with that nicca," Malcolm commented.

"Hey, yeah it is. What happened in there?" Chico asked.

Junnie looked back at Malcolm, waiting for him to respond.

"Everything went smooth, although he acted with us the same way he just did with you," Malcolm said. "Like he knows what went on with Kenny and a lot of other shit, too."

"Hmm..." Chico hummed. "So the question is, what does Marco know, or, does he know more than he's telling us about the whole deal."

"Hold up, Chico. I'm not saying that I think Marco's doing anything fishy. I'm saying that dude Daryl was trippin'. Might not be nuttin' to it."

Junnie flipped around in his seat again. "Damn, Malcolm! When you gon' wake da fuck up? Something ain't right with Marco, man." He looked at Chico. "I'm telling you, we need to check him. That's wassup."

Chico was quiet. The picture of Daryl's semi-playful finger shot at him kept racing through his mind.

"Yeah, maybe you're right. That's wassup."

Candy was late for their park meeting. Maybe she had decided she wouldn't come, Chico thought. He tapped his feet as he waited. Ten more minutes. That's how much longer he would wait and then he'd roll out. He wasn't sure why he had come anyhow. He had so many other things on his mind that he had fought to put the thought of Candy Rosas out of it.

Chico felt like a caged animal. Well, maybe not that bad, but close enough! He had all the freedom in the world, yet at the same time he knew he was prey. The street-element kind. But he didn't want to think about that.

He looked down at his watch again. He could admit to himself that Candy's father's words had hurt him. Hell, thugs cried, too, at times. Candy was a good girl, too good for him. In that her dad had been right. This had been obvious back when she had gone with them to D.C., and Big O got smoked. He knew even then that this was no life for her. Shit, it was no life for him either. But he had made a choice to do it, she hadn't. And although she knew he carried a gun, and that everything about him was not all on the up and up, she didn't really know what was going on. Chico made sure to never talk to her about it.

The Kenny situation had shocked her, but it had done more than shock Chico; it had awakened him. He had to find out who killed his cousin, take care of it, and then he would get out, make straight his path, and never look back. But in the meantime, Candy having dealings with him would only get her hurt. He had thought about all of this for days, and he knew it was the right thing to do.

During the week he had seen Candy a few times at school, but hadn't acknowledged her. Once when he saw her, he deliberately turned away while talking to Alisha. He knew that shit had hurt her. But he had to get her off him. Whoever was trying to hurt him wouldn't think twice about hurting her, too. This evening, he had to let her go.

Chico looked at his watch again and turned his music up a little bit louder. He had parked on the side street toward the lake, where they would sometimes meet up. He turned around as he heard a car pulling up behind him and instinctively reached for his piece. He let out a deep breath when he saw Candy.

"This jumpy feel has got to go," he whispered aloud to himself, opening the door for Candy.

"Hey," she said quietly, looking at him intently.

"Hey," he said back, picking up a joint and lighting it. "Took you long enough."

"Well, I had to wait 'til my dad left." Candy looked at Chico as he smoked, surprising him when she reached out for the cigarette. "So when you start smoking weed?" Chico asked her, with raised brows as he handed her the joint.

"When you stopped calling me."

"I never stopped calling you. You were never home when I did. So…what was the point?"

"There is no point."

Candy inhaled deeply, then let out a puff of smoke. "Anyhow, what are we gonna do, Chico?"

"Do?"

"Yes. Are you just gonna give up on us and start seeing other girls? I saw you talking to Alisha the other day. You kicking with her now?"

Chico was quiet, not really knowing what he wanted to say to her. No, he wasn't kickin' it with Alisha, or anybody else, but now that she had brought Alisha up, maybe that was a good way to break things off.

"Are you gonna answer me?! I heard that you messed around with her months ago, back in the summer. Was that true?" Looking up at her Chico, saw the glassy tears in her eyes, silently begging him to say it wasn't so.

"Is this what you wanted to talk to me about, Candy?"

Candy sighed in frustration. "Come on, Chico, were you with her or not?"

"It doesn't matter really. The fact is your father was right; we are too different, and I realize that now. I think I've always known it. I just felt like we needed to talk about it face-to-face, and make if final, you know?"

"Make what final? What! He wasn't right, and I can't believe you're saying this. I really can't," came her incredulous reply.

They were both silent. Chico felt this incredible urge to take Candy in his arms, to tell her they could work it out, to tell her that he didn't mean it. But his mind switched back again to what was real; they were too different, from two different sides of the fence.

Candy was looking away, sniffing quietly to herself.

"Candy?" Chico said softly.

"You breaking up with me?"

"No, just calling it off for now until I get some things straight. After I do, if you still wanting us…"

"I got to go, I gotta get outta here!" Candy took a deep breath, quickly opened the door and ran off in a rush.

He could've gone after her, but instead he took another drawl from his blunt, wishing the haze to come over his mind quickly. He had to forget about all this, and at this point the weed was his best friend. Almost.

CHAPTER TWENTY-SIX:
HEAVEN, I NEED A HUG...

Game time.

Everyone who had school spirit was there and cheering for JFK. Junnie had saved seats for Chico and Malcolm, who surprisingly had brought Jenene along. It raised eyebrows. Even though it was common knowledge among their group of friends that the two were kicking it, Malcolm rarely wanted anyone else to think he had a one-on-one with any chick. As he told it, that would kill his playa rep.

Chico raised his hand in a high-five as he approached Junnie. "Wassup, nicca!"

"Shit, man, you know wassup," Junnie said as he high-fived his two ace niccas. "We kicking Justice ass tonight! Tonight! Ya heard me!"

"Yeah, I knew that was gonna happen. John Marshall is slow." Chico looked over at the scoreboard and laughed. "Like I said, them niccas are slow!" He and Junnie gave each other daps again as they finally sat back to watch the basketball game.

Jenene looked at Chico after a moment, giving him a lil push with her shoulders. "So what up, cousin?" She gave him a knowing look.

Chico looked at her. "What you want, girl?"

"I just said, what up," Jenene said, smiling. "How come Asha didn't come tonight?"

Chico shrugged his shoulders. "I dunno. I think she was throwing up and shit."

"Ugg...Poor thing."

"Poor nuttin'. That's what she gets for fucking around with that sorry nicca." Chico frowned.

Jenene made a face. What Chico said was true, but he didn't know that his so-called dead friend Orlando could have been the one. That was a secret that she knew Asha wanted to keep secret, for-ev-er.

They watched the game for a while, jumping up and screaming when their school scored and booing, although they got the scowl of teachers when they did so, when the Justices scored on them.

"So…" Jenene prompted again, "What's going on with Candy? I heard y'all was splitso."

Chico gave a short bitter laugh. "You all up in my business."

"I'm not in your business."

"Yeah, right. I know you talked to Candy. I bet she told you everything you need to know, if you need to know."

"You ain't gotta be getting all funky about it," Jenene said, making a face. "I care about her, so when she comes to me saying some dude hurt her, whether it's you or whoever it is, I'm gonna say something, you *feel* me?"

"Whateva." Chico reverted his eyes, then looked over Jenene's shoulder as a semi-familiar face came walking through the double gym doors.

There were two guys, one who looked so much like a figure in Chico's dream, the same nightmarish one he had every night since that fateful day they had spent at Virginia Center Commons mall. That day they had come back to his place, that day that a guy who looked just like the one Chico was looking at had splattered his cousin's brains, and had taken away his life.

"It don't make no sense," Jenene was mumbling.

"Hold up," Chico shouted. He looked past her to Malcolm and Junnie, making sure not to lose sight of the dude who resembled Kenny's killer. "Junnie, take a good look at that nicca over there by the doors."

Junnie and Malcolm looked up. "You mean the brotha with the braids?" Junnie asked.

"Yea."

Chico could hear Jenene huffing and mumbling beside him as he and Junnie talked, but he blocked her out. He didn't remember this dude having braids the day Kenny was killed, but everything else about the guy fit. Malcolm sat on the bench in front of them, carefully eyeing their suspect along with them.

'What's up? Who's that nicca?" he asked.

"Who are you all looking at?" Jenene felt slighted.

The guy in question got up and started walking toward the exit doors with another familiar-looking guy.

"No, I don't think that's him. I know that muthafucca," Chico spat.

Junnie shook his head. "That ain't him, dawg."

"Like hell it ain't! Look at him!"

Junnie squinted his eyes. "Maybe it is," he said slowly. "I'm not completely sure about the other guy, but the one with the braids, he's got a limp. I shot that nicca in the leg, remember?"

"Let's go," Malcolm said, jumping up quickly.

"What? No, I don't think so! Y'all do not need to be getting in that kind of trouble." Jenene jerked on Malcolm's arm, as he, Chico and Junnie quickened their steps so not to lose the guys they were following. Looking out of the gym doors, Chico saw them standing by a car. The loud crowd around them seemed to have vanished. All they were concerned about were those two guys.

All four of them jumped in Malcolm's car, waiting for the two guys to exit the parking lot.

"I'm telling y'all don't do this!" Jenene cried again.

"I just wanna follow 'em," Chico said. "I just wanna know where this nicca live at."

"Ugg!" Jenene said.

They ignored Jenene, focusing more on the dark gray Taurus that was in front of them. He made a right turn off Cool Lane.

"Turn, Malcolm! Shit, you all slow; you gon' lose 'em!" Junnie shouted.

They ended up driving all the way to Southside, driving past Royal Avenue. They didn't want it to look suspicious to the two guys that they were being followed, so Malcolm U-turned, then connected back with them on the backside, heading toward the Afton apartments.

"You think they know we following them?" Junnie asked Malcolm.

"They shouldn't," Chico answered for Malcolm. "There's been a lot of cars around." He leaned over to Malcolm. "Nicca, you drive like Five-O."

"That's wassup," Malcolm and Junnie said together, laughing.

Jenene sighed. "What are we doing, y'all? Why do you want to follow these people anyhow? Take me home, Malcolm. This was not what I thought you had in mind when you asked me to go out with you tonight!"

"Shhh...Stop fussing, Jenene. I'm trying to concentrate."

Jenene sat back roughly against the seat. Chico observed the two guys carefully as they got out the car and walked into a project house. They watched as a loud girl who looked to be in her late teens to early twenties hollered a hello as the guys walked in and firmly shut the door.

Junnie pulled out his .38 and cocked it. "We can take 'em, take out every bitch in that house, 'cuz I'm one hundred percent sure they the ones."

"Hell to da fuck yeah," Chico agreed as he pulled his piece from his jacket pocket. "I swear to God I want to go in there and blow his muthafuckin' head off!" He swung the passenger door open, moving without thought to make his way to the project house.

"You mean hell to da fuck naw! Come on, let's just go!" Jenene looked at Malcolm. "I wanna go!"

Malcolm quickly got out the car. He walked up to Chico and grabbed him by the arm. "Man, wait, let's think about this," he whispered, pushing him back toward the car. "We don't know who's up in that crib, yo. We don't know if they saw us following, we don't know if that girl got babies and shit up in there. And then we got Jenene..." He nodded toward her. "I'm telling you, this ain't the right time, bruh."

Chico breathed deeply—shaking and steadily trying to calm his inner flex, and stamp out the blood he saw etched in front of his eyes, Kenny's blood, all over the ground, and shooting out of his head.

"You right, we'll wait." He inhaled the cool air in deeply.

"Damn straight I'm right. I'm always right!"

Malcolm and Chico got back in the car. "'Cuz I'm a 'bout it muthafucca, that's why!" Malcolm laughed.

"Y'all all crazy," Jenene said, still blasting them as they pulled off. "I'm not hanging wit' y'all no more!"

Malcolm's eyes met hers. "I'm sorry, aight?" He looked at Chico, who was still visibly upset. "We got the plate number; we got the address. We can talk to Marco tomorrow and see wassup."

"Nicca, you know what we gotta do! You always talk about Marco like you sucking that nicca's dick or something!"

Chico tensed up and looked from Malcolm to Junnie, who had said words you don't say to another brotha 'less you lookin' to be capped.

"Because Jenene is in here; because I know you're just upset about Kenny, I'mma let you slide on that foul shit," Malcolm said slowly. "This time..."

Chico closed his eyes as he sung the words of a new R. Kelly cut. He swallowed his off-key words and laughed a little.

"Is it cold down there, dawg?" he spoke, looking at Kenny's tombstone. He sighed, then stared blankly at the name engraved on the stone.

His Aunt Dee had gotten "Resting in a brotha's world" carved on it. Chico wasn't sure how much rest his cuz was getting, but it had to be better than where he was. He felt this freedom somehow to talk to Kenny, touch him in some way, and get him to help work out the puzzle that was the maze of his messed-up life. Hell, he thought, he had messed up Kenny's life, he at least owed him a peek into his own. As Mrs. Mayes said, let Kenny live on through him.

"Me and Candy, we called it quits. Hard to believe, ain't it?" Chico shook his head. "Man, I don't even know what I want. I was thinking about this college thing. Just seems like it made more sense when you were here talking about it. But now...I don't know—just don't seem real, or as important as it did before."

Chico stopped talking and zipped up his down jacket as a swift wind blew in his direction. He didn't know what caused him to ride down to Charlottesville to visit Kenny's grave. But it seemed as if some invisible force pushed him in that direction. This was his first time there since the funeral. It seemed so unreal. Almost like how could someone he had been so close to be cold and dead in the ground? Could he hear what Chico was saying? Was he feeling anything? Was he really dead, or in some ghostly place? Everybody seemed to have different ideas about what happens when you die. Where it seemed like a young boy of seventeen shouldn't have to worry about things like that, death was always on Chico's mind. So the thought of what would happen when it grabbed him, and where his dead friends were, shouldnt've been there. Yet the thought of where Kenny really was permeated his mind.

"Damn, Kenny...why did this shit have to happen?" Chico cried, feeling the wet sting to his eyes. Being in this alone, he refused to stop the wetness from falling to his cheeks. He felt more tears building, in huge globs, weeping like an old woman, and he didn't care. He wasn't just crying for Kenny; he was crying for it all. He was crying for all the shit that had grabbed control of his life for the past months. He cried for Wesley, the big bald Chamberlayne Avenue brotha; he cried for Orlando, seeing flashes of his face, smiling as they rode to D.C., then flashes of the bloody blown-off mug that used to be his. He cried for the drive-by killings that he had witnessed. He cried for the killings in York, the playground executions that he had taken part in. He cried for his mother. He cried for his Aunt Dee; cried for his sister Asha and her pregnant self. He cried for Candy and the pain he brought her. He cried for Junnie and Malcolm. But mostly, he cried for himself, for his lost opportunities, and for what he had allowed himself to become.

"I'm sorry, man. It should've been me. I should be there, not you. You didn't deserve it; I did. I didn't tell you the half, Kenny, the half of what I am, and what I've done. And the worse part about it? I don't even know why. And I know you, man, and I know what you would say. You would say, 'Let it go, don't get revenge.'" Chico wiped his eyes, fighting hard to see clearly. "But I got to. This is the one thing I have to do. And then I promise, I'll leave this thug life alone, 'cuz see I'm not even trying to be cool no more; fuck dat. And I can't even promise you where I'll go from there. But I think I'm gonna leave Virginia though, start over again somewhere, be somebody different. I'm gonna clean up, surprise all these muthafuckers. Everybody but you, 'cuz you always told me I could be somebody, and I will be that somebody."

Chico stood up and dried his eyes with the back of his hands. "When I become that person, Kenny, I'm gonna come back to see you, dawg. Shit, nicca," he said, laughing sadly. "You won't even recognize me. And that's real."

CHAPTER TWENTY-SEVEN:
AND THAT'S WASSUP...

Marco listened carefully as the guys explained what had happened when they followed the two guys from the game. He was extremely quiet though, which puzzled Chico.

"So y'all saying y'all did nothing?" Marco asked.

"Naw," Malcolm responded, "we figured we'd just wait it out. You know, wait for a better time and all. At least we know where they live or hang out at."

"Do not, and I repeat, do not, go over there fucking with them Southside niccas!" Marco stood looking Chico, Malcolm and Junnie in the eye, spitting out a toothpick after hearing their story. "This is way beyond what was s'pose to go down. So was York. And it's my fault for letting you all go up there. Had I known what it was really about then, none of this would've happened. I hate a double-crossing muthafucka!" he said, referring to the guys from the North-Clique.

"So, Marco, you saying I should just let these guys get away with killing my cousin?" Chico asked calmly, even though he could feel his face getting hot, just talking to Marco.

"Marco, you know we can't just let it go like this," Malcolm stated, actually surprising Junnie who looked his way and raised his eyebrows.

Marco walked over to his wet bar, poured himself gin and swallowed it down nervously in one gulp. "I'm not saying we won't do something, eventually; I'm saying *you* all do nothing. I'm telling you I know what I'm talking about. This thing is bigger than we are—this whole scene. If we get involved, we will have every type of shit coming at us from all angles."

"We already do!" Chico said loudly.

"I told you this whole thing started out as a gang hit, and that's the one reason I don't fuck with cliques and gangs. I like to do my shit independently."

Malcolm walked closer to Marco. "Yeah, but if that's the case, why did you have us selling to them? And why did you send us to Blackwell when you know wassup with them niccas?"

"That was business, Malcolm. Wassup with you, dawg? This ain't you." Marco put a hand on Malcolm's shoulder.

Chico and Junnie looked back and forth at each other as Marco talked. When Chico looked in Malcolm's eyes, he saw the same knowing look that he and Junnie felt. All of them were seeing for the first time that Marco was nowhere near the big Shonuff character, Mr. Gangsta godfather that he had put himself out to be. Instead, he was now giving off the appearance of being weak.

"Yea, okay; we hear you, man," Junnie said, looking over at Chico and giving him the eye when he seemed about to say something.

"So, you want us to just sit tight and see what your friends from North Carolina are gonna do. Is that what you saying?" Malcolm asked.

"Exactly. See now, you my boys, you feeling what I'm saying. Niccas like that? They always get what's coming to them. There's no use in us putting shit on our heads over this. There are other peoples who can take care of this for us, you know? I know these guys; I know how they work."

"Aight, man, we cool." Chico pretended to be settled for his plan, knowing that they were obviously in this one without the help of Marco's so-called expertise. They all gave Marco daps, promising him they would go home, chill, and wait for him to call Chico the following morning before he left for school.

"He's a punk, and all this time he and his Lil Cane getting us all wrapped up in this foul shit. And he's been just using us as his crutch. Whatever happened to all his, 'getting that respect' bullshit?"

Both Chico and Malcolm shook their heads in agreement with Junnie as Chico drove down Chamberlayne Avenue.

"Look, y'all," Chico took a deep breath as he began to speak, "I appreciate you two having my back in this. But I just can't let this go like you talking about, I won't. But from what Marco was saying, this could get ugly, and it's like y'all don't have to feel obligated gettin' up in this shit just for me."

Malcolm looked over at Chico as if he were crazy. "What! Man, check this out, we in this *together*. Kenny was my boy, too. Marco's scared about some gang; fuck a clique; fuck a gang. They got blood just like we do, and they can check out just the same. I'm behind you, Chico, hundred percent." He looked over at Junnie. "Junnie?"

"You don't even have to ask me where I stand. I was there. I saw and felt what they did to Kenny. I'm tired of the game but this is different. We owe now. It's not like doing it just because that simple ass Marco tells us to. Shit...y'all know I never trusted his ass no how."

Chico laid his head back against the rest as he stopped at the red light, then looked over at Junnie and Malcolm. "Y'all my niggas, you know that?" He put his fist out. The fists of all three joined as they gave unison daps.

"One love," Malcolm reminded him.

"That's right," Junnie agreed. "It's always gon' be one love with us."

In every situation in life, there are choices, choices that change you for the rest of your life. And as Chico and his friends made their way over to Southside with loaded weapons on themselves and in the cargo space of Chico's vehicle, they knew that they were about to make choices that would change them. The change wouldn't necessarily be for the best. This was different from what they had done for the past six months working for Marco. This was stepping over a boundary where there was no return. And in each of their individual minds, they all knew it.

They parked on a side street by the Afton apartments. They had scouted out the night before, just staring at the project house they had seen the guys go into. Tonight, they were ready.

"So, how y'all wanna do this?" Junnie asked his boys.

Malcolm sat forward in his seat. "See the thing is we don't know if he lives here or not. So maybe we should just wait it out for a few."

"Well, in the meantime..." Chico pulled out his piece and double-checked it, just to be sure. "I got something for that nicca."

"Yep, the last shot is yours, Chico," Junnie agreed.

Just as he spoke, a lone figure walked up from the alleyway. His hair was in braids, and he was coming right their way. "Bingo! That's our boy."

Malcolm jumped out of the car and walked right up to the guy as Chico and Junnie opened their doors.

"Wassup, man?" Malcolm asked him. The guy looked up at Malcolm curiously.

"Not much. Do I know you?" the guy inquired. He looked over at Chico and Junnie, instantly recognizing them, and went to reach at his back pocket, obviously for his piece. But Malcolm was quicker, pulling out and shooting him in the hand.

"Oh shit! Oh shit, wha' da fuck!" he cried, grabbing his bleeding hand just as Chico and Junnie grabbed him.

They muffled his mouth with a scarf. Malcolm looked around to see if they were being watched, but the pop sound of his gun was such a familiar sound in the projects, not a soul came out to see what had happened. They dragged the guy to Chico's Expedition. As he was pulled into the backseat, his head bumped hard against the side of the door. He screamed out in pain.

"Shut the fuck up!" Chico snarled, reaching around to the backseat and giving him three solid punches to the face. Blood squirted out of his nose with the last punch. "That's for my cousin, punk ass! And you better not bleed all over my ride!"

"Go down Jefferson Davis, man, down to the old Spaghetti warehouse," Malcolm instructed, as Junnie stuffed the scarf deeper into the guy's mouth.

They pulled up in the back part of the warehouse. Chico jumped out first and opened his cargo door to get some rope, a blanket and his CD player.

"What's that for?" Malcolm asked.

"So nobody can hear his ass, nah mean?"

He slipped a Nas CD in the player, but didn't cut it on yet. Chico laughed as the guy looked at the ropes. His eyes got huge. "Yeah it's for you," Chico stated. "It's your show, brotha."

Chico and his boys grabbed the dude, and walked up to one of the side doors, kicking at each one till they found one that was easy to open. Chico walked in, grabbing a chair that was stored in the room. The sounds of the traffic on Jefferson Davis Highway drowned out the noise Kenny's killer was making as they dragged him to the chair and tied him up with the rope. Malcolm removed the scarf from his mouth as Chico walked up to him and pointed his gun to his mouth.

"Who put you on me?"

"I...I didn't kill nobody, man. I don't even know what you talking about!"

"I asked who put you on me. Did I say shit about who you killed!" He slammed the gun handle into the guy's mouth, causing him to cry out.

"No...nobody!"

"Try again, nicca! Who put you on me?"

The guy was quiet except for his sniffling and crying at his busted mouth. His eyes read real fear and were wide open as he looked into Chico's eyes.

Malcolm aimed for his kneecap, firing once. He screamed loudly. "Man, I just dddid what I-I-I was to...told!" the guy stammered, moaning.

"Told by who?" Chico asked.

He was silent, except for the pitiful cries over his knee. Chico looked at Junnie, who pointed his .38 at the guy's other knee, pulling the trigger.

"Aww, man...God! Awww shit!" he cried out, blood shooting from both his knees profusely.

"Who told you to come at me, I said!"

"Marco! This New York nicca, Marco. He told us to do it! I shouldn't even be here, yo!"

The room was quiet except for the sound of Nas rapping in the background, Money is my bitch.

"Dayum!" Malcolm exclaimed, an incredulous expression on his face. "Marco?"

Chico looked at Junnie and Malcolm, all three in complete shock. "I can't believe it. He's been fucking us?"

"I'm telling y'all, it was him, it was him all along. He the one told Snoop and me where you live, man." By now, this brotha was bawling from the pain in his hand and kneecaps. "Just don't kill me, yo! I'm sorry! I don't wanna die, man!"

"Okay," Chico said calmly. "Why would Marco want me dead?"

"Because they fucked up when they sent y'all on the wrong guys in York. They blamed Marco and told him he either had to take y'all out cuz y'all pulled the trigger, or else he gets it!"

"Who are they? Who told Marco all this?"

"Daryl Roane. This nicca lives in Blackwell. But he runs shit around there, yo. I didn't have nuttin' to do wit' it. We just did what we were told!" The guy sniffled and moaned again at the pain in his knees. "Yo, I don't wanna die, yo!"

It took a minute for Chico to register all this new information in his head. He looked around, then at Junnie and Malcolm, who were looking at him to see what he wanted to do. Rage filled him, thinking about Marco, Daryl, this punk sitting here in front of him, and whoever else was responsible for Kenny's death.

Chico moved closer to the guy and looked him in his eyes. "You don't wanna die? Do you think my cousin wanted to die? Did you give him a chance to beg for his life before you took it?"

"Yeah, but I just told you the truth! You should be on Marco about this, not me! I'm telling the truth, yo!"

"And I believe you, but just like you told me, they want us dead cuz we pulled the trigger. That shit ain't fair, is it? But then with my cousin, you pulled the trigger. So my bad." With that, Chico aimed and shot him point-blank between the eyes. "That's for Kenny."

Chico closed his eyes. He didn't even realize the way he had been shaking the whole time. He looked over at Junnie and Malcolm, who also looked surprised at what he had just done. "Let's get the hell outta here…" Chico finally said.

He grabbed the blanket he had brought in, forgetting for a moment why he had thought he would need it. He wiped away the blood that had splattered on his chin when he had shot the guy. Chico and his boys walked out of the warehouse back to his Expedition. Once they had settled in, Chico grabbed his steering wheel and took a deep breath. The fight had gone out of him. He should be feeling better, shouldn't he?

"Man, I swear I want to get out Richmond, I'm so sick of this shit…" Junnie said quietly.

"You ain't the only one," Malcolm agreed.

Chico was quiet still, thinking about what had happened. He was thinking about what they were gonna do next, and mostly, about Marco, and the double-crossing bitch ass he was.

"Let's go to my place, get cleaned up and grab something to eat. My mom is at work, so it's all-good. We need to figure out what we gonna do about Marco."

CHAPTER TWENTY-EIGHT:
AND THE WALLS CAME TUMBLING DOWN...

Instead of going to his place, a tired Malcolm asked Chico to drop him off at home. They sat in front of Malcolm's grandma's house talking for an hour, trying to calm each other down and figure out what they wanted to do. Finally, they decided to just get cleaned up, and meet back in thirty minutes. For some reason Junnie had no desire to go home, so instead, he went home with Chico. When they got there, Asha was waiting impatiently at the door.

"Chico, I been looking all over the place for you! Where you been?" she cried. She stopped suddenly and gasped at the bloody clothes he wore, and at the spots of blood on Junnie's shirt. "Who's bleeding? What the hell happened to you two?"

Chico closed and locked the door to their place, looking around nervously. "Is Mama here?" he asked.

"No. You know she's at work. Where did all this blood come from, boy?"

Junnie and Chico paced nervously around the living room, ignoring Asha.

"Come on, Junnie, I got some clothes I'm sure you can wear. Maybe even something of yours you may have left over here," Chico said. He and Junnie turned to go down the hallway into Chico's bedroom, with Asha running down the hallway behind them.

"Listen, Chico, you gotta tell me something or I'm calling Mama. This don't look right. Now what happened?" Asha cried.

Chico started pulling off his shirt as he talked.

"We killed that nicca, that one that did Kenny. I killed that nicca."

"What?" She covered her mouth and shook her head. Her mind was racing. "How could you...how..." Asha's breath caught.

"Look, Asha, let me get showered and changed, aight?"

"What if the police come?" she cried. "What you gon' do, Chico?"

Chico jumped as the phone rang.

"It's for you," his sister said. "Somebody's been calling you all evening; I was trying to tell you before."

The ringing continued for a third ring. Chico swallowed hard. "You get it, Asha..."

She gave her twin another unbelieving look, then went over and picked up the receiver. "Hello? Just a minute." Asha looked at Chico.

"Who is it?" he mouthed.

"It's the same guy; Marco."

Junnie came walking back to the hall door, having gone into Chico's room already to change his clothes.

"It's Marco, man," Chico told him. "What should I do?"

"Just play his foul ass off. Act normal!"

"Yea, yea, you right." Chico took the phone from Asha. "Wassup," he said.

"Man, where da fuck you guys been?" Marco asked demandingly.

"You said you would call me tomorrow, right?"

"Yea, I did, but I've been paging your ass and you haven't been answering. We got trouble, boy. I've been trying to get Malcolm and Junnie and can't find those niccas either."

"What kind of trouble you talking 'bout?"

"I think you know what kind of trouble I'm talking about." Marco's voice got low, and even more demanding. "I told y'all not to fuck with them niccas over in Southside, didn't I?"

"And how do you know about that?" Chico asked suspiciously.

"Marco don' told you that before, haven't I? When y'all stupid asses pulled Lorenzo at Afton, did ya make sure nobody was watching? Fuck naw! Y'all just went on witcha dumb ass, young ass plan, not knowing what da fuck you were doing!"

Chico's face got hot. He didn't have to wonder now whether or not Kenny's killer was telling him the truth about Marco. Marco had just told on his self.

"You're a foul bitch, you know that, Marco?"

"What you talking about, fool?"

Chico snapped. "You know what I'm talking about, muthafucca! You set us up; you set me up. Now you sitting around acting all innocent and shit. You didn't want us to dig any further into this because you thought we would find your ass out!"

"What?" Marco exclaimed. "Man, what you talking about? Ain't nobody set you up. Why would I do something like that, and I'm the one that had your back; I'm the one who been warning you about all this. Those North-Clique brothas fucked me as well as y'all when they sent you to York. And now after this shit y'all don' pulled, I know that if you boys are responsible for this. They coming after you, they also coming after me 'cuz they know y'all my boys."

"Yea, then why the hell did he tell us, the dead ass at the warehouse, that you sent him and some nicca named Snoop to my house the day Kenny was killed? Wassup with that?"

Marco sighed. "Listen Chico, you have to trust me on this one, seriously."

"I ain't gotta trust nobody; trusting your ass is what got me in this mess!"

Chico suddenly heard a phone click.

"Hold up," Marco said. "Sounds like somebody's on the other phone."

"What you running for? And what do you mean somebody's on the other phone?"

Suddenly Chico heard muffled sounds, and what sounded like a phone dropping. "Marco! Where you at, punk? You ain't got shit to say? Marco!"

He heard Marco hollering, and then three loud pops.

"Marco, what's happening over there?" Chico shouted.

There was silence on the other end of the phone, and then a click, letting Chico know that someone had hung up the receiver.

Chico looked over at Junnie, who had questions written all over his face.

"What happened?" he asked as Chico hung up the phone.

"Man, sounded like somebody just took Marco out. I heard it, just now!"

Asha shook her head, her mouth moving like a fish out of water with no words coming out. "This is so bad! Chico, we need to call somebody. I'm calling the police!" she said, grabbing the phone from her twin.

"You ain't calling no cops, Asha. Are you crazy? I got this, I got it, and I know what to do!" Chico said wildly, looking from a crazy Asha to Junnie's grim features. "Let's um…let's just get dressed and go get Malcolm. Then we'll figure out something!" He dialed Malcolm's number and Junnie sighed again. His hands were shaking as he sat down on the couch beside Asha trying to comfort her.

"Malcolm? Meet me and Junnie in like five minutes."

"What's wrong, why your voice sounding like that?" Malcolm asked.

"Marco is dead, man, at least I think he is. I wanna go over there and find out. Look in the window or something. I don't know. But this is all just getting crazy. Meet us over there, okay? And park where nobody will see you."

"Aight, bruh, I got you. I'm leaving now!"

Hanging up the phone, Chico looked over at his sister. "I'm sorry, Asha. Just don't call the police, aight? I'll be back in a short. You keep the doors locked, and the lights low, and we will be back as soon as we can."

"What if somebody comes here looking for you?" she cried. "Chico, I'm scared…"

"It's gonna be okay. I wouldn't let nobody hurt you or Mama. Trust me, please?" he pleaded. Asha sat back on the sofa, rocking and wrapping her arms around herself as if chilled.

Chico didn't know what to say. He was scared, too. Scared because all of this was coming too close to home—scared because it was all getting too real. Especially with it appearing now like somebody had gotten to Marco. He slipped on a fresh shirt that Junnie had given him, then walked back into his room to grab another .38 from under his bed and a loaded semi. He then grabbed his keys and walked back into the living room.

"We need to bounce, Chico. If you said five we don't want Malcolm out there by himself for too long," Junnie said quietly.

"Yea, you're right. Let's go." He looked over at Asha one more time. "Lights out, and don't answer the phone, okay? If I call you, I'll ring you on your cell phone."

He hugged her small nervous form, and he and Junnie walked out the door.

After they left Asha sat in silent darkness. She was afraid to move, afraid to sit, afraid period. But she knew she had to do something—call someone. She thought about Jenene, and quickly got up and dialed her number. There was no answer, and then she remembered that Jenene and her mom and dad were going to her dad's acceptance ceremony from something with his job. She thought about calling her mom, but for some reason she felt that would be a big mistake. All her mom would do is come home from work upset, and feel just as scared as she felt. Finally Candy came to mind. She tippy-toed into her bedroom, grabbed her cell phone and dialed.

"Hello?" Candy's mother answered after three rings.

"May I speak to Candy, please?"

"Just a minute, hon."

"Hello," cooed Candy in a soft voice.

"Candy! Is your mom around? Can she hear you talking?" Asha whispered.

"No. What's wrong, Asha?" asked Candy with concern.

"Oh, girl! It's all crazy around here, and I don't know what to do!"

"What happened? What's crazy?"

Asha held her hand to her chest. Her heart was beating extremely fast and causing her to feel lightheaded. "That guy who shot Kenny? Chico killed him. Junnie and him came here with blood all over their clothes!" Asha held her stomach, feeling instantly sick at the memory. "I'm scared, Candy. I don't know what to do..."

Candy gasped. "Asha, maybe you misunderstood. I can't believe Chico would do something like that!"

"No, girl, he told me himself. I swear to God!" Asha put her hand to her temple. She felt a sudden ache coming.

"Okay, let's calm down. Is anybody there with you now? Where is your mom? And where is Chico?"

"He left with Junnie to meet Malcolm. They said something about somebody else they know just getting killed. I told you Candy, it's crazy, and I'm scared that somebody is gonna come here looking for him, and I'm all by myself!" Asha started crying in hiccupping sobs.

"Stop crying, Asha. It's not good for the baby," Candy whispered. "Listen, I'm on my way to get you, okay? I'll be there in a few minutes; just don't worry. Chico shouldn't have left you there by yourself."

"Okay," Asha cried.

"I'm on my way."

"Okay..." she cried again.

After hanging up Asha sat staring at the phone. She looked into her dresser mirror. Her face blanched, her hazel eyes were big, frightened and swollen from crying.

"Hurry, Candy," she whispered to herself, "hurry!"

CHAPTER TWENTY-NINE:
PAYING THE PIPER...

When Chico and Junnie got over to Marco's townhouse apartment all was quiet. The street seemed extremely empty for some reason. Chico couldn't decide if that made him nervous or made him feel a little bit better.

"You see Malcolm's car anywhere?" Chico asked Junnie.

Junnie looked around. "There it is," he said, pointing a couple of cars ahead of theirs. Both of them spotted Malcolm waving his hand at them. They ran over to his car.

"Damn, Malcolm." Chico breathed. "I was getting a lil worried that you had started snooping around by yourself for a minute there."

"I ain't no fool, dawg." Malcolm ran a pick through his wild bush of hair and stuck it in his back jean pocket. He never let his cornrows stay in long. "Let's see if we can get in from the back."

They crept quietly around the back of the building, trying to peep through the sliding glass door.

"Marco was on the phone when I heard the gunshots," Chico told his two boys. "So he could have been in the kitchen, unless he was upstairs. I mean he could have been anywhere in this house."

Junnie suddenly did something that none of them had thought of before. He tried the door to see if it was locked. It wasn't. They walked inside, carefully looking around to make sure there wasn't anyone still in the townhouse. The upstairs and downstairs were both empty and nothing appeared to be missing or out of place.

"Nobody's here," Malcolm noted.

"Wait," Chico said, suddenly remembering the basement.

The guys followed him as he walked quickly, taking two steps at a time down the stairs. Once they got downstairs, there was Marco; big bad Marco in a puddle of blood with a hole in his head. Shot execution style.

"Oh dayum!" Malcolm exclaimed, as he and Junnie came up behind Chico looking at Marco's dead body. "This is just...dayum..."

"We…have…we need to get outta here!" Chico said in a hurry.

"They coming after us next," Junnie said.

"I know! Don't you fuckin' think I know that?" Chico screamed, feeling panicky. "Let's go!"

They rushed outside.

"We can leave my car here and ride with you. Marco told me that we were spotted when we grabbed that Lorenzo dude. That means they're looking for my ride, just like they were when they killed Kenny."

Jumping inside Malcolm's ride, Junnie said with a shaky voice, "What about Asha?"

"Oh hell, that's right! They know where I live. Shit, Junnie, we shouldn't have left her there by herself! We shouldn't have left her there, man!" Chico cried, slamming his hands on the dashboard. He looked at Junnie and Malcolm. Both of their faces read the same panic as his.

"Just go, Malcolm!" Chico shouted, "Go now!"

Every light seemed to take extra long to change. All kinds of thoughts were flying through Chico's mind. *Had they gotten in over their heads? They had gotten in over their heads. Had they gotten in over their heads?*

"We um…we can just get Asha, take her to Jenene's or something."

"Yeah," Malcolm agreed, "good idea."

"Then what do we do?" Junnie asked.

"I don't know," Chico spat. "Damn, shit, man, I'm trying to think!"

"Then what do we do?" Junnie asked again in a loud voice.

"We could ride up to Maryland tonight, maybe call my dad. He may help. Hell, I don't know. He may come get us from Maryland. But I got to call my mama, too. I don't want her coming home," Chico mumbled. "Shit, I don't know what to do…"

He handed Junnie a semi as they pulled onto the street leading off Creighton Road. "Keep that close," Chico told him.

Junnie nodded, and then looked over at Malcolm. "Malcolm, you got your piece, right?"

"Yea, I do," he answered, pulling in front of Chico's house, behind what appeared to be Candy's lil Pontiac Sunbird. Candy got out of the car just as they did.

"Candy?" Chico said, jumping out. "What are you doing here?"

"To get Asha. She called me. She's scared, Chico." Candy walked up to him, slipping her arms around his waist, holding him close. "What have you done, baby?" she cried quietly in his ear.

"You need to get outta here, girl! I'm going in to get Asha and you take her with you, aight?"

Before Candy could answer, two cars rolled up on the other side of the street. Chico and Candy looked up, but Malcolm and Junnie had already spotted them.

"Run, Candy!" Chico screamed. It seemed to all happen in slow… fast…slow again…movie-style motion. The sound of bullets flying. Malcolm and Junnie shooting back. Running. But not fast enough.

Candy appeared to be frozen for some reason. Her eyes met Chico's. He grabbed her by the arm and started pulling her roughly behind him. Chico fell to the ground when a bullet hit his shoulder. The hot acid pain caused him to cry out.

"Chico!" Junnie screamed as he saw him get hit. He quickly turned around and steadily began to shoot at the gang of guys who he could barely make out once a flood of bullets invaded his body. He cried out, then fell, his body jerking out its last breath.

Malcolm had already made it to the door. Asha had opened it for them as soon as she heard the commotion outside.

"Go, Candy!" Chico screamed. He kept low, worming his way across the porch, trying to avoid the bullets. Candy got to the door, then turned around again to help Chico. The whole world seemed to flash before Chico's eyes as he saw Candy's body jerked. Her eyes looked into his, big with a disbelieving expression in them. She fell backward through the apartment door. Malcolm and Asha quickly dragged Chico in behind her. Once they had locked the door, Chico rushed over to Candy, falling to his knees when he saw she had been shot in the stomach. Her goose-down white jacket was stained with blood.

"Don't be dead! Don't be dead, baby!" Chico cried. He pulled her close to him, and then realized that she was still conscious and vomiting blood as he held her. "I'm sorry, baby girl…"

"Chico…" she said weakly. More coughs; gagging. Chico held her closer.

"God, this is so bad," Asha cried, trying to wrap a blanket around Candy.

Chico cried pitifully. He couldn't let Candy go as she fought to breathe with harsh puffs of air.

"Where is Junnie?" Asha asked.

"He gone, he's dead! He out there," Malcolm screamed, pointing toward the door. "Now stay low, everybody!"

Candy coughed again, and more blood spat out her mouth. Her eyes weakened as she looked at Chico. "It hurts, Chico…"

"I know, Candy. Just hold on; it's gonna be okay. Just hold on, aight?"

"Uh-huh…" she whimpered, tears falling down her face, coughing still.

"You call the police, Asha? You call an ambulance?"

"Yes! You know I did," she exclaimed, looking down at Candy's face. She covered her mouth with both hands, shaking her head. "I shouldn't have asked her to come get me…"

All the shooting outside had seemed to stop for a minute, suspiciously so Malcolm felt. He peeped out the window. Just as he did, more rounds were shot their way. Bullets flew through the windows, bouncing loudly off the walls. He started shooting back angrily through the broken glass. "Chico, I need you over here, man. Come on or they will bust up in this joint!"

Chico laid Candy close against Asha, telling her to stay low. His hands were slippery with Candy's blood as he pulled out his semi-automatic. He crawled over to a window to fire back along with Malcolm. The situation had him on a numb high. He had completely forgotten about the pain in his shoulder.

Asha screamed and covered her ears as the gunfire got louder and louder. "Somebody help us! Oh, my God!"

"Look at Junnie out there. Look what they did to him, Chico!" Malcolm looked over at Chico just as he looked back at his life-long friend. For reasons Malcolm could not understand, Chico stood up and tried to make the window open wider.

"Get down, man! Down!" Malcolm screamed.

Chico looked at him blankly, seeming crazed. He pulled his Uzi out, aiming it through the bigger space in the window. Suddenly, bullets flew back at him instead, conquering his body.

"*Chico!*" Malcolm screamed.

"No!" Asha cried as her twin fell to the floor.

Malcolm screamed again at the sight of his friend's stilled body. Still screaming, Malcolm loaded another round of ammunition in the Uzi semi he had picked up off the ground from when Junnie fell. He ran out of the apartment firing wildly, blinded by tears, fear and rage. The police pulled up just as he ran out, but not in time before he was ricocheted repeatedly by bullets, falling to his death.

Asha sat quietly, rocking Candy against her as she watched the zooming lights of the police vehicles. She listened to the sound of gunfire outside between the police and the group of guys who had come to cause havoc in their world.

She looked down at her brother's body lying still on the floor and felt herself crumbling inside—crumbling as her safety foundation was yanked from beneath her.

"Are you hurt, miss?" someone suddenly asked her. But she didn't respond. She couldn't see anything, only a glow of light as she continued to rock Candy in her arms.

"Young lady, are you hurt? Miss? Are you hurt?"

Asha kept rocking.

CHAPTER THIRTY:
TIME TO KILL...

Aileen felt as if she had just run a marathon as she rushed into MCV Hospital. The doors opened quickly as though they somehow knew she was in a hurry. She rushed to the front desk.

"Did they just bring in a young man named Sean Grayson?" she asked the receptionist.

"Are you a relative?"

"Yes, she is," Liz Grayson's voice cried out from behind them.

Aileen rushed over, hugging her tightly. "How are the kids?"

"Candy and Sean are back there. Both are in pretty bad condition." Liz looked shaken. Upset. Scared, and in shock.

"What happened to them, Liz? And where is Asha? Is she okay?"

Just as Liz was about to answer, the doors to the patient care area of the emergency room came flying open. Liz and Aileen could see a group of doctors congregating around Chico. The curtains to where he lay were wide open for all to see.

"What's going on in there?" Aileen mumbled, almost to herself.

Liz, however, automatically sensed that something was wrong. She rushed inside the doors with Aileen running closely behind her. As they got to Chico's bed two nurses fought to keep them away.

"Miss, you can't go in there."

"That's my son!" Liz cried. She saw the flat line on Chico's monitor screen. "Oh my God, save him please! That's my baby!"

"One, two, three, stat! Stand back," one of the nurses counted as the multitude of doctors worked, using the electric paddles to try to bring Chico's heart back to pumping. His body jerked convulsively as the electricity went through him.

"We aren't getting a response, doctor," one of the nurses said.

"This kid is seventeen years old. We keep trying!"

They repeated the procedure over and over. Liz cried in horror, and Aileen held her—praying that his young life would be spared...

Sit a spell as I tell u a once upon a tale…
The haunting story of a young boy waiting to exhale…
his life of ups and downs and twirls and frightening desolation…
of startling dreams and haunting scenes and a street wise education…
It didn't take him very long to sense the naked true…
to smell the stench of ghetto hood that smoked from every roof…

Jenene walked up and down the floor, fighting hard to calm herself. She had gone from one tense moment to another in the past week. Everything had taken its toll. The funerals and now the wait. Waiting to see if the doctor would come in with hopefully some good news; waiting to find out if Candy was out of danger. She looked up at Candy's mom and dad who were busy talking to the doctor.

"If all is well by morning, we might be able to move Candace out of intensive care. She was one lucky girl," the doctor said.

She sure is, Jenene thought to herself, *far luckier than the others.* She covered her face, shaking as she thought about Malcolm. She had loved him, and she never even told him. Now she never would be able to. She could still see that day when they were sitting on her living room floor. She was braiding his hair as he smiled up at her with his big, dimpled, cocky grin.

"Yo, check this out! I'm not afraid of dying…I know I'm gonna die young, always have known—like Tupac said I feel the depths and the shadow. But when I do go out, I'm gonna go out fighting like a mutha, that's fo sho."

She had looked at him angrily after his saying that. *"Well I'm sick of burying y'all, and I'm sick of going to funerals. And if you die, I ain't going to yours you hear me?"*

And I went anyway, she thought to herself. Went, and saw them bury Malcolm. Died young, just like he had said he would. Jenene sighed tearfully.

He grew up in a world of crack and beer can-coated streets…
where twenty-one was old and wacked and college was unique…
No, in his world of hoochie girls, the problems were immense…
he hid his fear and pain inside his electric homeboy fence…

"Hey, Jenene." Asha came and sat down beside her. They hugged briefly. They had been hugging a lot lately.

"I'm just sitting here thinking about Malcolm." Jenene sighed, wiping at the tears that starting fall again. The same tears had been falling since the moment she had heard the news about the guys.

"I know," Asha said sadly. "I'm just glad that Candy made it."

"Where's your mom?"

"She's talking to the doctor right now I think, but you know she hasn't left Chico's side. It's amazing that he's doing as well as he is, considering all the bullets he took. Mama said it was prayer. She never stopped praying through this whole nightmare."

After the police came, Asha had been in a frightened daze for hours, hardly able to talk even after she saw her mother. She had been sure that Chico was dead. And truth being the case he barely made it, suffering bullet wounds in his chest, shoulder and one kidney. But he was lucky; he was alive. This was far better off than Malcolm and Junnie. Candy had also been in ICU for the past week. They had almost lost her a couple of times, but by the grace of God she, too, had made it.

"How are you feeling, girl?" Jenene asked Asha, pointing to her belly.

Asha smiled sadly. "Oh, baby and I are okay."

"Have you heard from Peanut again?"

"Yea," Asha said, nodding. "A few days ago he called to let me know that he's joined the Marines. Ain't that some shit? Anything so he can get away from me."

"Well, you can always get money from him if he's in the military, you know? They would make sure he paid up. The same thing happened to my mom's brother. They took it out his check."

"But that's just it. I don't know if I want to even have him paying when I'm not sure the baby's his."

"But you don't know that it's not, Asha. Make that Negro pay, girl!"

"You know what? I don't even care anymore, Jenene. I really don't…"

Jenene couldn't help looking at Asha as though she had lost her mind. But she could see from her expression that she was dead serious. Before she could get out more info about it, Mr. And Mrs. Rosas came walking into the waiting room with a relieved expression on their faces.

"Candy will probably be going upstairs in the morning, and she's even talking, girls!" Mrs. Rosas said happily.

"Oh, thank goodness!" Asha and Jenene responded in unison.

"I know," she said, smiling. "You girls can see her once she's moved. I know she'll be excited to see you."

"Well," Asha looked at her watch, "I'm gonna go see Chico for a bit right now. I have some things from school that I need to leave in his room. Just some cards and stuff."

Candy's father got a hard look to his face when Asha mentioned Chico. He walked away going over to glance out a window. He blamed everything that had happened to Candy on Chico, feeling that they had not stopped seeing each other when he had told them to, and feeling that Chico had been nothing but bad news for his daughter. Her being in MCV with a bullet, and barely getting away with her life, was proof enough as far as he was concerned.

"How is he?" Mrs. Rosas asked. "I need to get in and see him. I saw him a couple of days ago but I didn't get a chance to talk being that I needed to get back to Candy."

"He's better," Asha replied. "He was a bit upset because he couldn't go to Malcolm's and Junnie's funerals. But then again, he's been upset about this whole thing, ever since he's been conscious enough to know what's happened."

Mrs. Rosas closed her eyes. "This has been such a nightmare, such a waste." She opened her eyes again. "Are you going in to see him now?"

"Yea, I am."

"Give him my love, okay? And your mother, too," Mrs. Rosas said kindly, giving Asha a warm hug.

And every time he ventured out to a society that shunned...
he held his head up high and proud, the way he held his gun...
It was his pillar, his protection...it gave him his respect...
a sense of pride and dignity that hadn't happened yet...

◆◆◆

Chico could see and feel the warm sun shining through his hospital room window. It was a far nicer room than the one he had been in before. The cold sterile ICU room he had woken up to that first time, and would see every time he managed to crack open his eyes again during the next few days that followed.

But as warm as that sun looked, his heart was freezing, and so was he.

"Are you cold, sweetie?" Liz Grayson asked, as if reading his mind.

He nodded his head yes. He instantly regretted that when hot pain shot through his shoulder, it caused him to gasp and breathe in air that sent pain rushing through the spot that once housed his left lung.

"I know it hurts, baby, but you are doing so much better, and you're going to be just fine. You'll be coming on home with me before you know it."

Chico panted in pain and opened his eyes to look at his mother. "Did you go to Malcolm's and Junnie's funerals?"

"Yes, I did, I went to Malcolm's. Junnie's parents had him cremated. You know about the memorial service," she said sadly.

Chico looked at his mother and saw her pain. It was as if they had turned to the cable horror channel by mistake, and couldn't switch it off. As she looked down at him tears were swimming in his eyes.

"Sean, you're going to make yourself hurt." She handed him a tissue.

Chico was already hurting; every damn where.

Malcolm and Junnie. Just the thought of them not being around anymore, just the thought of how they went out, how they died, was just... Now he couldn't even imagine his life without them, especially Malcolm. He felt a sick feeling come over him again.

The one thing he was thankful about, very thankful for, was that Candy had made it. He hadn't been conscious enough to know just how well she was doing. For now, just knowing she was alive was enough for him.

But in his mind it wasn't lost, the one undeniable fact...
that in a land of justice for all, he always would be black...
this vivid truth held him inside his self-inflicted prison...
afraid to peep out of his cave...afraid to share his vision...

The sound of the door opening caught his attention. His sister Asha and his cousin Jenene came in, with Asha smiling broadly.

"Chico, I'm glad you're awake. Ms. Mayes told me to give you some good news."

"What good news?" Chico asked weakly.

Jenene kissed him on the forehead. As his mom sat quietly beside him on the bed, Asha opened an envelope.

> *Dear Sean,*
>
> *We are happy to announce that your poem "Rainbow Child" has been chosen as our grand-prize winner for literary excellence. Also, it has been chosen as our Editor's Choice Award, and will be featured in our upcoming anthology of young and gifted writers.*
>
> *It is indeed a pleasure to see young people making an effort to succeed in an arena where so many others have excelled, and in our efforts to give you a push in that direction we are happy to award you the grand prize of a $2,500 scholarship to the college or university of your choice.*
>
> *We will be watching your future writing career with eagerness, and wish you the very best of success! Congratulations on your creative achievement.*
>
> *Sincerely,*
> *The International Library of Poetry*

"Oh, Sean, I'm so proud of you! See that, you are good, I've always told you!" Liz purred with pleasure.

Chico was speechless. He had actually won something. Someone outside of his mama, and Ms. Mayes felt that he had abilities and talent with the pen. As that thought washed over his mind, the door creaked again. A tall white man and a black man, both in suits and with badges, walked in along with his doctor.

"Sean Grayson?"

"Yea?" Chico answered curiously.

"FBI. We have a warrant for your arrest, for the torture murder of Lorenzo White," the white man said.

"What? What is this about? You can't come in here arresting my son with him in a hospital bed!" Liz screamed.

Chico's doctor, who had accompanied the agents to his room, shook his head angrily, sighing.

"There will be a twenty-four-hour guard placed by his door, Ms. Grayson. Believe me, nobody is planning on taking your son out of his hospital bed in handcuffs," the black agent said.

"But he didn't do anything! I know my baby didn't do anything. He didn't kill anyone!"

Chico closed his eyes as the voices rang out around him. *You're gonna end up dead or in prison, Sean*...Didn't his mom always tell him that? Paying the piper. God's gonna ask it back from you. *God's gonna ask it back from you*...Didn't it always come down like this?

More voices echoed around him. He could hear his mom crying and steadily defending him. He could hear his Asha and Jenene crying quietly in the background. And finally, he could hear the FBI agent, reading him his rights.

"You have the right to remain silent..."

The talents of this lost young man sadly remain unveiled...

"You have the right to an attorney. If you cannot afford one, one will be appointed to you..."

His gifts were hidden in the sand, his scars remain unhealed...

"If you give up these rights, anything you say or do, can and will be held against you in a court of the law..."

For just like other young black men, his prison became real...

"Do you understand these rights as they are explained to you?"

And now, he's number thirty-two eighty-nine, with too much time to kill...

A WORD FROM THE AUTHOR

When I first started writing *Ballad*, I had a unique concept in my mind. I didn't want to just tell another sad tale of the hood rats invading our streets. I wanted it to be told from their perspective. I wanted to humanize these young people and the situations they get involved in. There is so much talent that flows from the veins of our children. Yet many of them instead choose to hone in on the street violence that appears to offer a quick ticket to the American dream that they feel is out of their reach. Sean "Chico" Grayson, and his homeboys, instead of tapping into the well that already flowed from them, choose instead to be like Eve from the Bible, who by reaching out for more lost the joy and the beautiful prospect of life that she already had. That's how old this story is.

The raw street element of this novel may shock and upset some readers, but I wanted to keep it real. I didn't want to sugarcoat it. I wanted to appeal to the younger audience and to the older ones, so that everyone would see the dire need for our people to actually do something before—as what happened in this story—it becomes far, far too late. As Nas says in his poignant rap, "all it takes is one mic" and one voice to speak up and actually do something for our youth. Especially our young, Black men without fathers who need guidance from positive Black male role models in our communities.

This story was told from the urban streets of Richmond, Virginia, but the setting could be anywhere. That's how widespread this disease is that has contaminated our children. Yes, they are responsible for their actions, but are we not the ones raising these street children?

My final word to my readers would be this: Open up your heart, and listen to your conscience, so that we as a people can join together and do something to save our own. Because if we don't care, if we don't do it, who will?

A.J. White

ABOUT THE AUTHOR

A.J. White is a native Virginian who presently lives and works in Richmond, Virginia. Having a multitude of interests, writing has always been a first love, including poetry and song lyrics. A.J. White is a staff writer, co-founder and an editor for the popular online e-zine *The Nubian Chronicles* and is co-founder and web developer for TNC Communications, a portal on the web designed to assist new and established writers to create a web presence. A member of the Black Writers Alliance and R.A.W Sistaz, A.J.'s work has also graced the pages of the online e-zine *Timbooktu*. Writing under the pseudonym JDaniels, A.J. White is also co-author of the Strebor Books International release *Luvalwayz: The Opposite Sex and Relationships* and its sequel, *Draw Me With Your Love*. Writing as JDaniels, A.J. is also the author of the BET Sepia thriller *Serpent in My Corner*.

Contact A. J. White at www.jdanielsonline.com